Escape While I Can

WHEN THE FAMILY FORTUNE suddenly dissolved, the Brandons wrapped the threads of their former prestige about them and went into solitary confinement. Middle-aged, outwardly courteous but inwardly bitter and hateful, the three of them lived in a state of suspended animosity, pretending to ignore the fear that hung over them.

This was the family that greeted Elizabeth when, in her youth and naïveté, she married Thayer Brandon. She tried sincerely to fit into the curiously distraught household, but fear is contagious, and the time came when Elizabeth feared for her own life and fled. She returned eight years later when murder became an accomplished fact instead of a whispered fancy, and the words *insanity, revenge, motive* were flung around a courtroom.

Melba Marlett spent two years perfecting this first-rate mystery novel. She has always told a good story, but here she reaches a new high in suspense and characterization.

MELBA MARLETT

Escape While I Can

WILDSIDE PRESS

Escape While I Can

Published by Wildside Press LLC
wildsidepress.com | bcmystery.com

For
B. A. Grimes
my father

Escape While I Can

CHAPTER I

TODAY I found in the back of my bureau drawer an old letter from
Maggie Mitchell, and my first look at the fine, sprawling handwriting brought back last summer as clearly as the lifting of the lid of my
rose jar brings back last June's Killarneys and Talismans and Ophel-
ias. Just as I sometimes sift through the dried, spicy petals, seeking
the flowers I picked on such and such a day, so I find myself now
leafing through my old journals and hunting for my first glimpse at
the crimson thread that led us through the astounding maze, and I
am obsessed with the impulse to put down each tiny fact, to explain
our tragedy as sanely as I can, to absolve myself of the feeling that
I was to blame for letting death into our Northern gardens. *"S'excuse, s'accuse,"* the French say, and if they are right I defeat my
purpose in thus letting the old ghosts out of last summer's tomb.
But I am driven. I cannot help myself.

If I had met Maggie Mitchell before I met the Brandons, I might
have been spared the most miserable months of my life. It could
easily have happened that way. Maggie was in Harbor Springs as
often as was Effie, and Mother and I were plainly displayed every
morning and afternoon on the veranda of Harbor House, Mother
because the Northern air eased her asthma and I because I could
not bear to leave her for a minute lest her poor tired heart should
choose that time to fail. And Maggie had heard the Brandon plans.
She was a clever woman, actually, and there was little that she
missed.

"Yes, I knew," she told me once. "I heard Thayer say that he had
seen you, that he would like to meet you, and that Effie must arrange
it. She didn't like it too well. Thayer's wife had been dead a long
time and they had thought they were safe, that he wouldn't try it
again. But she never refused him anything, and I knew she'd move

9

heaven and earth to bring you out. I never thought—you being so young and all—that it'd come to anything."

"And when you saw that it was, Maggie, why didn't you warn me then?"

"By that time it was too late."

It was, too. From the moment that Effie Brandon came down from her porch in the summer twilight to welcome us, I was impressed. I was only nineteen years old then, very pleased with myself for having just precociously completed the work on my master's degree and full of the business of writing letters to boards of education throughout the state to discover a vacancy in some teaching staff that I might fill. In June, with my blue and gold hood over my shoulders, I had felt so confident of employment by September that I had persuaded Mother to use the last driblets of Dad's insurance money to give us a month's vacation in northern Michigan; but now, in the middle of July, my brashness was fading. No kindly town had stepped forward with a munificent offer of one hundred and fifty dollars a month, and I was hard put to it to conceal my disappointment.

"Never mind, dear," Mother would say. "You'll get something. I remember that in the early days, when your father was just beginning to teach, we didn't know from one spring to the next fall what we'd be doing or where we'd be."

"I'm not worried, Mother."

I was worried, however. Worried and afraid. In common with most people who go through school young and concentrate on maintaining a high scholastic average, I knew very little about people, their motives, or what to expect from them. Until that summer I had been thrown with students who were four or five years older than myself. After twenty, this disparity in ages does not matter. But when you enter a university at fourteen with curls still down your back, you cannot expect to be included in the activities of the other freshmen who have reached the ripe majority of seventeen or eighteen. And by the time you are a senior and of an age that would allow you to melt into the routine of your classmates without being pointed out as an anomaly, the parade has passed you by and the rest of your class has grown quite used to getting along without you. I did not have a single date in college, unless you count the evening sessions at the library where several young men would surround my table to copy my notes assiduously, murmur polite thanks, and sprint with all haste to the sorority house where dwelt the lovely young thing who would recopy the notes for herself to a fanfare of masculine beating on chest and, "Aw, it was nothing. Thought I might as well bone up on the stuff. No use you going to all the trouble."

Even now, eight years later, pleasantly entrenched in my post as English instructor in one of the best girls' schools in the East, firm in the poise that comes with the lecture platform and the disseminating of one's words to more or less attentive audiences, I quiver with humiliation when I think back to my undergraduate days. Always I was trying to scale the wall that would let me into the intimate circle where everyone else seemed to be having so much fun. And always I had to slide back into the outer darkness where dwelt the grinds, the social misfits, the hopelessly unattractive youngsters that make up the outskirts of any university circle. I could not adjust myself to this group either, and I was sick with resentment that I had been consigned to it. The crime that I had committed was Youth, and only time could correct that, a job which, by the way, time has done only too well.

It was on my return from one of my perpetual trips to the Harbor Springs post office for mail that I found Mother in the happy state of excitement in which she asked questions and answered them herself immediately.

"Guess who was just here, Elizabeth? Effie Brandon."

"Who's she?"

"Elizabeth! You know the Brandons. Their father made all that money selling—oh, oil fields or one of those early makes of car that ran on steam or water or something. They were always living in Europe or Africa or somewhere. I've read about them in the papers since I was a little girl. Their mother was Anne Thayer, from the stage, and a famous beauty. They said she had the most beautiful legs in tights—that was before she was married, of course. And then there were pictures of the animals they'd raise. Those big horses— Percherons—and deerhounds, or some such dogs. They're both dead now."

"The dogs?"

"No, silly. Mr. and Mrs. Brandon. You remember the trip to Alaska? No, of course not; it was years before you were born. Anyway, they took the three children. Thayer couldn't have been more than two years old, and I know Mrs. Powers, who lived next door to us then, said that it was a wonder that child wasn't dead the way he'd been dragged all over the universe ever since he was two weeks old. He must be over forty by now."

I had heard of the Brandons, naturally, although they belonged to Mother's era much more than to mine. They had been one of the fabulous families whose comings and goings had provided exhilarating reading to the plainer Americans of that day who had been much too busy making a living to think of travel. The good people of the Middle West gasped as the newspapers unwound the saga. Alaska. Europe. China. A yacht named *Westwind* that had toured all the Southern islands. The amount of duty that must be paid on a Russian sable coat. Squab was like chicken, only smaller. My land, then why all this fuss about it! Yet turkey seemed gross and corn on the cob and fresh Limas too hearty compared with the image of small brown birds on bone-china plates and tall crystal glasses whose hollow stems sent up fragile bubbles. There were thousands of people who knew as much about the Brandons as though they had been their next-door neighbors: what a good, charitable, kindly man Mr. Brandon was; how beautiful his wife, and what a temper she had; the last details on Effie's first ball gown; the names of the schools to which Thayer was sent; the fact that Anne knew three foreign languages. And, with the coming of the Golden Age of American prosperity, you missed them when they faded from ejaculatory print, the Brandon fortunes not being as securely founded as those of the Rockefellers and the Dukes.

"What are they doing up here?"

"They live up here. The year round. The three children, I mean, though you could hardly call them children any more. They own miles and miles along Lake Michigan, just above here, and there are two big houses. Thayer lives in one, and Anne and Effie live in the other one. We've been invited for dinner tonight. They're sending the station wagon for us. What shall I wear? My black chiffon."

"Why should they ask us to dinner?"

"Well, really, Elizabeth! We're not as unattractive as all that. Miss Brandon said that she had read your father's books and been a great admirer of them——"

"She's interested in organic chemistry?"

"She must be. That's what your father's books were about, weren't they? And I had been pointed out to her as his widow, and she felt she would like to know us. You wear your organdy."

Thus I came to Brandon Oaks for the first time in the early summer twilight, the green and orange lights in the sky reflecting faintly on my white organdy ruffles, Mother chattering incorrigibly to old Nathan, who drove grimly, as becomes a man whose profession is gardening, his knotted hands distrustful of the wheel, his face contorted to allow for his wad of chewing tobacco. For fifteen miles the road wound north of Harbor Springs. Sometimes the trees encroached on the very fenders; sometimes they dropped back and permitted us the sight of Lake Michigan tumbling and heaving on its beach a good hundred feet below; once a soft-footed Indian woman stepped from the gravel to the grass and watched us go by.

"An Indian!" Mother shrieked.

"Yes, ma'am. Quite a colony of 'em settled down there on the beach. The women help with the housework for the summer settlers. God knows what the men do. You never see 'em. Only the women and the kids."

"How much farther is it to the Brandons'?"

"Three mile."

Mother settled back virtuously. "I shouldn't care to live so close to heathen, myself."

"They ain't heathen, ma'am. They're Catholic. Got their own little church down on the beach. They keep themselves to themselves. You won't never see 'em unless you send for 'em."

"Do the Brandons——"

"No'm. Miss Effie and Miss Anne, they do some of their own work, Miss Maggie helping. They got a housekeeper, Jane Moss, does the cooking and heavy cleaning. I take care of the outside. Mr. Thayer lives alone in the other house, and between us all we manage to get his work done for him, too. Course he keeps a lot of his place shut off, not having any use for it."

Mother was shameless. "Seems strange he doesn't live with his sisters."

"He did, long ago. Wasn't but one big house there then. But Miss Effie got married, and they built the other place about a block away from the main house for Mr. Thayer and Miss Anne and Maggie to live in. Then after the summer that Miss Effie's husband died, Mr.

Thayer got married, so they all switched around again. After he lost his wife he just kept on living where he was."

"What did she die of?"

Nathan was inscrutable. "I can't say, ma'am. I wasn't there at the time."

Mother did not wince even at this plain rebuff. We had turned into a narrow, sandy road that led between two large stone pillars, and the pines had come back to line the road. The first star pierced the light blue of the sky, and, though the lake was invisible, its murmuring was loud in my ears. The road twitched to one side to slide between two of the largest oak trees I had ever seen, and we were in a tremendous clearing of lawn and garden. I had a fleeting impression of hundreds of roses, a stone wall covered with honeysuckle, a sundial set in the midst of Oriental poppies, and then we rumbled by a large white house whose windows were all dark.

"Guess Mr. Thayer's down at the other place already," Nathan said. "We'll go right on."

The road sloped gently through the terraced lawn; the breeze became fresher; we passed a flowering hedge, and there was another white house with every light ablaze and people sitting on the screened porch.

Effie herself came out to welcome us, and, as I have said, I was impressed. She was so much the lady, so much the daughter of wealth and ease. All the assurance that I so painfully lacked was in her light step and the confident poise of her ash-blonde head, now rapidly growing silver. She wore midnight-blue chiffon and a rope of pearls that would have been incredible unless you knew her family name. On either side of her, courtiers attending royalty, paced a gray Russian wolfhound.

Mother fluttered at her like an excited moth fumbling a candle flame, and I tripped awkwardly on my ruffles. She can't really want us here, I remember thinking, we're small town, we're middle class, there are many more prepossessing people who would be glad to come. A feeling of hopeless inadequacy swept over me, and I kept my head down through the introductions to the three other people on the porch, bending to pat Boris and Duke as soon as I decently could to hide my gaucherie. Even that was difficult. The big dogs were patiently tolerant, but their aquiline faces were bored and disapproving, their rounded backs sloped away from my shy touch, they bent their slender necks with the sterling-silver chains that served them as collars away from me.

"They don't like strangers," said a timid voice in my ear. Maggie Mitchell had perceived my embarrassment and come to sit beside me.

She could not have been more than forty-five then, but she looked older. Her figure was short and plump; there were lines around her eyes; her hair was a dim brown, worn long and bundled up any old way. Later in the evening I noticed that her black dress was a hand-me-down and had had to be pieced out at the seams with black satin. Her only jewelry was a big cameo brooch, a little askew. She kept her hands out of sight, a mannerism which was habitual with her, because there were calluses on her palms. But she looked beautiful to me at that moment, a kindred ugly duckling among the galaxy of Brandon swans.

"I'm afraid I didn't catch your name," I confessed.

"I'm Marjorie Mitchell. I'm—I'm a sort of cousin."

Which was not true, either, but it was the explanation she invariably gave to newcomers. It saved their having to listen to the Brandon story about how she had been adopted out of an orphanage by the senior Brandons when she was three, chosen deliberately—Mrs. Brandon was the authority for this—as the most unattractive child in the institution to test the power of money to effect a sea change in even the most hopeless individual. Perhaps if the Brandons had not already had three children of their own it might have worked better, or if Mrs. Brandon had been a more motherly sort of person. Maggie was twenty-six at the time of the sudden deaths of Mr. and Mrs. Brandon, and, with the concurrent dwindling of the family fortune, she had sunk back into the position of poor relative and household drudge.

"Please call me Marjorie," she said that evening in her quick, breathless voice.

The fact that after the first two days of knowing her I could think of her only as "Maggie" was a triumph for Effie Brandon, though one she had long since ceased to care about. Maggie never reproached me for the use of the ugly nickname. The real sting of it had left her years before when she was scarcely in her teens and had gone into sobbing hysterics every other day, insisting, "Marjorie! Marjorie!" while Effie stood over her and shouted, "Maggie! Maggie! Maggie!" Old Mrs. Deever told me about that much later.

At nineteen one senses no undercurrents. We went in to dinner, and my courage revived enough to allow me to look around. We crossed the forty-foot living room, and I had a fleeting glimpse of the huge fireplace that could take half a tree as a backlog and whose brass and irons stood as high as my head. The rugs were worn, but they were Orientals. The furniture had seen better days, but every piece belonged in a museum. I had never seen such masses of flowers. Vases, bowls, baskets, every conceivable kind of container held roses in florist-window-display bunches, tall spikes of delphinium and whole branches of flowering shrub. I heard Mother gasping over them, inquiring where they all had come from, and Effie's reply, "From the gardens," in the slightly surprised and amused tone that said, "Where else does one get flowers in summer?"

Thayer was next to me at the dinner table, and I risked my first direct look at him. He was a handsome man with beautiful manners that were, I was to find, so firmly ingrained that even his rages had a smooth, lucite quality. He was tall, and, in spite of a good pair of shoulders, thin. His hair was brown, shaping to a nice contour about his temples, and his eyes were rather shockingly light. They were amber, a clear translucent color through which you could not see his mind, but rather your own antics mirrored back to you in sardonic yellow glints.

Anne sat on the other side of me, a tall, dark, gentle soul who seemed to have difficulty paying attention to the mundane considerations of food and conversation. Maggie scrunched, a shapeless heap, in the most obscure corner of the table, directing the somber Mrs. Moss, who served us, with little apologetic signals, and eating as much as the rest of us put together. Effie caught me watching Maggie's plate, and her mouth made a knot of wry amusement, her narrow shoulders raised in an almost imperceptible shrug. "The proletariat. What would you?" said the shrug. Maggie caught it, turned scarlet, and refused dessert. I felt guilty, as though I had entered into some conspiracy for her embarrassment, and I had not meant to. The poor creature was entitled to whatever pleasures she could find, and eating largely was certainly a minor dissipation.

"Your older sister," I mumbled to Thayer, "I don't know what to call her. They said she had been married, but everyone calls her Miss Brandon——"

"It is Miss Brandon. She took her maiden name back after her husband's death." He leaned closer to me. "I suppose a great many people have told you that you're a very pretty girl?"

It caught me completely off guard. "No. No, they haven't."

"There's a refreshing quality about you. A certain innocence. What my sister Anne would call a favorable aura. She's a spiritualist of sorts."

I sought escape into the impersonal. "I don't know much about spiritualism."

"It wouldn't help if you did. Anne's system is all her own. However, she does believe that she has rather unusual powers as a medium. She spends hours in her own room conducting séances all by herself. Effie and I have never encouraged her, and she doesn't tell us much about it."

I am afraid that I avoided Anne more or less for the rest of the evening. I was not anxious to find myself sitting next to a table that had none of its legs on the ground. Long before eleven o'clock, when we prepared to take our leave, she had excused herself and gone upstairs. Maggie was not much in evidence either, and I imagined she was in the kitchen helping Mrs. Moss with the dishes and perhaps surreptitiously consuming her once-dismissed dessert.

Mother was breathing fervent thanks to Effie for a lovely evening while Thayer helped me on with my wrap. His touch was intimate and personal. He had not been more than a yard or so away from me all evening. I was flattered and confused and anxious to get back to our prosaic room at the hotel. And then there was the loud knocking at the screen door, and there were Mother and I with no choice but to overhear. Effie went out to the porch to talk to the man.

"Miss Brandon," said the voice, "you owe me for two more sheep. They're down in my south pasture dead as doornails, with the throats torn out of 'em!"

"That's absurd. The dogs have been in the house all evening, Mr. Lucas."

"These sheep didn't tear their own throats out!"

"Then the Indians have been after them. I paid you for the first sheep because we couldn't prove anything. But this time I'm sure. The dogs have been shut up in the kitchen."

"I'd like Miz Moss' word for that."

Effie turned and walked past us with a face like ice, but when she came back she had her purse in her hand.

"I'm afraid I've been mistaken, Mr. Lucas. The dogs were in the kitchen until Miss Mitchell decided to let them out to go for a run. I have no choice but to pay you. This time, though, I wish you'd bring the dead sheep up here tomorrow. I'd like to look at them. My dogs are not sheep killers."

"I'll cart 'em up first thing tomorrow, Miss Brandon."

He had barely gone scrunching down the path when Maggie came hurrying in, the two wolfhounds at her heels.

"They just came back," she said excitedly. "There's not a mark on them, not a drop of blood."

Effie cut her off. "We'll talk about it later, Maggie." Poor Maggie! "I'm sorry for the unpleasantness when our guests were here, that's all."

Old Nathan drove us home, and even Mother was subdued.

CHAPTER II

WITHIN FORTY-EIGHT HOURS of my first meeting with the Brandons, Mother was dead. Her heart, the fashionable Harbor Springs doctor said, and was careful to get his fee before he left. The hotel management was very sympathetic, very helpful, even when it became apparent that I was not a good financial risk.

"Brown is the nearest undertaker, miss. You'll want the body taken there, no doubt, and they'll take care of all the details, seeing that it's sent back home, wiring on ahead in case you want the funeral service at your own home——"

"There's no place to send it. She'll have to be buried here." Father lying far away in the cemetery at Ann Arbor. Our little house sold. The town to which we were to move and where I was to teach still as ephemeral as ever. It had been too long a chance to take.

The management cleared its throat. "That'll cost money, then, miss. There'll be a burial lot to buy, for one thing, and—— Well, I'll send Mr. Brown in to talk to you. He'll know better than I."

Mr. Brown said that for five hundred dollars a very simple funeral could be arranged and a fitting grave provided. I did not admit that three hundred dollars was all I had in the world. I said that I would have to talk it over with friends. In the meantime, if he would take the body and do whatever was necessary, except seeing about the lot . . .

Thayer Brandon came to see me that morning. Mother had been taken away, and I was sitting in our little room watching the yachts nuzzling into the harbor. There is a stage in sudden sorrow where one is sacked of emotion, where thought lies idle, and the only things that prick the brain to action are the demands of the importunate senses. Smooth wood of window ledge under the hand. Unclench your fingers. Dazzle of sunlight on water. Half close your eyes. Cool breeze against your face. Breathe deeply and long.

Blankness is frightening. I had a problem to solve; I had thinking to do. I must add and subtract and multiply factors that had nothing to do with the dearness of the clay that must now be committed to expensive earth. All I could summon were little stereotyped, bromidic thoughts that came along the oldest, easiest paths. Everyone must die. Your mother would not have wanted you to worry so. People have lived through things like this before. And when I looked up and saw Thayer standing in the doorway, I thought, "Old friend of the family," without measuring the phrase. My mother had spoken well of the Brandons; I had had dinner at their house; they were the only people I had any personal connections with in this foreign land. Ergo, they were old friends.

He came in and sat down and took my hands.

"Elizabeth," he said.

Like a tidal wave the flood of my dammed-up feelings swept over me. I was weeping and coughing and strangling and biting my lips and writhing in the quiet sunshine against the pretty blue and white background of the view of the bay. I was my mother's Elizabeth and she was no longer anywhere in the world. Run to the ends of the earth, little sister, and call, and nowhere shalt thou be answered, for the warmth of the bosom you seek is no more and thy mother is inscrutable with God.

Thayer kept my hands and pulled me through the maelstrom. Sodden and exhausted, I sat again in the chair by the blue and white window.

"My sisters sent me to ask you to come out to stay with us. Is there anything we can do?"

"Nothing at all." I was not sobbing, but the tears kept coming and I did not bother to wipe them away.

"We thought—the expense and everything—you might not have enough money readily available——"

"I don't have enough. I'll think of something."

"As I understand it, you have no home at present. You must consider our place your home."

"You're very kind. There's no reason why you should be."

"Yes, there is. I fell in love with you the first time I saw you walking on the beach two weeks ago."

"Did you?" I said.

"I wanted you to know so you wouldn't feel that we were just being polite. My sisters know. You will be doing me a favor if you come."

"I can't. I have to work at something right away. I need two hundred dollars that I don't have, and cemetery lots are——"

"We have our own private cemetery out at the Oaks. Let us bury your mother there. Will you come and see it? It's a beautiful place."

It was, it is, a lovely place. Half a mile away from the two houses by a path through the woods you come upon a clearing. On three sides the big trees bend and rustle. The fourth side gives to the edge of the cliff that overlooks the lake. You are not conscious of the drop-off and the stretch of white sand far below. You imagine that the blue ripples of the great inland ocean come within inches of these white stones. Far to the left and below you there is the tip of a white spire. It belongs to the Catholic church in the Indian village on the beach.

Thayer left me there to think. I sat down near the top of the cliff, and the peace of the sun and the lake and the warm earth began to draw my soreness out of me. It was so quiet there. The stiff breeze whipped my hair and tore vagrant leaves from the tall trees. The odor of sweet dried grass and distant pines came with it. Below me on the beach a little girl skipped past, her tuneless song rising faintly to my ears.

Mother would love it here. I had never seen a place so beautiful, so eminently suited to the peace and dignity of death. I got up to go back to Thayer's house and tell him so. The little girl on the beach was building a sand castle.

There were six headstones in the little cemetery. Two of them had fresh roses placed by the stones. The biggest white block was marked "William Brandon, 1862–1914. 'The Lord is mindful of His own.'"

And below that, "Anne Brandon, 1865–1914, beloved wife of William. 'He remembers His children.'"

Thayer's father and mother had both died in the same year, then. It was embarrassing not to know more about the Brandons. They had been a rich, much-publicized family, and highly respected, too. I had heard their name mentioned only a few times, never without a deferential little pause before and after it. Their history, or at least the part that made them conversationally holy ground, I did not know, and it seemed stupid to have to ask. Especially I would not ask Thayer. We were a generation apart, and I was not tactless enough to remind him of it.

At one side was a small white stone with a circle of pansies growing around it. "Melissa Brandon, Baby Dear, June–September, 1910." Melissa had been the last Brandon baby, born when her mother was forty-five, and she had scarcely had the strength to last out a summer. Six months later, when I stood in the same spot, looking out over the gray, heaving water, leaning against a raw wind, and feeling the snow crystals melt against my mittens, I knew that Melissa was the luckiest of all the Brandons.

The next stone was marble with an ornate design of roses wreathing the epitaph. "Alice Norris Brandon, beloved wife of Thayer. 1902–21. 'Remember now thy Creator in the days of thy youth.'" Nineteen when she died. Certainly she could not have been married long!

A big marker and a little one huddled together. There were no inscriptions on these. One said "Robert Warren"; the other, "Robert Warren, Junior."

The last square of polished granite stood alone, and someone had laid a bunch of red roses at its foot. "Margaret Thayer, 1868–90. Our Sister. 'Her sun is gone down while it was yet day.'" Thayer had been a family name, Mrs. Brandon's maiden name, and Margaret had been her sister.

I walked to the edge of the cliff and looked at the lake and the white ribbon of sand so far below. The little girl had gone. The light was beginning to flare red in the west, and from the Indian church two faint bells began their sweet monotonous plaint. The beauty lulled me, and I thought dreamily that I must get back to Mother at the hotel, she would be worried about me. Then the strangeness of the huge incontrovertible Fact broke upon me, and I knew that I had no one to go back to.

Thayer was waiting, though, at the other edge of the wood, just beside his own garden. I almost hurried past him, he stood so quietly in the dusk. The sky was vivid with streaks of lemon and green above the red fire at the horizon, and I was hurrying so I would not see the first star come out and be reminded that just forty-eight hours before——

"I'm here," he said.

"If your sisters don't object, I would like Mother to be buried there."

He did not say any more. He took my arm and led me past the stone wall and the night-blooming stock and the glimmering roses down to the other house. Effie and Anne were sitting on the porch, and they rose to welcome me. A frantic figure I must have been: crumpled seersucker dress, white coat with grass stains, eyes swollen from crying and sleeplessness, my throat still so constricted that I could barely speak.

Anne spoke first. "You are very welcome, my dear," she said in her gentle voice.

"Quite the best thing you could do." Effie was more brisk. "We'll send Nathan down for your things, but just now we had better get you to bed. Heaven knows when you've eaten last. We'll bring you a tray."

I trudged through the great, impressive living room and up the stairs, down a hall lined with pictures, and into a bedroom that was a queer composite of modern and mauve decades. The bedstead was massive brass; the highboy and lowboy were mahogany scrolled with a Greek key design. A large square mirror perched over the latter, framed in the same wood carved into flying birds which seemed momentarily about to swoop out. The rug was pretty, but old and faded. It had been used in a dining room once. There was the unworn spot in the exact center, the narrow path, most worn, where many feet had rested, the wider path, less worn, where the chairs had scraped. Windows with frilly white curtains made up three sides of the room. The fourth wall contained the door leading to the bath which I would share with Anne, whose bedroom was on the other side of it. A puffy lavender chaise longue was placed near the windows, looking for all the world like a fat lady who has fallen suddenly backward, her arms stretched plumply before her, her feet a little higher than her waist. There was not much wall space, but covering almost every inch were photographs and photographs, and photographs, all of people, all autographed.

Thayer and Anne had disappeared. Effie alone led me into the room, snapped on lights, began to get out extra blankets.

"I'll give you a nightgown and a robe of mine," she said. "They'll do you for tonight. Mrs. Moss will bring your supper up to you. Just get into bed to eat it and then try to fall asleep as soon as you can."

"I hope I'm not putting anyone out of this room."

"Indeed no. This is a guest room. We have little company these days, so it doesn't get much use. In the old days we could sleep twenty-five people in this house with no trouble at all. Father built it like that on purpose. It was our summer place, and he liked to have lots of people around him. For a month each year it was turned over to the society for underprivileged children. It would take weeks to get the house and grounds back in shape again afterward, but Father never minded. We can't afford to do that sort of thing nowadays, of course." She turned and looked directly at me. "We lost all our money except a very small income from certain investments, and some land which has as yet been unsalable. We live in what might best be described as genteel poverty."

It was the warning note on Thayer's behalf. I muttered "Unfortunate" and "So kind." I went on undressing, peeling my things off and dropping them on a chair, my eyes half shut with weariness. She left for a minute and came back with a white cambric nightdress with hand-ruffled neck and sleeves and an old-fashioned black kimono. It was not the kind of gown I would have associated with the fashionable Effie Brandon, but it was very comfortable and cool and I said so, timidly.

She stood facing the twin lights on the lowboy, not looking in the mirror, not looking at anything, especially not looking at me.

"I must tell you," she said, "that we have certain rules in this house. It is not very often we have guests to hamper with them, so you must forgive us. I imagine that wherever one goes one runs into necessities—or, perhaps, prejudices—that cannot be explained and that must be borne with." I am sure she thought she was motionless, but her hands were moving, and I watched them. They were strong, slender hands, very pale, with the blue veins noticeable even at that distance; and they were wrapping themselves around each other, clinging to each other, the dry skin rasping faintly, the fingers agonized. Had she been wearing rings, they must have cut into the flesh with the tremendous, secret anxiety of that wringing. "You must never leave your room unless you are fully dressed. In here, you may do as you please, but I suggest that you wear a robe and slippers until you get ready to get into bed. We have a lovely beach farther down, but we do not swim or bathe in the lake. We have objections to bathing suits and sun baths. If, later on, you wish to swim, there is a public bathing beach ten miles away, and you may go there. Nathan will always be available to drive you." The hands sprung into each other and clasped. She turned and smiled at me. "We sound very old-maidish, I know. But we are glad to have you with us, anyway."

She turned at the door. "I hate to trouble you, but I really think you should get up and lock this. All of us lock our doors at night, and I should feel better about it if you would follow the custom of the house." She laughed shortly. "A little superstition, if you like."

"But if Mrs. Moss is coming up with a tray——"

"She may not be here for twenty minutes yet. Lock it until she comes."

I was not sleepy any more. I got out of bed, and, so impressed had I been by the excessive earnestness of the conversation, I dutifully put on the plain, unattractive robe and slippers she had left at the foot of the bed before I crossed the room to lock the door. The key turned easily. Everything else in the room was old, but the lock was not. It was new and sturdy. I went into the bathroom. New locks there, too. Gently I tested the one on the door that led to Anne's room. The door did not move; it had been locked on the other side. But a second later Anne's voice called, "What is it?"

"It's only I. Elizabeth. I'm trying to get the lay of the land. I hope I didn't frighten you."

She opened the door six inches, her gentle face peering around it apologetically.

"I am never frightened," she said. "We are all in the hands of God."

"Your sister seemed so careful about locking doors that I wanted to be sure they were all——"

She smiled, and I noticed that her upper teeth were false. "Yes, we are careful in that regard, but not for our own protection."

There was nothing to say to that unless I wanted to turn childlike and shout, "Why, then?" The quiet assumed proportions as we stared at each other. Then her thin hand—the same hands that her sister had—came round the door and handed me a key.

"Let's each leave our key on the inside. Then whichever one of us has the bathroom can be assured of privacy. Good night."

I went back to sit on the edge of my bed and try to remember. When Effie had led me to this room had she had to unlock the door there that opened on the hall? I rather thought she had. And it seemed to me she had taken the key out of her pocket to do it. The key had not been in the outside of the lock. The door had been locked and the key in Effie's pocket! Then when she had gone into the room before me, turning on lights and giving the little tugs that pull a room to attention for company, hadn't she unlocked the bathroom door too, again with a key she carried? She had made little fussing motions near the door, but the room had been dim and I had paid small attention.

Well, grant that the two doors had been locked. And add to them the locked door on the other side of the bathroom. That meant that before my arrival Anne had needed three locked doors between herself and the rest of the house. Four, if you counted the one I had not yet seen, the door from her room to the hall outside. "We are careful, but not for our own protection." That was plain, simple maundering.

Outside my windows the night had come with an eerie half-light. Black, rolling clouds had smothered the last trace of color in the sky. Dimly I could see the big black trees wave and bow to the wind, and over there, where it looked as though the world had dropped away into thin gray air, was the great lake.

I unlocked the three windows and threw them open, and the rushing sound of the trees and the lake filled my room, ballooning the curtains and shaking the small crystal lamps on the lowboy. Directly below was the garden with its low stone parapet; that narrow edge of roof covered the screened veranda; that light must come from the living room downstairs. No one could see into my room unless he stood far out in the garden near the edge of the woods and craned his neck. Yet here I was, bundled into an uncomfortably warm robe which covered me from my neck to my heels.

Wooden doors were banging somewhere, and old Nathan came slowly around the corner of the house and followed the flagstoned

walk out of my sight. He did not look up. Presently the banging
stopped, and the wind and the trees and the lake had the stage to
themselves again. After you became accustomed to the heady movement of the elemental sounds you disregarded them, your mind refused to take them into full consciousness, and the place seemed very
quiet. Brandon Oaks was always very quiet. When I came back eight
years later the sounds of air and water thrilled me only for an hour
before they were shoved to the periphery of my mind and ticketed as
silence.

I unlocked the door for Mrs. Moss and my supper. She stayed
with me while I ate it, and when the wind shook the door slightly
and it swung open, she went over and closed it.

"The dogs have the run of the house," she said. "You don't want
them coming in here."

"I wouldn't mind. I like dogs."

"They're uncertain animals. Miss Effie is going to have to get rid
of them. She won't like it, either, because they're the last of the
strain her father bred. But they've killed I don't know how many of
Mr. Lucas' sheep. A sheep-killing dog's no good."

"They don't look at all vicious."

"No, they don't. They're nice as pie, gentle and obedient. It stands
to reason, though, that they've got a bad streak in them somewhere.
We keep them in the house most of the time. Shame, too. They love
to run."

"Miss Effie doesn't think they kill the sheep."

She sniffed. "There's not another dog for miles around, unless you
count those mangy Indian curs that slink around the beach. They're
little dogs, and the Indians keep them pretty close to home."

I locked the door after her, turned out the lights, and got into bed.
This was the moment I had been dreading all day, the time when
no practical daytime trivialities could hold off the realization of my
grief. It must have been very late when I finally slept. Once the
wind broke off bits of someone's voice and threw them in my window. "Terrible," the voice said, and "all we can" and "in the morning."

Toward dawn I half awoke. The door to the bathroom was shut,
and someone was moving beyond it. It sounded as though Anne were
taking a bath. I could hear the water running, and above that a low,

dreadful sobbing, not gusty or impassioned, but dreary and hopeless, as though it were a commonplace thing for the weeper.

"Someone is crying," I thought hazily. "Someone is crying terribly."

Reason, judgment were not awake. Exhaustion pressed me back into sleep before I could stir.

CHAPTER III

THAYER AND I went back into town the next morning to complete the arrangements for the funeral. We visited the undertaker's, and they took me in to look at Mother. After that I was no good to anyone any more, and Thayer sent me over to the hotel to pack my clothes. It was almost as bad there. Mother's things were still in the room: her white handkerchiefs stacked neatly in the corner of a drawer, her powder chamois—she always refused to use a puff—on the bureau, her dresses and shoes looking questioning and forlorn as I opened the closet door.

I don't see how people live through moments like that. Strictly speaking, I did *not* live for the next few days. My only thought was to put time behind me, to climb over the minutes, to shove the hours into the past, to keep my mind numb and formal. I packed all her belongings into two of the suitcases, and it was months before I dared to look at them again.

After all the harshness there was between us later, I am still grateful to Thayer for those few days. He paid all the bills, on the flimsy pretense that there would be a future business arrangement between us; he saw that there were flowers; he planned that the funeral service would be at the parlors the next morning and that the procession would then wind out to Brandon Oaks for the burial; he went through the legalities that are necessary before a body finds private interment; he secured the proper minister. In all this he gave no impression of magnanimity. He was simply doing the things that must be done on the behalf of a friend of his who was incapable of doing it for herself.

Looking back, I think that I was never in love with Thayer. If his kindness and courtesy and consideration had persisted, I might easily have been, despite the difference in our ages. Remembering him as he was that day, I forget about the erratic, violent man he became, through no fault of his own, but not through my fault either.

When we got back to the Oaks, Sergeant William Stark was on the veranda talking with Effie and Anne and Maggie. It was the first of so many visits that always followed the same pattern. The state police car would come down the sandy drive and stop at the door; William Stark, in uniform, big and rangy, would unfurl himself from the front seat, and the minute the heel of his black boot touched the porch, a tight constraint would settle down on the house: Effie would grow politely defiant; Maggie would dart like a hummingbird from unfinished task to unfinished task; Anne would sit white and rigid in her chair.

Today he was looking for a little girl, a Sue Kennedy, aged seven, who had been missing from home for almost twenty-four hours.

Effie knew no Kennedys.

"They're summer boarders with Mr. Lucas," Sergeant Stark said. "They came about a week ago. Sue got up early from a nap yesterday afternoon and slipped out of the house without anyone seeing her. She's the child we were hunting when we came by last night. She was crazy about the lake, but she was pretty sensible about it. Her mother doesn't think she would even go wading in it by herself. Of course there's no telling what kids will do, and it's natural that her mother would rather believe her lost than——"

Thayer broke in smoothly. "Have you been down to the Indian village, Stark? If they found a little girl, they'd be apt to take her in and they wouldn't tell anyone about it. They'd just wait till somebody came to find her."

"I was there first thing this morning. There are only ten houses and the church, and they let me look everywhere for a trace of her. She wasn't there, and I don't think she'd ever been there."

I came to with a start. "I saw a little girl. Yesterday afternoon at about five o'clock. She was skipping along the beach below me."

Yes, I thought her hair had been light. Yes, she might have been wearing a blue-and-white-checked pinafore. Yes, she had been alone. I hadn't noticed a hair ribbon.

Trooper Stark wanted to see the very spot where I had stood and looked down. Thayer went with us, across the warm, lush garden, into the talkative woods and, half a mile later, into the clearing with the white stones. I walked to the edge of the cliff.

"I stood here, and she was running along down there. She stopped once to play in the sand. I didn't see which way she went, but when I first saw her she was going that way."

"She was on her way home, then. The Lucas house is down that way, on past the Brandons' and down nearer the beach. The Indian village is the other way, where you see that spire. She probably didn't go down that far. Wait here for me, will you? I'm going down to see what I can see."

He was hardly out of sight over the steep bank when Thayer took my hands.

"I'm sorry about this. You're in no condition to go through all these questions. Let me tell Stark who you are and why you're here. He seems a decent fellow. He'd let up, I'm sure."

"It's no trouble to me. I'm glad to do it. Poor Mrs. Kennedy must be frantic with worry. Where could a child like that go, Thayer?"

"There isn't any place she could go. Stark knows that as well as anybody. Outside of the Indians, who are secretive but wouldn't hurt anybody, there isn't a house that wouldn't have reported finding her. We all have phones, and there aren't so many of us, at that, in the distance she could walk. The Warrens live a mile farther down past the church, and the Lucases half a mile beyond us the other way. There are houses up on the rise in back of us, but they're too far too."

"Maybe she came up the cliff and walked on back to the main road to town?"

"There aren't so many ways up the cliff for a little girl like that. The Indians have built a wooden ladder, but they'd see anyone who used it. We have a wooden steps that starts in our front yard and goes down. And the next way to get up is right by the Lucas house. No matter which way she used, somebody would have seen her."

I couldn't face the logical alternative. "She could be lost in the woods."

"Bless you, Elizabeth, these aren't woods. More like a park. The grass is tall, but there's very little underbrush. We've worn paths through them that even a little girl couldn't miss. No, only two things could have happened to her, and one of them didn't. If she had tried to climb up the embankment anywhere along, she might have fallen and hurt herself so that she couldn't move; in that case they'd have found her when they searched the beach last night. I think the lake got her. Grown people have been drowned around here, and Stark says the child was wild about the water."

The trooper was down on the beach, waving. "Whereabouts did she play in the sand?" he called.

I motioned him back and forth until he had reached the approximate place. He bent over the white sand, knelt in it, brushed it carefully.

"He won't find anything," said Thayer. "The lake was high last night. Every inch of that sand was covered."

I didn't want to look any more. If I had not been so taken up with my own misery the day before, I might have called to Sue. I might have helped her scramble up the cliff, and we could have walked home together and her mother would have been scoldingly glad to see us. And today she could have been down on the beach again, instead of a tall man in an official uniform who combed the sand and studied every move of the peaceful lake. I turned to the white stones.

"Who was Robert Warren? You said the Warrens lived up that way. Is this one of them buried here?"

"Yes. There were two brothers. This one married my sister Effie. He died before the baby came, and the baby lived only three days. Effie nearly died too. She's never been the same since. You should have known her when she was a girl—beautiful, spirited, proud, and capable of immense devotion. She could have married almost anyone, and God knows she had plenty of chances. This was only one of our summer houses then. We didn't spend one month of the year here. But after Mother and Father died and the money began to go, we sold everything else and moved up here. That was twenty years ago. It doesn't seem possible."

"And she met her husband here?"

"Yes. I never could understand it. He was kind and solid, but he wouldn't ever have set the world on fire. Wouldn't have wanted to. Effie, of us all, had the biggest pride in the family; the Brandon reputation was almost a religion with her. Still is. But she married this undistinguished gentleman after knowing him only six months. I didn't have any idea how much she had cared for him until I saw what she became after he was dead. All her youth and spirit went with him. Only the pride was left."

Sergeant Stark had begun to climb back to us. He was a powerful young man, and his grasping and swinging and pulling were effortless and graceful. Thayer watched him wryly.

"I can't do that any more," he said. "I don't think I ever did it that well. One flatters oneself that the proletariat may have the shoulders but the moneyed aristocracy has the brains. Then you turn around someday and find out that they have the brains too. It's discouraging."

The trooper was waving a small spade. "This is hers," he said. "It was wedged down there between three stones. I couldn't see the red tin pail anywhere. She had that with her too."

Thayer faced him directly. "You're not kidding yourself, are you, Stark? You know as well as I do that the little girl is drowned and that the body, chances are, will never show up. You've patrolled this neck of the woods long enough to know about Lake Michigan and what it's like when it's stormy."

The policeman was turning the toy spade over and over in his hands, studying it abstractedly. "Sure, I know," he said, "but also, Mr. Brandon, I know that if you could see the Kennedys you'd try to find some hope for them."

Thayer had begun to tremble a little. I could feel his arm quiver through his sleeve. He was as taut as an arrow at the bowstring.

"The Kennedys!" he said. "If they'd have kept proper watch on their daughter they wouldn't have to worry now. This riffraff comes up from the cities and rents a room with that skinflint Lucas and right away they own the lake. Then something like this happens and they go around wailing and peering and making you think it's your fault for being alive and that if you had scolded the lake when it was younger it wouldn't be so vicious now. What else do they expect when they let a child that young stay out on the beach after dark in a storm!"

The sudden spurt of words left the trooper imperturbable except for a faint contempt that wreathed itself around his mouth. I felt apologetic for Thayer. There had been no excuse, no provocation, for the trembling or the words.

"In the first place, Mr. Brandon," Stark said slowly, "the Kennedys aren't riffraff, even by your apparently exalted standards. He teaches English in a Detroit high school. His wife is an educated and *pleasant*"—he accented that—"woman. They have only the one child. I'm pretty sure none of them thought that they owned the lake, although I have met people—not summer visitors, either—who did think just that. In the second place, Mr. Lucas is not a skinflint. He's a hard-working farmer who has lived up here all his life and has managed—*out of his own efforts"*—the accent underlined the words again—"to build a large house for himself into which he is perfectly free to take paying guests if he likes. In the third place, the Kennedys did not purposely turn Sue out into the storm. She woke up from her nap and slipped out the back way. Yes, I'm afraid she's drowned. But she had been carefully schooled to stay away from the water unless someone was with her, and I'd like to bank, as long as I can, on the chance that the training held."

He strode on ahead of us, and by the time we reached the house again he had already driven away, Maggie waving at him politely and abortively from the porch. The sight of her seemed to be the last straw to Thayer. He walked off to his own house without a word.

Maggie fussed over me delightedly. Effie and Anne had driven into town, and Mrs. Moss had gone upstairs to lie down. Maggie shepherded me into the dining room, brought a salad and iced tea and rolls, and sat down opposite while I ate. She was a different person when none of the Brandons were present. It was only then that beneath her nervous bustling showed a calm poise, a congenial social manner, and even a sly and acute wit.

"What happened to Thayer?" she asked. "I've never known him so surly this early in the day." There was no harshness, no criticism in her voice. It was tolerant and factual.

"I think he was annoyed that the police were asking so many questions."

Maggie broke a roll and poured herself some tea. "Well, you can't blame him in a way. They've had the police here so many times. Not Sergeant Stark. He's new. But the police, anyway."

I sat back in the heavy carved chair and raised my chin to catch the cool breeze from the veranda. Outside Nathan was mowing the lawn. Through the windows the lake glinted and the hundreds of roses sent up their fragrance. There were bowls of them in the room: on the old mahogany table before me, on the long elaborate sideboard, on the tea table in front of the heavy silver service. The setting was dim and elegant, the characters—Maggie and I—commonplace. Yet all of it was firm lacquer over something tremulous, a veneer over a past that had died and was still putrefying noisomely. The police had been to Brandon Oaks many times before!

Munching and sipping, Maggie blinked at me like a cheerful little dormouse. "Oh, foolishly, you understand," she said. "I wouldn't want you to mention—to think that there had been anything wrong. There never was. And it's been a long while since the last time. Twelve years."

"What happened then?"

Maggie fumbled at a wrinkled package of cigarettes. "I don't smoke when They are home," she said, "and I suppose it looks silly, a woman of my age, but"—recklessly—"I enjoy it occasionally. Will you have one?"

Maggie was a poor smoker. She was conscious of the cigarette, fussed with it, took short puffs and brushed desperately at every falling ash, but the thrill of downtrodden Marjorie Mitchell smoking in the Brandon dining room sustained her, made a daring cosmopolite out of her.

"What happened twelve years ago?"

"Thayer's wife died. Seeing you reminded me of her. She was a pretty young thing too, with red hair, and they had been married such a little while. Her digestion was never good, she ate like a bird, and she had had colitis the winter before. Sick the whole time she was married, as a matter of fact. One night she had a worse spell than usual, and in an hour she was dead."

"Of what?"

"I don't remember what Dr. Day said it was. A long name for stomach trouble. Anyway, she had screamed out while she was dying, and sounds carry so far up here. The Lucases heard it and called the police, so they came. Dr. Day explained it all to them and they went away again. That was all."

"Does the doctor live near here?"

"No. He lives in Cleveland, but he visits here. He's an old friend of the family's. I think they sent for him to come and see if he could do anything for Alice—that was her name—but he was too late, of course. His father was physician to the elder Brandons, and he inherited the next generation. I don't like him myself. A forbidding, sharp kind of man."

"And before that when were the police here?"

Maggie squirmed uncomfortably. "I shouldn't be telling you all this ancient history. It's all past and gone. Effie will be furious, and it doesn't amount to anything anyway."

"It won't go any further."

She moved to a chair nearer me where, through the arch, she could keep an eye on the drive and the front door.

"The other time was four years before that when Robert Warren —he was Effie's husband—hanged himself in the barn."

The shock was as great as though she had suddenly slapped my face. "But I was told—I understood from something Thayer said— that they had been so happy together!"

"I thought so too, and no one ever knew what went wrong. You see, when we knew they were going to be married, the other house was built, and Thayer and Anne and I went to live in it. We saw a lot of them, naturally, but it isn't the same as when you're living under the same roof. There might have been—must have been— trouble of some kind, but we didn't know about it. I can remember the evening she came running up the drive to us, screaming. She had been hunting him to tell him that dinner was ready, and she had found him. Like a mad woman she was, and she was sick in bed for months after that. Wouldn't talk to any of us. Just turned her head to the wall and wouldn't eat or sleep. That's when Mrs. Moss came to us. She's had some nursing experience, and after Effie got well she stayed on as housekeeper."

Her small, flabby hand was cool and emphatic on my arm. I looked at the scratches on her paring finger, the burn, the two small cuts, the stains from weeding. "I think you're the real housekeeper here, Maggie."

She turned pink with pleasure. "I do my best. My heart isn't in it, though, I'm afraid. I'd rather be up in my room with a book. Aunt Anne—that's the children's mother"—Maggie constantly referred to Effie and Anne and Thayer as "the children," though two of them were older than she—"always used to say I was such a bookworm. 'If you can't find Maggie,' she'd say, 'look for the nearest book and she'll be behind it.' I didn't have the education the children had, but I love books."

"Wouldn't your aunt and uncle help you through school? Mother said they were very wealthy."

Maggie stood up and concentrated on removing the last trace of ash from the cloth. "They weren't really my aunt and uncle," she said. "Mr. Brandon adopted me out of an institution before I was three. Mrs. Brandon didn't want him to, and she never liked me. The children could see how their mother felt about me—and, well, you know how bullying and aggravating youngsters can be with a child they don't like."

"When you were old enough why didn't you find a job and get away?"

"I wasn't trained for anything, you see. Mr. Brandon was terribly nice to me, took me to Europe with the family and wanted me to have everything his own children had. But Aunt Anne had direct charge of us, and she saw to it that I was snubbed and left out and that my clothes weren't as nice as her daughters' and that the governesses slighted me." She brushed her eyes with the same handkerchief she had used to flick ashes. "Old as I am, I can't find it in my heart to forgive her. I wasn't an attractive child, and my health wasn't good until I was thirty, so I daresay she had some excuse for resenting me. She died when I was twenty-six, and I've just never had the gumption to get away."

"I would!" I said hotly. "I'd leave and I'd find a way to support myself, and I'd let them see how well they could get along without me!"

She was standing like an obsequious maidservant, holding the ash tray and a stack of dishes, but her face grew cheerful and animated. "Do you really think I could—at my age? I'm forty-five, you know, and I don't know anything but housework. I've already told you I'm not very good at that. I have a little money of my own. If I were to take a business course, for instance, would anyone hire me?"

I felt a qualm. She was so small and dumpy and earnest. "I think they would," I said firmly. "If a person is really good at something, he usually gets a chance to do it."

The gravel spatted as a car came up to the veranda steps. "I'll talk to you more about it later," she said, and ran out to the kitchen. There was a light crash, and I knew I would have to hold Effie off until Maggie had time to sweep up the pieces and hide them. If the casualty had been the Spode salad plate, there would be questions sooner or later, and I decided that if the matter came up I would say that I had broken it. In spirit I was already in conspiracy against the Brandons.

Effie came into the dining room lightly and quickly, before I could rise. She smiled coolly at me and began to set her packages down on the table. Poor Maggie! There were telltale smudges of ash there, and Effie saw them. For a moment she seemed to forget I was there. She looked toward the kitchen with an expression of the most acute hatred I have ever seen, a nasty half-smile, a so-you-think-you-have-fooled-me-you-loathsome-little-thing look. She put the last package down and faced me composedly.

"You've been talking to Maggie," she said. "I hope she gave you a nice lunch."

"A very nice lunch, thank you."

"I thought you would be longer with Thayer and Sergeant Stark. I meant to be back here before you. It was rude of me to be away."

"Not at all. Maggie looked after me."

"You must have found it tiresome. Maggie is hardly a conversationalist."

"I found her very interesting. We were talking about jobs."

She looked suddenly relieved and amiable. "Jobs! You must have been telling her your plans, then. Maggie has never done a decent day's work in her life."

I equivocated. "She said she wasn't good at housework, though she seems to do a great deal of it." I hoped my tone added, "While you play the fine lady."

"She does a great deal of it because she has to do everything three times: once wrong, once half right, and once right. But let's find a more comfortable place to talk, my dear. Where's Thayer?"

I told her he had gone to his house, and we crossed the hall on our way, I thought, to the living room. Suddenly she tugged at my arm and motioned me up the stairs. I followed her quietly up to my room, where I stood like a naughty schoolgirl while she closed my door and leaned against it.

"What I am going to say will sound strange to you, Elizabeth, but I can't help that. It must be said, and it cannot be explained. You will have to take my word for it. It's this. You must not become too intimate or friendly with anyone in this house. Like us if you can or will, but keep your distance from us, in public and in private. Don't confide in any of us. Don't link arms with us or pat our shoulders or be demonstrative in any way. You must take it for granted that we like you. You will have to believe that, without any outward display on our parts. With Thayer you may behave as you please, since he has seen fit——" She stopped and bit her lips. "I'm sorry," she said, and was gone. I could hear her going down the stairs, undoubtedly to find Maggie.

I locked the door after her. Already the habit was growing on me. It seemed natural to lock it, to me who had not locked a door in my life before I came to Brandon Oaks. I went into the bathroom and locked the door that led to Anne's room. Then I looked at my face in the bathroom mirror to see what the last eight hours had done to it.

Inwardly I was seething. Effie had made me sound like an over-enthusiastic puppy who had had to be rebuked. Try as I would, I could not think of a single instance when I had gushed or been offensively familiar. Did she think I was being so with Maggie, behind her back? I would be stiff and formal until after the funeral. Then I would leave—God knew where to, but I would not stay here.

I turned on the shower. The tub did not seem as immaculate as it might have been, and I got down to clean it. A few faint little ribbons of pink dissolved and ran clear. A few deep red specks rinsed away. I sat back on my heels with a jerk. Blood! I was washing away blood! Here was a spatter on the tile, and here was another toward Anne's door, and up there on the molding was a smudge of it. The room dimmed and receded and came back again, and I was kneeling with my forehead against the cool rim of the tub.

This was not the time to be silly and melodramatic. Anne had hurt herself—her hand, I judged by the smudge on the molding—and had let the water from the shower run over it. The night before, of course, when she had been crying! Anne would cry easily, gentle, middle-aged infant that she was. I ignored the facts that she had not mentioned hurting herself and that I had not seen the trace of a bandage that day.

My mind formulated it into a primer-simple formula: Anne hurt her hand; she washed it; the pain made her cry.

That was logical, and that I would believe. I washed the last bloodstain away.

CHAPTER IV

MOTHER WAS BURIED the next afternoon. Only two cars followed the hearse out from Harbor Springs: Thayer and I and the minister in the first; Effie and Anne and Maggie in the second. Only the five of us stood in the sunny clearing while the Reverend Loring spoke gently on the transience of man and the infinity of divine goodness. I did not want to turn away when the others did. I had the feeling, which I suppose many others have had, that the beloved dust might wake and find itself strangely lonely in this new place and that I should be there to explain and comfort. I walked back to the house between Thayer and the minister, went up to my room, locked the door, and lay quietly on the bed for a long time.

It was almost dusk when I began to pack. I had no idea where I would go, but I could not stay and feel myself a kindly borne burden in this house. The first thing next morning Nathan could drive me into Harbor Springs, and I would go on from there by myself. I had three hundred dollars: two hundred I would leave for Thayer with a request that he let me know the full extent of my indebtedness; the other hundred would have to last me until I found a job.

When I went down it was dark and they were sitting on the veranda. They rose, they spoke gently, they were thoughtful, they hoped I would not be ill, they had saved a supper for me. Yet, with the exception of Thayer's taking my hand, no one touched me. I am not gushy, and I particularly dislike being handled casually. Though I was eight years younger then and rather remote, I knew that under the same circumstances most women would have patted an arm or put a hand on my shoulder. "You must not become too intimate or friendly with anyone in this house."

Maggie went in to set the table for my supper in the dining room. "It's a cool evening. Shall I make coffee for all of us?"

"You make abominable coffee, Maggie, as well you know," Effie said. "I'll make the coffee. Thayer, run down and see that the barn is shut up properly. Nathan may be in town until late, and I don't propose to have any of those Indians snooping into our things."

I was left alone with Anne. "Barn?" I said.

"You haven't seen it. It's down that way. It isn't a big one. Father used to keep his horses there, but we have no horses now. We've made the second floor into living space for Nathan."

"I wondered where he stayed."

We were quiet. The breeze from the lake was blowing stiffly now, and out in the dark the trees rustled and a windy moon was rising.

"You must not feel that your mother is gone forever, Elizabeth," Anne said. "The dead are with us always, as living presences. I learned that a long time ago, and I have talked to Father and Mother many times. It's a great comfort to me."

The nape of my neck prickled suddenly. "I'm sure it must be," I said politely.

"Of course you must Believe. That's the hard part. And it will be harder for you because you are young and your life will be full of interesting diversions and a variety of people who will seek to enlist you in their worldly pursuits. I suppose that Faith comes easiest to those who find little in humanity to love and trust."

"My faith might be very different from yours."

"Yes. Perhaps each of us is driven to the kind of faith we need. Father and Mother were my world. While they were alive they kept a golden enchantment around us. It spoiled me for facing the bleakness after they were gone."

"They made you too dependent on them."

"In a way. They were a fortress, as all parents are, against trouble and time. My father was a big, hearty man with a laugh that could shake the house. He would have faced the devil himself to get whatever he really wanted, but he was kind and generous too. Mother was very much in love with him. She was good to us children, but her first devotion was to him. She might have been a little jealous of us if she had thought that Father liked us too well, but he was hardly ever with us. Restless, you know, and full of boundless ideas. We worshiped both of them as if they were demigods."

"They both died in the same year."

"Yes. They were killed in an accident. We were too young and too inexperienced to hold the empire together, so it crumbled. And now we are three middle-aged relics brooding on a past glory. You don't find it pleasant here, Elizabeth."

"It has been wonderfully kind of you to have me here at all. I don't know just why you have."

"Thayer wants to marry you."

"That's absurd of him. He doesn't know me."

"From the first time he saw you he has talked of nothing else. I think it must be because you are very like Alice was." Her voice fell to a musing half-tone. "That, of course, makes it worse than ever."

Headlights came round the corner of the house, and the police car stopped at the steps.

Anne went to open the screen door. "Sergeant Stark," she said loudly and clearly. "It's late for official callers."

"I thought I might get a chance to speak to Miss Elizabeth," he said. "I see that she's downstairs now." He came over to my chair, his heavy black boots shaking the old flooring. "I know it's almost unpardonable for me to intrude at such a time. Believe me, I wouldn't have come to see you twice on such a day if it hadn't been important."

Anne gave me a frantic look and rallied her forces. "She was in no condition to talk to you earlier," she said.

"So I was given to understand. I thought it possible that she might be composed more now."

Effie spoke sharply from the lighted doorway. "She's going to have her supper now. Really, Sergeant, this is ruthless of you."

"I don't mind," I said meekly. "I'll talk to him."

"As you wish," she said briefly. "I daresay he won't object to your eating while you talk. The two of you can have the dining room to yourselves. The rest of us will have our coffee out here."

Maggie fluttered into the light. "Shall I pour a cup for Mr. Stark too?"

"I suppose so." Effie was grudging but polite. "I don't know much about your routine, Mr. Stark. Have you had dinner?"

"Yes, thank you. Just coffee will be fine."

There was an odd expression on Effie's face as we passed her by in the doorway, a grim, reluctant smile, the look a strong person might give to an objectionable but respected adversary. The sergeant had certainly won his point.

The dining room was lighted with six candles in two silver candelabra. The large blue bowls held fresh roses, and on the sideboard in a vase were towering spikes of white and orange lilies. My place was set at the head, and the trooper sat down beside me. Maggie

rushed at us with cold meat, sliced tomatoes, lettuce, bread and but-
ter, and angel-food cake.

"If you'd like some of this, Mr. Stark, I can get you a plate in a
minute."

"No, thank you, Miss Maggie. Run along now, like a good girl."

Her exit toward the porch was a blushing sidle.

I found that I was hungry, but I wanted to be helpful too. "What
do you want to talk to me about?"

"Time enough after you've eaten. If what they've been telling me
around here is true, you haven't eaten since breakfast."

"That's true."

"Did anyone come up to you at five o'clock and tell you I wanted
to see you?"

I quibbled. "I might not have heard them."

He grinned. "I thought as much. They're a stubborn outfit. Nice
as pie, but they'll have their own way just the same. What's their
connection with you?"

"There isn't any, really. I met them only the day before Mother
died. They knew I was stranded and they took me in."

"They have the reputation in these parts of people who like to be
left strictly alone. Unusual, isn't it, that they should have gone so
far out of their way for you?"

I couldn't say that Thayer thought he was in love with me and
that his sisters were being nice about it. "It's very generous of
them."

He drank his coffee, pushed the cup away from him, and sat staring at the candles. He was nice-looking in a Roman-gladiator sort
of way.

"I didn't know policemen were like you," I said.

He laughed. "Oh, I'm the newfangled kind of policeman. Went
to the state university and took courses in it. I not only know about
guns and bullets and fingerprints, they beat some literature and
psychology into me too. The literature didn't hurt me, but I wish I
hadn't taken the psychology."

"Why?"

"Because sooner or later I was bound to meet people like the
Brandons, and there are only two ways to deal with a bunch like
that. Either you take them at their face value and believe what they
tell you and not try to peer over the wall, or you chart the under-

currents and end up by understanding what makes them tick. I'm not dumb enough for the first or smart enough for the second. There's something very wrong with them, you know."

I didn't say anything, and he watched me like a big tawny cat eying a confiding mouse.

"You do know," he repeated.

"They're—they're not like other people."

"That's a classic understatement."

I was glad that I had finished eating. This man had a confident warmth and strength that invited shoulder-weeping and trouble-telling. I had difficulty keeping Anne's crying and the locked doors and Effie's strange advice to myself.

"You haven't found Sue Kennedy?"

"No," he said curtly. He got up and went out to the kitchen and came back and went out into the hall. "They're all out on the porch, all right. I wanted to be sure. When are you leaving?"

"Tomorrow morning."

"Have you told them?"

"I was just going to when you came."

"Good. Now as I understand it from the hotel manager, you haven't any definite plans for a while. Would you be willing to stay on here a while longer? They've asked you to, haven't they?"

"I don't think they would object, but——"

"You don't want to. But suppose I put it that you'd be doing the state a favor. What about it then?"

"I don't see how my staying——"

"I'll tell you. I don't think Sue Kennedy was drowned. She was a bright little kid for her age and well trained and obedient. She knew the lake was dangerous for her when she was alone, and she wasn't going near the water when you saw her. She was playing on the sand. Now if she isn't in the lake, somebody knows where she is, and the people in this house are our best bet. They're not going to tell us and they're not going to tell you. But you might notice something that would give us a clue. Mind you, I have no hope of saving the little girl. I think she's dead. To put it in a nutshell, I think she died accidentally, that the Brandons know about it, and that, not being able to bring her back to life, they see no reason why they shouldn't do everything in their power to avoid publicity about it."

"Maggie knows everything that goes on here. She could tell you what you want to know."

"I haven't a doubt that she could. But she won't. I've given her plenty of chance. She loosens up for a while, and just when I think everything is going merry as a wedding bell she closes up on me. She's scared to death of something."

"Effie's had her under her thumb for forty years."

"You're not under Miss Effie's thumb. That's why I'd like you to stay here."

"I couldn't stay here and spy on them."

He sighed and tilted back in his chair. "All right, then. Let's put it this way. Stay, and if you happen to notice anything you think might interest me and that wouldn't interfere with your scruples, let me know."

"I could do that, I guess. For a week."

He lowered his chair gently. "Don't be lavish," he said. "Thanks for that much, anyhow."

I walked with him to the porch. Thayer had come back, and the farewells were subdued. As the police car drove away someone gave a long sigh in the darkness.

"How foolish!" said Effie sharply, and there was quiet again.

Thayer said that it was only ten o'clock and that I hadn't seen his house yet. Wouldn't I care to come with him for an hour?

"I think that, under the circumstances, it will be perfectly correct," he said in his courtly way. "We can take a dragon along with us if you insist."

Maggie looked hopeful, but in the end the two of us walked back the sandy drive alone. Thayer had a flashlight and was very solicitous about my footing.

"Stark is getting a bit above himself," he said, "forcing himself on us to ask you questions about an accident you couldn't possibly know anything about!"

"I didn't mind. He was nice about it."

"He'd better not be anything else!"

Out of the darkness to our left came a throat-rending howl. I clutched Thayer's arm.

"It's only the dogs," he said. "We've kept them locked up lately, and they love to run. It's breaking their hearts."

"Are they vicious, Thayer?"

"Boris and Duke? Two milder animals never lived."

"Except for sheep."

We were climbing his front steps now, and a light from his living room picked up the annoyance on his face.

"If you will," he said. "Personally I'm inclined to think that Mr. Lucas is killing his sheep himself and charging them up to us. Here we are."

Architecturally the house was much like the other one. The furnishings, however, were more modern and less worn and there was an exciting note of gaiety about them. A tremendous pink velvet pouf in front of the fireplace, for instance. A dainty rosewood piano. Trim wing-backed chairs in a colorful print. The rugs were broadloom from baseboard to baseboard. The other house had big Orientals thrown on waxed floors.

"It's lovely, Thayer."

It was the best I could do to express the feeling of relief the room gave me. It was not overwhelming or grand or pretentious. The tight expectancy that lay over the other house was absent here.

He beamed. "I thought you'd like it," he said. "Sit down over there and I'll bring some coffee. You couldn't have enjoyed yours before with that Gargantua hanging over you. Will you have a cigarette?"

"I'd like one. I don't smoke down at the other house, of course."

"Why not?"

"I thought your sister objected to smoking."

"I can't imagine why you would think that. They've both been known to smoke on occasion, and my mother did, long before it was fashionable."

"Something just made me think so," I said lamely.

"Well, you must smoke whenever you like. We want to make it pleasant for you here." He pressed my hand. "So pleasant that you will never want to leave us."

He went for the coffee, and I sat back and tried to figure out what there was about this room that raised my spirits so phenomenally. It wasn't only the colors, and the modernity of the furniture. The room sparkled and was alive.

Perhaps that was due to the lack of photographs. In the other house there were hundreds of them, lining the walls, frame to frame, from the upper molding to within two feet of the floor. They climbed up on tables and prevailed upon every flat surface. Faces of forty years before stared out above the writing that sometimes crouched in an obscure corner and sometimes dashingly covered half the picture. People who had been authors or musicians or actors or poets or royalty, all with a tender or admiring word for the Brandons. And because most of these people were now dead, or at least old, it was sad to contemplate them in their vigorous and famous heyday with their queer coiffures and their old-fashioned clothes.

In this room there was but one picture. It hung over the davenport, and it, too, was a photograph—in color: the profile of a lovely young woman with red hair in demure coronet braids. The head tilted back on the slender neck and she smiled up into an unseen light. By any standards, in any era, she would have been a beauty, and not in the careless sense in which the word is used today. Besides the fine texture of the skin, the gold overlights on the hair, the perfection of the nose, the connotation was of poise, of sweetness, of a young dignity that hinted at a future stateliness.

Thayer put the coffee tray down before me and gave me my cup.

"I debated taking that picture down before you came," he said. "That was my wife, Alice."

"She was beautiful. You must have cared for her very much."

"I thought I did. It's hard to remember now. She's been dead twelve years." He filled his own cup, sat down on the pouf, and stared reminiscently at the picture. "I can remember the first time I saw her. It was in New York in 1917, and she was only fifteen then, the younger sister of a girl I was taking around. Even then you could see what she was going to be, and though I was thirteen years older than she I decided to wait and see if she'd have me. We were married when she was nineteen, and she was dead within the year."

"Of what did she die?"

He leaned over to help himself to the cream, and I could not see his face. "Stomach ulcer. No one had suspected it was there, but the lining of the stomach was pierced and peritonitis set in. Dr. Day said it would have been a miracle had she lived."

I had no thought other than consoling him, but I made a mistake. "It's seldom you hear of stomach ulcers in so young a person," I said.

He looked at me quickly, and his voice was sharp when he spoke. "She had one," he said defiantly.

I drank my coffee in silence. The tenseness that belonged to the other house had begun to seep in faintly here too, like a white mist swirling about my ankles. Presently it would rise to my throat and choke off all the natural things I might say.

He went on more pleasantly. "She chose the furniture for the house. Everything here is as she left it. We can change anything you don't like, though we can't be extravagant. I have an income of about four thousand a year, and I own this house. You could be comfortable, Elizabeth."

I had had no experience with men; I had not had a proposal before; I was too young to know what to do without seeming impolite.

"We hardly know each other, Thayer."

He put his cup down and took mine away from me. Then he leaned forward, holding my hands, his brown, distinguished face only inches from mine.

"I have always known what I wanted the first minute I saw it," he said. "We wouldn't have to stay here the year round. We could travel a little. Where would you like to go for a honeymoon? It's hot for New York. Quebec would be better for this time of year. We'd have a grand time."

His hands were warm and persuasive on mine, and his amber eyes were intense. "Am I too old for you, my dear?"

"I don't think of you as being older."

"That's good. That's the main thing. I've been telling myself that it wouldn't be fair to hurry you into marriage with a man old enough to be your father. But then again, you're young and alone. You have no place to go. You need an anchor, a foothold. And I— I'm so terribly lonely, Elizabeth."

"I wish Mother were here," I said childishly, and began to cry.

He sat back immediately. "I'm a brute," he said. "I shouldn't have brought this up tonight. Time's so short, though, and I have a dreadful premonition that you'll whisk yourself away and that I'll never be able to find you again. You'll think about it, anyway, won't you? And you won't go away without giving me a chance?"

Faintly I could hear the dogs howling. "I can promise that, Thayer."

"Good!" he said.

He took me through the rest of the house. There was a white-paneled dining room with a Duncan Phyfe table; a large kitchen; a pantry on whose glassed-in shelves shone rock-crystal and china and sterling services; a large library downstairs; a smaller library up-stairs; and five bedrooms, only one of which was kept open.

"I'm my own housekeeper," he said, "and there's a little too much here for one man to handle. Anne or Mrs. Moss give me a hand once a week, and sometimes I'm not here for ten minutes out of the day. I'm afraid I've turned into a bit of a fussy old bachelor."

He was so eager to please, so anxious to show me his treasures, that I smiled more warmly than I had meant. "You do very well," I said.

For a moment I thought he was going to kiss me, and I was in two minds about that. I didn't want to be too encouraging, but it might be exciting. The moment passed, and he walked me home sedately and gave me his flashlight on the front steps of the other house.

"You can light your way upstairs without having to find light switches," he said. "Good night, dear."

I went up to my room and locked the door. I was feeling kindled and ravishing, like the heroine of a movie. I did not turn on the lights. I went to stand by the windows where the moonlight was streaming in. Through the trees and down the cliff I could see the beach, white as paper in the brightness.

Far down on that whiteness something moved. Someone was walking along the beach. At first I thought it was Thayer. Then I saw skirts blowing, and I knew it was a woman. I could not make out what she was doing. She would walk a few steps and then crouch down, and once she crawled on her hands and knees for a few yards. Perhaps one of the women of the house had gone for a moonlight stroll and had hurt herself and could not get back to the cliff.

I took the flashlight and left the house quietly. I found the place where the winding rustic steps left the lawn and I followed them down and down until I was above, but only yards away from, the black figure.

It was Anne and she wasn't hurt. She had not seen my light, so I turned it off and stood there watching her. She was evidently looking for something, and she was crying as she did it, and talking to herself.

"Oh God," she said over and over again. "Oh God."

Her face was contorted grotesquely, and she bent and walked and crawled like someone bereft. I was afraid to talk to her. I was afraid to go back up all those dark steps, but I did. I ran across the lawn and back to my room. I turned the key again and leaned panting against the wall. What I needed was Mother, who had expected nothing but the commonplace and ordinary from the world and who had had the magic faculty of turning everything into one of those two categories.

"Why, Miss Brandon was just looking for something she had lost," Mother would have said, "and she was crying because it was valuable or because she was afraid to be down there alone at that time of night, and I don't blame her. She had a great deal of courage to do it. We'll mention it in the morning and she'll explain. Now go to bed, Elizabeth, and don't be a silly child."

I went to bed, but again I tossed and turned for hours. I heard Anne come creeping up the stairs and go into her room, and I heard her voice and Effie's. Anne was still crying.

"I can't help myself," she was saying. "I have to do it. I can't help it."

I could not hear all that her sister answered. I caught "police snooping around" and "all these years" and "dangerous" and then, roughly, "asylum."

The sobs and voices subsided, and I finally slept.

CHAPTER V

AT THE BREAKFAST TABLE Anne was much the same as ever. Her full, pale, sensitive lips quivered occasionally, and she kept her eyes on her plate, raising them only when she was directly addressed.

Effie, though, was in much better temper than usual. She smiled often, asked with interest how I had liked the other house, and took me into the household by graciously wondering whether I would take upon myself the daily chore of filling the vases. I accepted eagerly, and Maggie's pathetic little company smile vanished. I guessed it was a task she had asked for once and been refused.

"You can help me, Maggie," I whispered to her as she began to clear the table.

She picked up my cup stolidly. "I'm not allowed to set foot in the garden or touch the vases."

I went out and found Effie sewing on the front porch.

"I noticed Maggie's face when you spoke about the flowers," I said. "I think she'd like to help me."

The fine white hands poised a needle and sought it with a thread. Effie's head was thrown back, her eyes half closed, her underlip caught between her teeth. The thread went through the eye smoothly and accurately.

"I'd rather she didn't, Elizabeth. She doesn't know a rose from a hollyhock, and she's so awkward that she tramples over everything. Once we set aside a corner for her to plant as she wanted, and I wish you could have seen it! Nothing came up but dandelions and sunflowers."

It was no use. I started off for my walk. Sorry and depressed and anxious to be alone.

The garden had been planned to serve both the houses and lay between them along one side of the drive. You could see Thayer's house through the trees, and I hurried lest he catch sight of me. The day was cool and sunny; the lake moved in small white waves; the air was brisk. I hurried past the roses and delphinium, through the woods, and out into the little cemetery. Someone had been there before me. Some of the funeral flowers had been removed—the faded ones, I suppose—and someone had laid an armful of white roses on Mother's grave. They were so fresh that the dew was still on them, but so badly, so hurriedly arranged that I knew they must come from Maggie. She must have stolen into forbidden ground before the sun was up, risked a tongue-lashing by cutting dozens of a cherished rose, run out while she was helping Mrs. Moss get breakfast, all because she had known that I would be coming here and that newly turned clay and wilted flowers would have made me feel worse than I did. So she had done her unskillful best, and I was touched and grateful.

The sun was much higher when I left the clearing, but I didn't want to go back to the house. Instead I took the way down the cliff that Sergeant Stark had taken. I arrived on the beach scuffed and torn and breathless and started down toward the church spire. I wanted to see the Indian village.

The sand was hot and firm under my feet; the sun warmed my back; the lake murmured restlessly at my side; the wind whipped my hair straight back. For the first time in four days I felt warmth creeping back into my blood, and the half-mile walk seemed very short. All of a sudden I was upon it. Ten small wooden houses, un-painted, huddled together, with the white sand serving as a road between them and the lake. The square white wooden church with its lovely spire stood a little apart, closer to the water. Beside it was a little fenced-in space where gravestones tilted crazily and weeds grew high.

I think there must have been a hundred Indians moving about the village when I first caught sight of it: black-eyed women moving with a slow grace and smiling; fat, chubby babies sitting stolidly on the sand in the sun, engaged in the solemn business of trying to put the beach into a bucket; older children, slimming out with growth, running and calling and making their dogs wild with barking. In the next instant they were gone, and as I walked past the houses there was not a woman, not a child, not a dog. The dilapidated houses looked at me blankly and silently, even though I knew that in each one there was at least one woman and several children and a dog.

I had meant to spend a little time at the church, but now I felt that I was an intruder. I would not keep these people shut up in their houses for long on such a lovely morning. I would simply walk in, take a look around, and go back the way I had come.

The church door was open, and when I stepped inside I was sur-prised. The village might be rickety, but the church was not. The floors were wood scrubbed white. The pews were plain wood, but solid. A hundred people could be seated there. A jewellike red lamp burned before the altar and several candles guttered in a low bracket at one side. There was a statue of Christ holding out his hands with the marks of the nails on them and one of the gentle Mary in a blue robe. Three walls were blank, but the third held a large stained-glass window through which the sun came only as blobs of blue and green and red. The writing on the bottom pane said: "This window given in gratitude by Margaret Thayer—1889." The place was dim and cool and smelled of incense.

Outside there was not a sound. The village held its breath and stilled its children's cries while a white alien walked heavily and awkwardly in its most cherished place. A bit of blue ribbon lay in the corner by the door. Because the floor was so neat otherwise, I picked it up and shoved it in my pocket. I went quickly out the door into the sunshine, past the quiet houses, and around the curve of the sand out of sight. Faintly behind me I could hear the laughter and talk spring up again, the shouts of children and the barking of dogs.

Sergeant Stark was sitting on a white stone under a crooked pine.

"Saw you go in," he said. "Knew you wouldn't be long coming out. I'll walk back with you."

"Are they always that way? Do they vanish like that for you?"

"Especially for me. The men hunt out of season, you see, and to them a uniform spells trouble. We've not been hard on them. I guess old Mr. Lucas comes and goes as he pleases. They like him and trust him. He's gone bail for some of them at one time or another, and I will say one thing: they remember favors a long time, longer than white people do."

"They seem to be so dreadfully poor."

"They are. I know the state tries to look after them, and the padre comes over to teach the children. They're the last remnant of one of the most warlike tribes of the North. A long time ago their forefathers had it out with the whites on this very beach. This whole area was a battleground, and it was soaked red. The Indians lost out at the last. They always did. But this bunch is cleaner and healthier than any other group of red men you could find."

"You like them."

"I like them better than that white outfit you live with. When an Indian wants to hide from you, he goes in his house; when a Brandon wants to hide, his body stays right there and the rest of him goes away. I'm too simple a man to care for that kind of psychological hocus-pocus."

I kicked at a stone. "Anne was looking for something on the beach late last night."

"Whereabouts?"

"Down here at the foot of their steps. I don't think she found it."

"I'll come down later and look. Too many people apt to be around now. That gardener has eyes in the back of his head."

"Oh, and I found this in the church." I handed him the bit of ribbon ceremoniously.

He took it and stood still. "You found this where?"

"In the church. In the corner by the door. Surely it isn't important."

"It's a piece of Sue Kennedy's hair ribbon."

"Then she had been down to the village!"

"At least I'm supposed to think so. That ribbon hasn't been there before today—that I'll swear."

We began to walk again. "Do you think that Anne——"

"No. She's afraid of Indians, and, strangely enough, so is Miss Effie. They wouldn't come down here on a bet."

"I don't think Effie is afraid of anything."

He shrugged. "You could be right."

"Does the ribbon mean anything?"

"It means one of several things. This ribbon hasn't been in the water, so either she wasn't drowned or she lost the ribbon beforehand. Somebody found it somewhere—that's obvious. As to why they cut off this piece and left it in the church, I can't say."

"To make it look as though the Indians knew something about it?"

"Anybody who knows what's been going on knows that the church was searched the first day she was missing and that we'd know this clue wasn't bona fide."

"An outsider wouldn't know."

"No outsiders are involved in this. It would be someone we know. It's my business to know about strangers. There haven't been any around."

"It seems silly to go about leaving bits of ribbon that don't mean anything to anybody."

"I think somebody knows more than they're telling and wants to give us a lead without coming right out with their story. Things like this make the police look harder, on general suspicion."

"Do you think we'll find more of them?"

"They won't mean anything unless we can find out who's scattering them around and why."

He left me at the foot of the stairs going up the cliff, and I did not see him again for three weeks. He told me, much later, that he had repeatedly asked for me at the house only to be told blandly that I was sleeping or out.

The days went by quietly, and I waited still for the letter from a little town that wanted a teacher. There was not much time. July was almost gone, and since I had not left immediately after the funeral, I had no excuse for leaving now. I saw very little of Maggie. Effie and Anne had their own routines, and I met them at mealtime. Thayer I saw every evening. Sometimes he walked with me when I took flowers to Mother's grave. Often we sat in his living room and had coffee. Suddenly the roses were thinning and I was filling the vases with early asters and chrysanthemums. The time for flight was almost run out.

One hot afternoon I did a forbidden thing. I took my bathing suit, hid it in my knitting bag, and went down to the beach. I walked for a mile on the sand, the other way from the Indian village, before I felt safe enough to climb into a nest of big stones and put on the suit. For an hour I swam and splashed and let Lake Michigan tumble me, and I climbed out waterlogged but exhilarated. An elderly man in overalls was sitting on the sand, chewing on a straw.

"Now that I see who you are, it's all right," he said. "Came down to see who was trespassing on my property. You're the girl who's staying at the Brandons'. I'm Jed Lucas."

"I'm sorry to be trespassing. I didn't know——"

"Perfectly all right. It's a big lake. I'm just wondering why, when the Brandons own the biggest stretch of beach along here, you should come down this far to swim."

"I—— Well, none of them go in swimming."

"I know that."

"I—I just feel queer about it."

He was silent, and I began to despair of getting my hair dry and my dress back on before dinnertime.

"I guess one thing's as easy to understand as the other," he said. "The Brandons used to be great hands for the water. The old man, he'd drive a horse in and splash around and laugh like a crazy man. All the kids went in too. Now all of a sudden they don't. Haven't for years. Set down."

"I have to be back by six o'clock."

He cocked an eye at the sun. "It's only about five now," he said. I sat down obediently.

"They're keeping the dogs locked up," he said.

"Yes, they are. I hope your sheep——"

"Right now they're doing fine. Sorry about your mother."

"Thank you."

"From what I can make out from the people in town, she was a fine woman. Too good to be resting next to the heathen. Old Mr. Brandon and his wife were cremated, you know."

"I didn't know. I don't object, though."

"Well, I don't hold with it. Seems a strange way for a Christian to want to be buried—just a handful of ashes. Course I might be doing them an injustice. They might have been pretty badly marked from the accident. Then again, I heard it was done by his own request, and he couldn't have known he was going to be having that accident, now, could he?"

"What sort of accident was it?"

"Automobile. He and she was out driving their car. Not around here, you understand. Down in Florida somewheres. Something went wrong with the steering wheel; the thing crashed, and they were both dead when they pulled them out."

"How dreadful!"

"Well, I don't know. They'd had a lot out of life. Now you take this little girl that got herself drowned a little while ago. She had all hers before her. That's worse yet."

"Have her father and mother gone home?"

"Left this morning. The mother still won't give up hoping, though it stands to reason the little girl's dead by now, whether she went in the lake or lost herself in the woods. I was sorry for them, I can tell you."

He got up suddenly. "Any time you want to come down here to swim, it's all right with me. You can change your clothes at my house, if you want. My old woman'll look after you."

I ran all the way home, hoping to slip upstairs and arrange my hair, but when I got to the porch Effie was standing there.

"I've been looking for you," she said. "You've been swimming."

"Yes, I—— Down at Lucases'."

"Nathan will drive you to the public beach next time."

I was a guest in her house; I was accepting her food; I did nothing in return.

"Very well."

There was no more swimming that summer. The whole thing seemed so odd to me that I spoke of it to Thayer.

"They're nervous about your going in alone," he said, "and there's nobody here to go in with you."

Which was such a poor and oblique answer that I did not push the matter.

Then a letter did come for me, but it was the wrong letter. The hotel in Harbor Springs was forwarding my mail to rural delivery;

it was left in one of the two white mailboxes way down at the road, and Thayer picked it up once a day. This was from the dean of women at the university.

DEAR ELIZABETH,

The papers here carried an account of your mother's sudden death, and all your friends on the faculty were grieved for you. We thought, perhaps, that the funeral would be here and that we would have a chance to express our sympathy, but I can understand that you might have decided against that because of the length of the trip and financial complications.

I had hoped by this time to have news of some opening in the state for your teaching. Nothing has appeared, and I am afraid we must assume that nothing will, unless some contracted teacher falls ill or changes her mind at the last minute. It may be that some board has communicated directly to you. I pray that this may be so, but the year is a bad one for new teachers. While the universities have been busy turning out new teaching personnel, the schools have had to retrench. Perhaps you will have to do some other kind of work for a while, and this will be especially hard on you, for you are much younger than most of our graduates and you have no family to see you through the first hard year of adjustment.

Consider us your family, Elizabeth. Let us know what plans you are making, and, if you need a helping hand, let us know. Have no compunction about turning to us, my dear. Your father was one of us, and the university is mindful of its own.

Affectionately,
SARAH WILSON

Pride is an extravagance that Youth can ill afford; yet it is Youth who most often digs deep for a last coin and throws it down as if it were a trifle. I did that now. I could not go creeping back to the university to be my father's daughter, to take kindness and grade themes and help in laboratories, or do the small scholastic jobs they would have to rack their brains to find for me.

I walked out to the cemetery. In the past month I had worn a path of my own through the woods, and I was so familiar with each stone, each blade of grass, each tree that I could have walked it with my eyes shut. I sat down, and my thoughts came like spoken words, clear and terse.

"Well, it's done. No use hoping any more. There's a year ahead I don't know what to do with. I could clerk in a store. I could be a cashier at a theater. I could take care of someone's children. All jobs that unskilled people can hold, so they won't pay well. I'll have to live in some little furnished room, and I'm afraid. I don't know anything about people, except young ones, or students or teachers. I wouldn't know how to get along with them; they know so much more than I about the practical side of living; they seem so sure of themselves when I see them on the street; they know just what they're doing and where they're going. I can't face it. I'm not ready to be on my own yet. I need time.

"I can marry Thayer. I like him. He's handsome and friendly and considerate. I don't feel about him the way the girls in the movies seem to feel about men, but I don't notice that married people feel that way either. If they do they don't show it. He's quite a bit older than I am, but I get along better with older people. I've always been with them more, and they give me the confidence I don't have. I wouldn't mind if he kissed me. I don't know whether that's love or not.

"His sisters are peculiar, but he says they won't bother us. When Alice was alive they came to the house only when they were invited. I wouldn't mind that. They're intelligent—and nice some of the time—and we wouldn't be here always."

After eight years I can still remember how I figured it out that day, and I know now that I was a coward and rationalizing to cover it.

Below me on the beach Effie went by, the two wolfhounds racing and jumping around her. When I turned from watching them out of sight, a tall brown man with white hair and a smooth face was standing by one of the stones.

"Don't be frightened," he said. "I'm Dan Warren. This is my brother's grave."

"I—I didn't see you come."

"We live down that way. Anne has told me—you're Miss Elizabeth."

"Yes." I was uneasy. He had come so quietly. "I must be getting back."

"No hurry. How is everyone at the house?"

"Very well. You—you could come back with me. They'd be glad to see you. We don't have many callers."

He smiled. "They wouldn't be glad to see me," he said. "As a matter of fact, I was forbidden the house years ago by my brother's wife. Occasionally I see Anne in the stores in town. I wanted to marry her once."

The subject of marriage was interesting to me that day.

"Why didn't you?" I meant no impertinence. I wanted to know very badly some reasons why people married or why they didn't.

He rubbed his chin musingly. "I don't really know. I meant to, and she never definitely refused me. I flatter myself that she liked me. I met her for the first time the day my brother married Effie. I was best man and she was bridesmaid, a lovely, dark, slender girl —timid and gentle, too, which I hadn't expected in a rich man's daughter.

"Well, I courted her off and on, whenever I could get away from my business in Detroit. There was something wrong about the courting, too, but I couldn't put my finger on it. She liked to have me there, I'll swear to it, but once I'd sat down I had the feeling that she'd give a million dollars if I'd go away.

"Then my brother died, and about a month after that, when I called, she told me that she couldn't leave her sister, that she and Effie had made out that I wasn't to come again. I went away hurt, naturally, but I was pretty busy then, and I drifted out of the habit of coming up here."

"But that's a long time ago. Surely if you went there now——"

"There's no reason for me to go there now. I married a Detroit girl, and we spend our summers here at the old homestead. You must come and call on us. My wife's an invalid and doesn't get around much, but she loves visitors."

I felt as though cold water had been poured over me. Love, according to books and the movies, lasted forever.

Effie was coming back along the beach, and he was diverted. She did not look up, and the dogs did not sense us.

"What a woman!" he said. "Made of steel. Keeps herself to herself and the rest of the world can go to the devil. Not many of us have the courage for that. Doesn't make a person easier to live with, though. If she weren't so damned proud, she'd turn around and say to somebody, 'I need help. I'm in trouble. Thus and so is what it's about and can you do anything for it?' But no. She's got to solve the whole thing herself."

"What trouble?" I asked.

He shrugged. "I don't know. Nobody knows. But if you can look at Effie Brandon and not know she's got trouble and plenty of it, you're foolish, that's all!"

I married Thayer that afternoon in Petoskey. We packed our things quickly and secretly, and when we drove away we left a note saying that we would be gone on a month's tour of Quebec and the Gaspé Peninsula. I said that it wasn't a very polite way to treat his sisters, not to invite them to the ceremony, but he said they would want it that way. I think now that he knew how much they had been counting on my refusing him, and he wanted to give them time to make their faces polite again.

CHAPTER VI

I had not traveled before, and it was fun traveling with Thayer. He had been every place, and he knew the exactly correct thing to do at the correct time. The hotels where we stayed were lovely, and our rooms always had the prettiest views and the coolest breezes. I ate more delicious food then I had known existed, and I began learning about wines, correct service, and accurate tipping. Each place we saw was more romantically lovely than the last, and between the meals and the moonlight and the pride in Thayer's eyes when he looked at me, I began to fancy that I was madly in love.

We had sent cards home, giving each new address as we moved on, but no word came back from Effie or Anne. Instead there came one day a note from Maggie, her fine sprawl showing the faint tremor of her hand.

Dear Elizabeth,

Even though your marriage was sudden, I cannot say it was a surprise. Indeed, it was what everyone had expected, and I know you will be very happy. Thayer is a fine man and he deserves better fortune than he has known.

We were up at your house cleaning it against your arrival, and I found this on Thayer's desk. It is addressed to you and it has not been opened, so I thought perhaps you had forgotten it in the rush and might like to see it, even though your thoughts must be above such mundane things as casual correspondence.

Everything is going as usual here, except that Anne is not well. She spends a great deal of time in her room and she cries often. I try to do what I can for her, but Effie keeps me away as much as she can. I think that Anne would be glad of any company, even of mine.

I shall be glad when you are back. We never had the talk we planned to have, and I am looking forward to it when you have the time to spare. Sergeant Stark has been here and he gave me a message for you. He said that he had not meant that you should take him so literally. When I asked him what he meant he laughed and said that you would know. I think he is a fine man and certainly a very handsome one. All love and good wishes from

Affectionately yours,
MARJORIE MITCHELL

The enclosure was a letter from the Board of Education in Adrian, offering me the position of third-grade teacher in one of their schools, and the postmark was over three weeks old!

I went from the hotel desk out to the veranda where Thayer was sitting in the sun and handed it to him. I did not mean to make a fuss. As a matter of fact, happy as I was, I was glad he had held back the letter, glad that I had married him instead of going off somewhere to teach; and so smooth was his usual manner that it took me some moments to realize that I had brought on the first of his famous—or infamous—rages.

"Where did you get this?" he asked.

I explained, laughing a little. "And I suppose," I finished, "that I've had a hundred or so of these, that without knowing it I was the most sought-after teaching candidate in Michigan, and you let me go on feeling unpopular, you determined wretch!"

"I give you my word this was the only one," he said crisply, and it was then I saw how furious he was.

I tried to tell him that I didn't mind, that I was even a little flattered that he had thought enough of me to do something that must have been distasteful and worrisome to him, but he was beyond listening.

"Maggie did this on purpose," he said, so sharply that several of the other people on the veranda turned to look at us. "She's always doing natural little kindnesses that turn out to be horrors. And you're just young enough and silly enough to be taken in by them!"

Acutely embarrassed, I started to walk away, but he caught my arm and dragged me back. By this time all traffic in and out of the hotel had stopped and we were playing to a growing and attentive audience.

"I won't have it!" he shouted. "I'm telling you right now. I won't have it! You stay away from Maggie and see that she stays away from you. I won't have her writing to you and I won't have her whispering sweet nothings in your ear that will turn you against us! We've had to put up with her prying and snooping and chattering for years. The woman's a cancer and I won't have you contaminated by her!"

He was glaring down at me, his hand tight on my arm, his body shaking. I don't know where I found the nerve to do it, but I turned a little so that I was facing most of our listeners.

"This is my husband," I said clearly to them. "He's in a temper because an elderly woman who has lived with his family for years has written me a very harmless letter. I married him just three weeks ago. I'm beginning to wish I hadn't."

The audience gasped, murmured, stood rigid again. Thayer came to his senses. He looked around the porch and dropped my arm.

"I'm sorry," he said. The grossness of the situation struck him and he began to smile. He spoke to the porch. "I'm very sorry. I apologize both to my wife and to you." Then he sat down in his chair and rocked with laughter. "Elizabeth," he gasped, "you're an archfiend in a very pretty, demure disguise."

The porch was pleased. It nodded and smiled and dispersed. A big, beefy man with athletic shoulders muttered to me as he passed, "That's the way to handle 'em, sister!" One of the women pressed my arm. We had to leave that hotel the next day, because we had become the most popular people in it and were swamped with invitations from strangers for dinner, tea, supper, and cocktails. There is nothing that makes you feel you know a couple better than to see them fight and make up. We had become the property of our audience.

Thayer referred to the matter only once. "I would have apologized to you later, when I came out of it," he said. "I have a bad temper, always have had, but I do have the good grace to be sorry afterward."

I felt cool and amused, the complete mistress, for once, of a situation. "It's one thing," I said, "to insult people in public and another thing to apologize to them in private. I think the apologies should be made where the trouble begins."

He looked at me with a queer smile. "I'm beginning to believe I've married a tiger under the impression that it was a kitten." Then, later and inexplicably, "You're going to be all right, Elizabeth. You're going to be all right."

The fact remained that, since it seemed to annoy him so much, I had decided to give poor Maggie a wide berth. I would be pleasant and polite, but I would stay away from her.

This I did, all too thoroughly. We had been home two weeks—it was the middle of September—and Effie, of all people, spoke to me about it.

I met her in the garden early one morning. Thayer had just left for Petoskey to be gone for the day. She stood, straight and silver, her cool dignity triumphing over the old garden hat, the heavy gloves, the worn gardening shoes.

"Elizabeth," she said, "I have no wish to offend you, but I must offer you a word of advice. We are situated peculiarly here, and it is difficult for a young person to grasp the ramifications of our social situation. Maggie is very hurt that you seem to be avoiding her."

"She was included in both dinner invitations," I said defensively, "and I was as nice to her as I could be."

"I know, and that was very proper. But she seems to have developed a genuine fondness for you, the first I can remember she has ever shown, and it is a shame to have it discouraged so obviously."

I had to come out with the truth. "Thayer doesn't want me to have anything to do with her. Personally, I rather like her."

She was snipping chrysanthemums and laying them in her basket. I could not see her face, but her voice was patient and reasonable. "I think Thayer is wrong," she said. "I don't think you should have her at your house in the evenings. Those belong to you and Thayer to do with what you choose. But he's away a great deal in the daytime and will be away more now that our properties are beginning to sell again. I think you should ask Maggie up for an occasional lunch or tea. She loves special events and makes a great deal of them. You need not have her alone. In fact, it would be better if you included one of us—not both, or she would think it was a group affair—but either Anne or myself. Then, certainly, Thayer could have no objections."

It was advice I was glad to follow. I hurried to ask Anne and Maggie for tea that very afternoon, and I ran back to my own house to fill vases, set furniture in a conversational group around the bay window that faced toward the garden, and bake a cake that was a frosty delight, albeit somewhat unlevel.

Strange how a thought, apparently from nowhere, can suddenly spear and impale the brain. I had not seen or heard the dogs since I had been back.

I was setting the silver tea service on the table and glancing out of the window to watch for my guests to come up the path when that occurred to me. I left the napkins in a heap and walked out to the porch. Far down to the right, where the kennels and the wired enclosure had been, there was nothing. The place was level and clean, and the grass was beginning to lap at the edges of the sandy paths the dogs had worn clear.

I was still staring when Anne and Maggie came up the steps and opened the screen behind me. I wheeled on them.

"Where are the dogs?" I asked, in what Maggie told me later was an accusing tone.

Anne took a step backward, and Maggie huddled down farther into her faded, shapeless print. "They're gone," Anne said.

"Gone where?"

"Effie—we gave them away. We felt we shouldn't let them run, and it was too hard on them being kept in all the time."

Then I realized that instead of being the gracious hostess I was acting like a cross schoolmarm, and I dropped the subject. It was too late. For Anne the tea was not a success. She sipped politely and broke a piece of cake with her fork but did not touch it again. Finally her chin dropped and she was dozing in her chair. Maggie motioned me out to the hall.

"I'm afraid you were too sudden with her," she said. "Her nerves are bad, and the slightest shock makes her sleepy. Poor soul, let her sleep. She was very fond of the dogs. Effie shouldn't have sent them away—so suddenly, too. One day they were there and the next day they weren't."

"I'm terribly sorry. I don't know why I attached so much importance to them. It was just that I hadn't noticed they were gone till that very minute."

She smiled and patted my hand. "You couldn't know. It wasn't your fault. One of us should have warned you."

I burst out with exactly what I thought. "You're so sensible, Maggie. I don't know how you stand this being so careful all the time, about what you say and how you act. You're the only level-headed one of us all, actually."

She colored with pleasure, and when I showed her over the house, pointing out the few small changes I had made, she walked a good two inches taller the whole time. She approved of everything.

"I'd like to do my own room over," she said. "We'll all have a little more money now, things are going so well. Mr. Brandon left me a little property, too, you see, though I never expected it would amount to anything. Now it looks as if"—she leaned toward me and almost whispered—"as if I'll have five thousand dollars all my very own soon. Isn't that wonderful?"

"Then you won't have to stay here any more. You can go wherever you want, do things you've wanted to do. Oh, Maggie, that's grand!"

"That's true," she said slowly. "I hadn't thought of that. Thayer had me sign the papers for the sale only yesterday, and I've been so glory-struck ever since it's a wonder I've been able to walk and talk and eat. Of course, I'll go!" She looked at me timidly. "Where?"

"There are lots of places. We'll talk it over when you get the money. I'm so happy for you, Maggie."

A new thought had struck her. "What—what if they won't give me the money?"

"They'll have to give it to you. It's yours!"

"Yes, but they wouldn't have to give it to me all at once. They could see that I got it in dribbles, enough to make me comfortable, but not enough so that I could go away."

I was indignant. "We'll see about that when the time comes!"

Then we stopped being serious and giggled and both talked at once, and bounced on the bed with our eagerness to spend Maggie's five thousand dollars.

"I could almost furnish a place of my own," she said. "I have a lot of my old things stored in the attic."

I had not thought of attics. "Where's my attic, Maggie? I haven't seen it."

She led the way into the hall and pointed to a steel loop in the ceiling. "You pull on that and steps come down," she said. "You'd better wait, though. Thayer might not want you to——"

"Nonsense!" I said, and pulled on the loop.

The dusty boards resounded under my feet, but Maggie tiptoed like an arch conspirator. Most of the attic was bare, but to one side, before the eaves came down, there were partitions that enclosed a room. It was a small room, plainly furnished with a brass bed, an old dresser, and a chair. A tiny but efficient bathroom opened from it.

"They used to keep a girl," Maggie explained. "She slept up here."

"An Indian?"

"Oh my, no. She was a girl from Harbor Springs. May Elliot, I think her name was. She stayed here during the week and went home over Sunday. They only had her a few months. It was too quiet here, she said."

I had been opening and closing drawers. "She didn't leave anything behind her, anyway."

Maggie was shocked. "My goodness, we've cleaned up here since then!"

There was broken furniture on the main attic floor and old trunks. I opened one. It was full of old dusty clothes, a woman's, carefully folded, wrapped in tissue papers and scented with moth balls.

"Those were Alice's things," Maggie said awkwardly. "We thought Thayer had sent them back to her folks, but he hadn't. There's a gray squirrel coat in there, and it seemed a waste to let it go. I offered to buy it from him once, and he was very rude about it. Look, over here's the little rosewood sewing table she brought from home. There's a tress of her hair in it, that he cut off after she was dead. See. It's dreadfully tarnished now. It was a lovely reddish gold. A real Titian, I think. Here's something I haven't seen before. It looks like a bunch of old newspaper clippings."

I had just taken the old bits of paper in my hand when all bedlam broke out below us. We could hear Effie calling and pounding, a little shriek from Anne, and then footsteps hurrying through the downstairs.

Maggie grabbed my hand and we ran. We achieved the upstairs hall, shoved the steps up behind us, and reached the head of the stairs just as Effie came panting up.

"What on earth's the matter?" I said.

She stopped, and color began to come back to her face.

"They'd been here so long," she stammered, "that I thought I'd better come and see—then I knocked and no one answered. I didn't know what might have happened. Anne woke up and came to open the door for me." She turned to Maggie crossly. "You shouldn't have left her, Maggie."

"We thought we'd let her sleep."

"You should have stayed with her, nevertheless, as well you know."

She whisked them both off with her, leaving me gaping after them. It was only four-thirty then, so I brought hot water, made a new cup of tea for myself, and sat down to look at the newspapers I had been holding ever since our flight from the attic.

Most of what I know today about the Brandons I learned that afternoon from those old bits of paper. Whoever had compiled them had made a small but complete history of the whole family. The earliest date was 1910 and told how the Brandons had just returned from abroad, where, it was rumored, Miss Effie had caught the eye of an English duke. There were pictures of their home in Florida and an account of Thayer's sailing his own boat to the Hawaiian Islands. There were reproductions of Brandon Oaks, too, with Mr. Brandon at the head of a prize Percheron, pictures of wolfhounds like Boris and Duke with blue ribbons pinned to their collars and the Brandon yacht *Westwind* that had won a silver cup. Mr. Brandon had owned servants and boats and miles of rolling country and farms and houses and oil wells and prize animals, and then—

"William Brandon and Wife Die When Machine Crashes."

They had been living in the Florida house at the time, and they had gone for a "spin" after dinner. Something had gone wrong; a farmer had heard a crash; the car had slid over a steep embankment into a wall, and the Brandons were dead. There were pictures of Mr. Brandon, stocky and blond, in a duster; of Mrs. Brandon, tall and stately in hat and motoring veil; and a sickening one of a heap of crushed metal that had been a car. The papers surmised that automobiles would never be really safe.

Then came what must have been a crushing surprise to a public that had liked marveling at the money-making powers of William Brandon and the lavish scale on which he lived. Mr. Brandon had owed money, and much of his fortune was on paper. Things were sold and picked over and raked together and marked down, and when that was done so was the Brandon splendor.

After that there were but four clippings. One told of Effie's marriage to Robert Warren: "A quiet home ceremony. The bride was attended by her sister, Anne Brandon, wearing cream lace and carrying a bouquet of delphinium and roses. The best man was Daniel Warren, brother to the groom. The couple will make their residence on the beautiful estate of Brandon Oaks."

The next was a full-page spread from a Detroit Sunday paper, one of the kind that revels in old scandal and dishes up wild surmises to whet the emotions of the superstitious and ignorant. The headline said: "Effie Brandon's Husband A Suicide." The theme was the old and favored one of an evil spirit presiding over what should be a fortunate family. It began with Thayer's father's father, James Brandon, who had perfected an invention, had it stolen from him, and died at Sunny Hill Home. The article spoke as though everyone in the world knew about Sunny Hill Home, and perhaps they did then, but I had never heard of it. There was a rehash of the automobile accident and the dwindling of the family resources. And now Effie, this young woman, married only two years and, daintily, "expecting," happy in her home, content to have found refuge at last in commonplace, everyday living, had walked out to the barn to call her husband to dinner and had found him there dead "by his own hand." There were more pictures, of Robert Warren, of Effie, of the Oaks, of the barn where the "fateful incident" had taken place.

The next two were more modest. One told of Thayer's marriage to Alice Norris of New York. The other announced her "untimely death" of peritonitis. She was survived by her husband, Thayer Brandon, and her father and mother, Mr. and Mrs. Fred J. Norris of New York City.

I didn't want Thayer to come home and find his family's misfortunes staring at him from the tea table, so I scurried out to the wire basket in back, stuffed the papers in, and set a match to them. When I came back Sergeant Stark was standing on my front steps.

"Alone at last!" he said grimly. "I hope that you're never a fugitive from justice. I'd hate to be the one who had to try to catch up with you!"

I asked him in, and he told me that he had tried repeatedly to see me while I was at the other house.

"I hope you'll be very happy," he added punctiliously, with just the faintest accent on the "hope."

"I'm sure I will be."

"That's good." He sat down wearily. His hat had left a red line on his forehead. "We've had a little excitement since you went away."

"You found——"

"The little girl? No, I've given that up for now. This time it was prowlers. At the Warrens'."

"Who on earth——"

"Mrs. Warren calls me one night about eight o'clock. It isn't quite dark yet, she's sick in bed, and she can hear someone creeping around outside the house. Her husband ought to be there any minute, but he isn't, yet. So I drive over, expecting the whole thing to be imaginary, but it wasn't. There was a prowler. Anne."

"Anne Brandon?" I almost shrieked it.

"That's right. She was standing by the front walk, a little bit back in the shrubbery, when I drove up. Said she had wanted a word with Dan and hadn't wanted to disturb anyone if he wasn't there. I drove her home, and that's all there was to that."

"That wasn't very exciting."

"Another of the Lucas sheep was killed three nights ago."

"Oh dear!" Boris and Duke had been such pretty animals.

"You knew there had been others, then," he said. "You never mentioned it to me."

"Surely dogs killing sheep doesn't necessitate the presence of the state police."

He leaned his head back and closed his eyes. "It's been going on for quite a while, Mr. Lucas says. He'd not told anyone about it. Miss Effie always paid him. And he wouldn't have mentioned this one, but I found it myself. Throat torn right out of it."

"But why should he——"

His eyes were still shut. "We don't think dogs killed this one," he said. "That's why I came up today—to have a look at the dogs."

"They're not here."

His eyes opened slowly. "Then where are they?"

"Effie sent them away without telling anyone she was going to."

"When?"

"I don't know. Yesterday, maybe."

"Guess I'll go ask where she sent them."

I watched him from the porch, and in ten minutes his car came slowly back up the drive. This time he did not get out. He cranked down the window and leaned toward me.

"She won't say," he said. "Says she sent them to a friend of hers and doesn't want him bothered with questions."

"Perhaps I can find out."

"You let this alone," he said. "You stay out of it. And lock your doors at night. And don't go romping over the landscape very much by yourself. If a dog killed that sheep, he did it with a knife. Somebody's trying to kid us."

He drove away and left me shivering in the red of the sunset.

CHAPTER VII

THAT EVENING marked the turning point in my relations with Thayer. We were never the same with each other again. From that day on there was no keeping a check on his frightful, spasmodic temper, and during the next month I passed through all the stages of heartsickness to emerge on the bleak plane of absolute indifference. I was, finally, beyond anything he might do or say.

He must have seen the transformation, but it was beyond his power to rally his forces, to control his tongue, to suppress the steadily mounting fury he felt. Perhaps he honestly wanted to drive me away at the last, although that is hard for me to believe. He was in love with me, he would say he was sorry, twice he even wept, but the unspeakable scenes would spring up like mushrooms, in a quiet hour, and the harm would be done all over again.

To other people he must have seemed the same as usual. His business acquaintances saw him as a poised, intelligent, immaculate, rather reserved man who sold excellent lands in a deprecatory, off-hand fashion and with a careful courtesy that eschewed every trick of salesmanship. I knew him as a man who was strung on tight wires, whose hands would begin to shake at a word, whose face would remain placid while he shouted and ranted and threatened. Even that was not the worst, though I grew to detest him for it. What frightened me were the periods that came later, the quiet spaces when he would stare at me appraisingly without saying one word an hour.

That evening it was a question of Maggie's five thousand dollars, and he was cross immediately.

"Of course she'll get it. Don't be foolish, Elizabeth."

"When?"

"She'll get it as fast as I do. The thing was arranged on a term-payment plan. So much down and so much a month."

"How much?"

He got up from the table and threw his napkin down.

"Really, Elizabeth," he said, "you force me to the rudeness of saying that it is none of your business. Since you have chosen, in spite of my request, to make a confidante of that woman——"

"Effie suggested that I have her up here."

"Effie was wrong. Though if you had conducted yourself properly there would have been no harm in it. Instead you sneaked off with her and the two of you ransacked the house. One doesn't take casual friends to one's attic."

I was angry. "You've had a complete report on the whole day, I see. Doesn't Effie find it hard to carry on her own work and spy on me at the same time?"

He was shouting now. "Leave Effie out of this! She has troubles enough of her own without having to cope with a disobedient youngster!"

I swallowed that, because he was white and shaking. I even tried to be soothing. "I know she has troubles. She was fond of the dogs."

He stopped in mid-rage. *"Was* fond?"

"She sent them away—yesterday, it must have been. Right after they discovered another sheep had been killed."

He sat down heavily. "Poor girl!" he said. "Poor old girl! She needn't have done that. Boris and Duke never touched those sheep."

"That's what the police think."

His eyes glittered yellow again. "Just what do the police think? You're so cozy with them. You should know."

"I don't know that I'm cozy with them. When they come to ask me questions, I don't see how I can refuse to talk with them at least. They think the sheep were killed by a person and then hacked to make it look as though the dogs had done it."

"The fools! The crazy fools! Why don't they go and look at the Indians and their dogs? They're the most likely people to know about it. But no! It's fun to annoy the Brandons. In the first place, it gets you in among a better class of people. In the second, you might get your name in the papers if you managed to turn up some little detail that the reporters missed the first time."

I tried to be calm and fair. "Sergeant Stark doesn't seem to be the kind who particularly wants his name in the papers."

He stood up and leaned across the table at me. His face was only inches away and he was panting a little. "Effie and I may have our differences of opinion about Maggie," he said, "but we have no difference of opinion at all about Stark. You are not to talk with him again, do you hear? He is not to set foot inside this house unless he has a warrant. We don't have to be bothered with him unless he chooses to be legal about it, and he has no grounds for going that far. He's a climber, and we are not going to offer ourselves as rungs in his ladder. Tell him that the next time you see him!"

I began to gather the dishes. "You tell him," I said. "I don't feel that way about him, and I shall certainly be polite to him whenever we meet."

He stamped off to the other house to spend the evening, and I did the dishes and went to bed. It was late when he came back and turned on the light in our room. I wasn't asleep.

"Would you prefer that I sleep somewhere else?" he said stiffly.

"Not at all."

He came over and took my hand. "I shouldn't have married you, you know. I didn't do you a favor. You'll have to be patient with me. I do my best, under the circumstances, and when things come up that seem inexplicable to you, you'll have to take them—and me —on faith. That's a hard thing for a person as young as you are."

"I can try."

He was right, though. I couldn't do it. Once or twice I might have risen above curiosity and suspicion. But the incidents came too thick and fast. I was forced to think and pass judgment, and it was never in the family's favor.

Thayer had spoken to Sergeant Stark, for his manner at our next meeting was cool, to say the least. I had been shopping in Petoskey, and as I came out on the street he was just stepping out of the police car. I had to block his path before he would notice me.

"Good morning," I said firmly.

"Hello," he said. "We won't be bothering you again. The sheep has been paid for, and it doesn't matter what I think about homicidal maniacs."

"Did you find out where the dogs were sent?"

"No indeed. As a matter of fact, I could swear that they weren't sent anywhere at all. In short, this time it won't work, Mrs. Brandon."

"What won't work?"

"Your fetching technique of telling me a little so that I'll tell you a lot and the rest of the Brandons will be kept well informed."

I climbed into the Oaks station wagon in tears. It was not a week for amiable conversation, and I said so to Nathan when I got home. He was raking leaves from the lawns; there was a huge pile of red and yellow and brown beside him; the cool wind would lift a few and scatter them again.

"Why is everyone so cross this week, Nathan?"

He leaned on his rake and smiled at me. "I hadn't noticed any difference."

"I've had my head snapped off twice, and it isn't Wednesday yet."

"You've been keeping indoors too much. What you need is a long walk. Nothing like exercise to cheer you up. Might walk down Lucas way. He seems to think pretty well of you."

"He's the only one."

Nathan chuckled and bent to set a match to the gay heap. It burned quickly, the aromatic smoke twitching this way and that as the wind came round. Then, tantalizingly, a few leaves fluttered up and I caught sight of a little piece of blue ribbon just as the flames seized and ate it.

I jerked his arm. "There was a ribbon in there!"

"Sure. Just a little piece, though. Didn't amount to much. I noticed it when I raked it up with the leaves. Was it yours?"

"No. Where did you find it?" It had been a bit of the same ribbon I had found in the Indian church. I hadn't a doubt of it.

"Over by the garden wall, I guess. I was raking there when I first noticed it, anyway."

He pointed the exact place out to me, and there right beside it was the print of one of Maggie's low, stub-toed little oxfords. Nathan saw it too.

"I wouldn't be surprised but what she might wear a bit of ribbon in her hair even yet, if The Girls"—Effie and Anne were always "The Girls" to Nathan—"weren't looking."

If I had not been angry with Sergeant Stark, I might have risked Thayer's anger and called him up. Still, he already had one piece in his possession. What could two tell him that one could not?

I was interested in the ribbon, nevertheless. I walked carefully back the drive, scrutinizing the grass on either side. I paced my own lawn to the very edge of the woods. I did not quite dare go down as near the other house as where the kennels had been, but I sat in the hammock, which was stretched beneath two oaks, and stared down that way as hard as I could. The ground was bland and uninformative. All I saw was Anne, dressed in a light green wool dress and looking almost pretty, hurrying away from me through the garden. I called to her, and she turned and came scuttling back to me, her finger to her lips.

"Maggie's doing the luncheon dishes and Effie and Mrs. Moss are fall cleaning upstairs," she said. "I thought I'd take a little walk. Isn't it a glorious day?"

Looking at the color in her cheeks and the animation in her big, dark eyes, I said that I thought it was.

"If you'll wait till I change, I'll go with you. I was thinking of taking a walk myself."

She was already backing away. "Oh, I have only a few minutes. They'll be needing me for something. I shouldn't be away even for this long. I just thought . . ."

Her words trailed away, and she almost ran through the garden and into the path through the woods.

Impoliteness Week, I thought, and went into my own cool, open, sunny house.

I noticed then, for the first time, what I noticed afterward many times. The living room was not exactly as I had left it. The changes were minor. A book open at a different page. A cushion fluffed up where it had been flat. A chair shoved slightly to one side.

I might have been frightened had I not been so enraged. All of us left our houses wide open in the daytime, whether we were there or not. Someone was always about, and we were too far from the main road to attract strangers. This was an arrant breach of confidence. Even in my bedroom there were the same slight signs.

Grimly I walked out to the hall, pulled down the attic steps, and went up. From the marks in the dust on the attic floor, a herd of people had been walking there. The activity had centered around the trunks and the rosewood cabinet, but when I examined them both they seemed unchanged.

Well, Thayer's sisters were probably welcome in Thayer's house whether his wife was there or not. I changed my clothes, ate a peanut-butter sandwich, and started out, leaving the house open as always. There was no use in trying to change an old order, and I was intruding, not they.

I did not purposely go the way that Anne had gone. I took my familiar route to the cemetery and sat down in the sun on the edge of the cliff, as I had sat the day I had seen the little girl on the beach. The air had a cool bite to it. I turned up the collar of my gabardine jacket and wondered how it would be here in the winter with all this color and sparkle gone, lost in a monotone of white and gray and black. The snow drifted deep up here, I had been told, and for weeks one ventured no farther than to replenish the feeding stations for the birds. And the people who walked around my attic and sat in my living room when I was away, picking up my books to see what I was reading, riffling through the music on my piano, would have to be careful lest I see their tracks in the snow.

I heard Anne and Dan Warren talking together, and I did not know what to do. Their voices came to me clearly in snatches, but I could not tell where they were. Walking one of the paths through the wood, probably. It made a pretty dilemma for me. If they did not eventually come to the clearing, everything would be all right. If they did, would they know that I could hear them long before they saw me, would they resent it that I had not made my presence known? And just how could I do that, short of rolling a stone down the hill or bursting into song, both such silly and obvious expedients that they were worse than sitting still?

" . . . can't get away," Anne was saying. "Oh, Dan, you've no idea how they . . ."

" . . . dangerous," he said. "You must see that it's for the best. Even though it means . . ."

" . . . your wife. And then the police came. I've done the same thing many times. I know I shouldn't. I can't seem to help myself."

"She'll be getting suspicious. She must be suspicious already. She's not at all stupid."

"You've met her?"

"Once. We talked for a while. You must try to get her away. If anything . . ."

" . . . tried at first, but Thayer was wild. He held back a letter of hers that would have sent her away to teach. Just think, she would have been gone long ago . . ."

" . . . Maggie day and night. There's no telling what she might say to her and give the whole show away. Though it needs to be given away, Anne. It should have been given away long ago."

Anne was crying now. "If I can only talk to you now and then, Dan. They watch me all the time, but I have to talk to somebody. If I didn't have my faith to hang on to, I'd kill myself. Do you think I'll ever be better, Dan?"

"It's your faith that worries me. I wish you'd never dabbled with that stuff."

"You're wrong, Dan. At first I couldn't get anything through unless I went to Mrs. Topping. She's such an encouraging woman. She said she thought I was a natural medium and if I kept trying, I'd succeed. And so I did, and now the messages come through directly to me and very clearly. I haven't been in to Mrs. Topping's in over a year."

"I thought it took a group to work that sort of thing. A bunch of scared people sitting around a table in the dark, feeling ghostly hands brushing the backs of their necks while other spirits played an accordion or a trumpet. Funny thing, I've never heard of a spirit playing a violin, in spite of all the good fiddle players who have passed over. The violin is a difficult instrument. No doubt the spirits don't have time to keep up with their practicing."

"You shouldn't scoff. You don't know anything about it, and it's hard to explain. Just sometimes—not always—when I'm sitting quietly, I get a feeling that someone wants to talk with me. Then I close my eyes and concentrate very hard until I'm sure I'm in communication. I ask questions, and the answers come to me by different voices. It's usually Father or Mother. Once it was your brother."

"It's your imagination—you must see that. You're lonely, so lonely that you've had to resort to this kind of stuff. I don't mind your play-ing with it, but I hate to see you taking it so seriously. Amuse your-self if you want to, but, for God's sake, don't regulate your life by it! If there were spirits who could talk to us, don't you think it would be wrong to disturb them for our worldly purposes?"

"I don't disturb them. They disturb me. There are things they want to say, and they find it easier to say them through me because I haven't built the barriers around myself that other people have."

Dan was getting vehement. "Damn it, Anne, can't you see that if anyone in any way could really foretell the future the world would beat a path to his door and he'd be worth millions? If I could, this minute, get a copy of tomorrow's newspaper with just the stock-market page and the race results, I could make a fortune. Yet you sit there and tell me that you have a whole corps of unseen persons reporting to you and telling you what's going to happen——"

She was patient. "They don't tell me what's going to happen really. They tell me of dangers that might come up, but they're no surer than I am of those things. What they tell me is what's hap-pened in the past, things they had experience of when they were alive and that I know nothing about. We've found I don't know how many things that had been mislaid or lost, that way."

"If that's the case," he said bitterly, "you might try to get in touch with Alice and find out what she thinks she died of!"

There was a tramping and a crackling, and I thought they had both gone away. I stretched out on my face and thought. There had been something peculiar about Alice's death, and now they wanted to get rid of me, peaceably if they could, and how if they could not? And if Anne could find out from spirits what had gone on before, did she know what had happened to the little Kennedy girl? Or did she know without an unworldly agency to tell her?

I turned and looked up. Anne was standing almost over me. She had a heavy rock in her hands and her face was set and very pale.

"Oh," she said. "I thought you were—a stranger. I didn't recog-nize you." She looked down at the stone in her hands. "I thought I'd take this home for the rock garden."

"It's pretty heavy to carry that far. I'll help you."

"On second thought, it's too big; we need smaller ones." She put it down, and I was relieved. "Have you been here long?"

"I was asleep. I don't know how long I've been here." I had to think of something natural to say. I pointed to the gray stone that stood alone. "Was Margaret Thayer your aunt?"

She sat down beside me. "Yes, she was my mother's sister. I scarcely remember her. I was only four when she died. Nurse said she was a very beautiful woman. When Mother left the stage and married, Aunt Margaret came to live with them."

"Margaret never married?"

"She was only twenty-two when she died of pneumonia. I believe she was engaged to someone at one time, but I don't really know. Effie would. She's the family historian."

"I've seen pictures of your mother. She was lovely."

Anne smiled. "Yes, she was. She wasn't the easiest person in the world to live with, though. Thayer inherits his temper from her. She was mad about Father, and she made a better wife than she did a mother. If Father paid too much attention to any one of us, Mother would cloud up a little, fond as she was of us herself. Jealous, even of her own children, and we knew it. We used to tease her by climbing all over Daddy when we were with him, not letting her get a word in edgewise, monopolizing him for hours. Then, when we saw she couldn't stand it another minute, we'd laugh and Daddy would laugh and she'd have to too. She was ashamed of being that way, but she couldn't help it. As children we were all nice-looking, and Mother was proud of that. She admired good looks more than she did brains or character, I'm afraid."

"Was Maggie a good-looking child?"

"No, and that was partly the trouble. That, and because she was a whim of Father's. He was on the Board of Directors of the orphanage. Mostly that meant that he just contributed money to it, but one day they took him through it and he saw Maggie and was sorry for her. He had adopted her legally before he brought her home. Mother never forgave him for it and she begrudged everything Maggie ever got, even though there was plenty in those days for a dozen children. I guess"—she stumbled painfully —"I guess you'd have to say that my mother was not a generous woman."

I was honest about it. "I guess I would," I said firmly. "Anybody who would beleaguer a child for something it couldn't help——"

"But she's dead now," Anne said queerly. "Mother's dead."

"You can't set all the wrong things you did right by just dying. If, suddenly, she could be alive again, she wouldn't be any different. She'd go on acting just as she did before."

"I know. She—she might even be worse."

She got up suddenly and ran toward the house. I walked home slowly and alone. My living room seemed to be just as I had left it, but I hooked all the screens before I went out to the kitchen to get dinner.

Thayer brought the mail with him when he came, and he was jubilant.

"The Days are coming for a week's visit," he said. "You'll like them, Elizabeth. There's Mike—that's Dr. Day—and his wife Norah and their little boy, young Mike. The kid must be five years old by now. They're sailing their boat up to the Springs, and I'll pick them up there."

"They'll stay with us?"

"Yes, if you don't mind. She's a good sport and she'll help out. She knows we can't keep servants here."

He was happy and considerate and pleased with me when I said I would be glad to have the Days. He helped with the dinner dishes and did an elegant waltz step on the kitchen floor while he put them away.

I felt guilty. "It's nice to have you gay," I said. "I'm afraid I haven't been too cheerful."

He hugged me exuberantly. "You're a darling," he said, "an absolute darling. I've been dull and stodgy myself. We've been in a rut. Let's drive in to Petoskey and see a movie."

We saw the movie and had chocolate sodas and sang along with the radio in the car on the way home. Effie was waiting on our porch. She wanted to talk to Thayer, and I went upstairs blithely. Then I thought that I hadn't been hospitable, that I should have offered to serve some coffee. I went down again, but they weren't on the porch. They were walking slowly down the drive, and I turned to go back into the house quickly. I did not want them to think that I was prying, that I resented family conferences that excluded me.

"They'll find out!" Thayer said. "That was foolish. They're bound to find out."

"What can they do about it? And I had no choice, Thayer. You can see that, can't you? I had no choice."

"What happened to the knife?"

"I think Stark must have it. I've been through everything. It's gone."

I stopped my ears and ran upstairs, but the lightness of the evening was gone. For Thayer, too. He came up the stairs slowly, and his face was old. He sat down and watched me brushing my hair.

He spoke only once. "You're a pretty thing," he said, and his voice had no inflection. "Too pretty. Too pretty to live."

I knew then, and I know now, that his speech was not a compliment. It was simply a reflection of what was passing through his mind, and he nearly came out into the open that night.

CHAPTER VIII

MAGGIE WAS NOT PLEASED to hear that the Days were coming.

"Whenever he's here there's trouble," she said. "I've never met his wife. He wasn't married the last time he was here, six years ago, so she may be all right. His father was the Brandons' physician in the old days, and a fine gentleman he was. Married some fly-by-night out of the social register, though, and his boy took after her rather than his father."

"He can't be a very old man."

"He's younger than I am, though, goodness knows, that's not saying much. He ought to be good at his job. They sent him to the best schools here and in Europe, and he has some newfangled notions. Won't even prescribe for a sore throat unless you tell him your history from before you were born. Don't let him pry anything out of you."

"Such as what, Maggie?"

"Such as—well, that you're not happy here."

She said it so simply that I had no thought of subterfuge. "No, I'm not."

"Thayer gave me a thousand dollars. It's the down payment on my lots. You can have it if you want it."

I leaned over and kissed her faded, soft cheek.

"Thank you, Maggie, but I'll get along."

"I'd hate to see you go. We don't see each other very often, but I have the feeling that you prefer me to either Effie or Anne, and that has never happened to me before. I may just be flattering myself——"

"No. You're right."

She went away beaming, and Effie spoke to me about it that evening.

"You're having a wonderful effect on Maggie," she said dryly. "She's been a great deal easier to live with lately."

"I think it makes a difference when you know that someone is really fond of you."

"I don't know. My father was fond of her, doted on her in fact, and I don't see that it helped her any."

"It's a shame your mother didn't feel the same way."

For a minute I thought she would slap my face. "We'll leave Mother out of this," she said, and walked back into her house.

Anne was sitting in a deck chair knitting, and I sat down to watch the last of the sunset over the lake. The nights came much earlier now. It was completely dark at nine o'clock. Thayer was having dinner in town, and I kept listening for his car to come in the drive. Meanwhile Anne and I chatted casually; the lights in the kitchen wing came on; Maggie was singing a funny lagging tune as she helped Mrs. Moss with the dishes.

I don't know how long the needles had stopped clicking when I noticed that Anne was lying back in her chair, her eyes shut, her breathing heavy. It seemed suddenly cold on the porch; the curtains at the windows billowed and a gust of wind rattled the screen. I thought she had fallen asleep and rose to go; but she spoke, and her voice was high and strange.

"Of course," she said. "I remember. I shall tell her. I didn't know she was going to leave us, but I shall tell her. In the rosewood cabinet. Exactly."

I couldn't move. She sat up and rubbed her eyes.

"I have such a headache," she said in her normal tone.

"I—I thought you had fallen asleep."

She seemed dazed. "Oh no. I was speaking to Mother. Strange, she's never come to me before unless I was alone. She gave me a message for you. You're to go to the rosewood cabinet in your attic. Down at the bottom you'll find a gray pottery horse wrapped in tissue paper. I haven't seen it or thought of it since I was a child, but I remember now that it used to sit on Father's desk. Mother wants you to have it."

She's making this up to frighten me, I thought. Aloud I said, foolishly, "Thank you."

She spoke like the girl at the cashier's desk in a restaurant. "You're very welcome," she said briskly.

I ran all the way up the dark drive, hoping that Thayer had come home without my hearing him. He had not, and I stood in the living room, undecided. Anne was having a joke at my expense. If the pottery horse was where she said it was, it would be because she had seen it and knew perfectly well that it was there. If it wasn't there, I would have showed myself a credulous idiot by going up and looking.

The horse was there. It was tucked way down under everything else, and the paper that wrapped it was old and yellow, its folds looking as though they had not been disturbed for years. I brought it down to my bedroom, set it on a table, stood off to look at it, and caught my breath.

This was no ordinary pottery figure. There was a low ebony base, and on it stood the gray shiny horse, saddled but riderless, one delicate foot pawing the ground. The whole thing was only eight inches high, and from whatever angle you looked at it, it was perfect: the alert, aristocratic head; the sheen of light along the smooth flanks; the small detail on the saddle. I have not been separated from it since, and it stands on my desk before me now. A friend of mine who knows a great deal about art objects tells me that it is Chinese and very old; that he would give me a thousand dollars for it any time and that he could make a profit on it at that price.

I showed it to Thayer when he came home and told him how I had come by it.

"May I keep it, Thayer?"

"Anything in this house is yours."

"How did she know it was there?"

He shrugged. "I don't know. Perhaps she had seen it there once. Perhaps these things do come to her as she claims. I don't maintain that I understand these things. Maybe she's fooling herself, but she's not deliberately lying or pretending. When she says she's had a message from Mother, she really thinks she has had."

"She said that she'd forgotten all about this thing, that she hadn't seen it since she was a child."

"Neither have I. To tell the truth, I thought it went at the auction of our New York house." He ran his hand over the smooth gray. "I'm glad to see it again. It brings back old times."

His face was smooth and peaceful, his hands were calm and relaxed, and I dared to approach him on a subject I was afraid would be touchy.

"Thayer, let's move somewhere else."

He set the figurine on the table and pressed one hand to his eyes. "You don't like it here?"

I was tactful. "It's rather dull. I'm alone so much, and there's no one around who has much time for me."

He laughed shortly. "You sound like the hired help we used to have. 'Rather dull here.'"

"I can't help it if I do. You said once we wouldn't have to stay here all the time. You said we could travel, though I'd rather stay home, if we can find a place where I feel at home."

"There's no reason why you shouldn't feel at home here. Is there?"

"I'd like to be able to ask people in, and not always the same people. I'd like to be far enough away from everybody so I wouldn't have to think about every move I make. We're—we're too close here. It's not healthy. And they're all so much older than I——"

"Including me."

"I didn't think so until you began treating me like a child."

He began to pace the room. "You are a child. Pandora with a box, trying to yank the lid off and set the troubles buzzing around your ears. If it were only your ears, it wouldn't be so bad, but other people are going to be stung much worse than you."

"You're talking in riddles. If you'd explain just——"

"Damn it, there's nothing to explain! Nothing that concerns you, anyway. You're living a nice life. Not much work to do, no responsibilities, everything handed to you on a silver platter. Why can't you let well enough alone? This is a better life than you've ever had before!"

I thought of Mother and Dad and the little house near the campus where we had lived and the perpetual coming and going of young and old alike, each contributing his bit of mosaic to make up the lovely pattern of my childhood.

"No, it isn't," I said. "Mother——"

"Your mother!" he shouted. "Your mother was a foolish, feathery woman with a marriageable daughter to dispose of, and, though she didn't live to see it, she did dispose of her. Your mother would be happy about you!"

"No, she wouldn't," I said stanchly, and burst into tears.

The rest of the week was a patching-up, Thayer groveling and infuriated in turn, I polite and aloof and somewhat frightened. The breech had widened so suddenly and unnecessarily, and I could think of nothing to do or say that would alleviate our mutual resentment. I tried to put the incident out of my mind and busied myself with getting rooms ready for the Days and planning menus and shopping.

I liked the Days, especially Mrs. Day and young Michael. She was a tall, handsome woman with ash-blonde hair, and her son was sturdy and dark, like his father. About Dr. Day I was of two minds. He had an alert, active brain that peered at you through his sharp black eyes. His manner was pleasant, but short. He wore a black Vandyke, which I thought was a little pompous and affected of him. My later and more mature theory about beards is that they are always grown to compensate for some weakness, if not in physiognomy, then in character.

There was a little trouble right at the first about where they would sleep. Dr. Day had made reservations at the hotel in Harbor Springs.

"I told you so in the letter," he said. "We're not intruding on a couple who haven't had time to tell each other their right names yet. We'll stay at the hotel and taxi out here every day."

Thayer and I joined in a chorus of how glad we would be to have them, how their rooms were ready, how we had been looking forward to their company. I believe that he would have remained adamant had it not been for Norah.

"Then we shall be very pleased to come," she said suddenly, and her husband shrugged, a little ungraciously, and climbed into the station wagon.

"I don't mind so much if we're to stay at your house," he said. "I don't want young Mike to get in the habit of running down to the other house, though. He'd be an awful nuisance to a bunch of middle-aged spinsters."

There was no keeping young Mike away from the garden and the lawn that was closer to the lake than ours, however. He was a good child and obedient, but the temptation was too much for him. Norah and I would sit on the porch in the sun; he would begin by playing almost at our feet, and then his circle would widen gradually until he had strayed too far down the drive to call to without being obvious. It was a good city block between the houses, but the other place drew him like a magnet.

Norah was annoyed with her husband. "I don't know why he's so insistent that I keep Mike under my nose all the time," she said. "You'd think the other place was in quarantine. I know that they feel it. When we had dinner there the other night, didn't one of them say how much she liked children and what a treat it was to have one around?"

"That was Maggie."

"Well, I felt like a criminal. All they want to do is feed him cookies and pat him on the head. That couldn't hurt him. The oldest one had a baby and lost him, didn't she? She couldn't have disliked children so much."

Nevertheless she kept him with her, and he was not too unhappy. We went for long walks on the beach, we showed him the Indian village, we sat through two-gun movies in Petoskey for him. And by the middle of the week old Nathan had taken a fancy to the boy, annexed him and took him everywhere.

"No chance I'll let him out of my sight, ma'am," he said. "There was a little girl drowned here this summer. I'll be mighty careful."

Norah swallowed hard, but she let Mike go along.

The doctor was always with Thayer, and since I was not particularly at ease with him, I was glad. When he did find me alone on the porch one afternoon, I felt that he had made a point of cornering me and making conversation.

"I've just been telling Thayer how we stopped on the way up to visit his old nurse, Mrs. Deever. She's in her late seventies now, but she remembers all the Brandon children very well. A remarkable woman, healthy as they come and in full possession of all her faculties. Thayer was her favorite. Because he was the only boy, I suspect."

"Did you know him—as a child?"

"Not very well. I'm younger than he is, for one thing, and his family were hardly ever in town for very long at a time. Dad used to take me along on his calls occasionally, and I'd see him then. I knew Mrs. Deever, though, because she was a friend of my family's. Used to come to the house and drink tea with Dad once in a long while. Lord, how Mother used to fume and fret! But whenever any of us were sick we borrowed Mrs. Deever from the Brandons in a hurry, and Mother was glad enough to get her."

"I don't know who we'd get if anyone was sick up here."

His teeth showed white above the black beard. "With all this fresh air and sunshine nobody could get sick up here!"

"Who took care of Alice?"

"Alice? Oh, you mean the former—— Well, that was a very sudden thing, my dear. We'd have moved her to a hospital had there been time. As it was, we had to make out amongst ourselves. I believe Mrs. Moss took over. She had some nursing experience. Yes, that was a dreadful tragedy. A girl so young, so pretty, newly married——"

"Just like I am now," I said.

His heavy geniality almost failed him. "Yes. Yes. There's a great similarity of circumstance. Hadn't thought of it before. Of course the chances of your falling seriously ill at your age are slight. Things like that aren't likely to happen twice."

"I hope not," I said.

It was fun to see his dignity wobbling, his professional façade crumbling. I had not meant to do it, I had not known that I could, but, since I had discovered that he was in terror of personalities and the Brandon past, I could not resist going on.

I kept my eyes wide and innocent. "What is Sunny Hill Home?" I asked.

It was cool, but he took out a handkerchief and wiped his hands. "Where did you hear about it?" he asked.

"I read the name somewhere. It seemed to be a place for invalids, and I thought you might know about it."

"It doesn't exist any more. At one time it was a famous—rest home. It catered to wealthy clients."

"Why should wealthy people go to a place like that for a rest? Couldn't they rest at home?"

"Well, they weren't well, you see, and Sunny Hill had some of the best medical and nursing facilities in the country."

"Like the Mayo Clinic?"

"No, not exactly." He had to give up, and he did it with poor grace. "They handled only mental cases," he finished abruptly.

I felt as though someone had driven a fist into the pit of my stomach, but I tried to keep my face composed.

"Mental cases?" I repeated stupidly.

"Sunny Hill Home was a private insane asylum."

And perhaps I had not fooled him at all, for he leaned toward me and spoke earnestly. "Insanity, as far as we know, is not an inherited characteristic. Certain tendencies—an unstable nervous system, a lack of self-control—may be passed on and, if the environment is unfavorable, may lead to insanity in the next generation. But babies are not born insane, and there are no insane children. It takes a certain background, bad attending circumstances, depressing surroundings, to produce madness." He got up. "I wouldn't mention this conversation to Thayer if I were you."

I said feebly that I wouldn't, and he started jauntily down the drive to the other house. "Tell Thayer I've gone to have a chat with Maggie," he called back.

Yet when Thayer and Norah came back from their walk and I told him, he looked displeased and sullen. Even Norah noticed it.

"I know," she said, patting his arm, "Mike will be late for the fishing this afternoon. When he gets with the ladies there's no telling when he can bear to tear himself away."

"I don't think he'll be so long," I said. "Maggie's no Venus and she doesn't care for doctors."

Thayer said nothing. He walked away after the doctor, and neither one of them came back for lunch.

"I must say," said Norah, cutting young Mike's chop for him, "that if I'd been married only two months or so I'd take it hard, this walking off without a by-your-leave or if-you-please. You'll have to put your foot down, Elizabeth. Good husbands are trained, not born."

"Thayer's been by himself for so long he forgets I'm here some of the time, I think."

"And part of it is that he always was a selfish, conceited boy who'd fly into tantrums if he didn't get whatever he wanted. Mrs. Deever told us."

"Your husband told me that she said Thayer had been her favorite."

"Well, that's true, but Mike put it mildly. What she said was that he was the best of a bad lot. She didn't like any of the children, nor their mother either, for that matter. She said they were a bunch of snobs that expected the earth with a little red fence around it without lifting a hand to get it. Mr. Brandon she liked. Everyone seems to. He's the only rich man that I've ever heard referred to as 'saintly.' Mrs. Deever says she doesn't know how he stood his family."

"He didn't see much of the children. His wife monopolized him."

"It's too late to make them over now, that's true. But you might as well make up your mind that you'll deal with them with a firm hand. Effie snubs you outright, sometimes; Anne just stares like a cow that's lost her calf; and Thayer's about to fly off the handle any minute. I should be ashamed of talking like this, but I wouldn't want to be in your shoes."

The last two days of their visit were unpleasant. Thayer and the doctor spent scarcely any time with us, and Norah was outraged.

"A vacation!" she said. "I see more of him when he's working!"

They quarreled in their room at night, and I could hear the rumble of the doctor's voice trying to soothe while Norah set up an indignant treble. Thayer did not make any explanations to me. He was thoroughly exhausted every night and went to bed without a word. I think that, wherever he and the doctor went, they must have talked constantly. Always, when I saw them, their heads were close, their lips moved rapidly, their hands made short, emphatic gestures.

It was young Mike who hastened their departure. He had been out with Nathan burning leaves in the dark of early evening, and when he came in his eyes were shining with excitement.

"Look!" he said. "Look what I have!"

He held out a thin silver chain with a silver tag on it.

"What's that?" his father asked.

"It's a dog collar," Thayer explained. "We gave the dogs away, but one of the collars must have been left behind somehow."

"It's Mr. Brandon's, dear," said Norah. "You'll have to give it back to him."

Mike's face puckered and he put the chain behind him.

"It was given to me," he said.

"He can have it," said Thayer. "We have no use for it any more. Nathan probably found it on the lawn."

"Was it Nathan who said you could have it, Mike?"

The child's eyes were bright again. "We had a wonderful fire, Mother. And then Nathan said he'd stand down by the other house and I could run on home and when I got to the front steps I should holler that I was all right. And just before I got here a low lady came out, and she said, 'Would you like this, little boy?' and I said, 'Yes, ma'am,' and I took it and she went away. Then I came up the front steps and hollered I was all right and came in."

"A low lady?" said Norah. "What do you mean by that, Mike?"

"It was a lady," said Mike patiently, "all low, like this."

He bent double and walked a few steps. Sturdy and small though he was, he conveyed vividly the impression of a stealthy, hidden, creeping thing. He had not seen the lady's face. It had been dark and he had not been curious. As far as he was concerned, someone had stepped out of the bushes to give him a lovely present and that was all there was to it.

"I'll see who it was," said Thayer tolerantly. But when he came back he was puzzled. "They're all down there, ready for bed. Mrs. Moss hasn't come back from town yet, but she'll be there any minute. Nathan says he didn't see anyone either."

Dr. Day kept looking steadily at Thayer, and Thayer was avoiding his eyes. Norah had gone to put Mike to bed.

"I hope it wasn't a lady burglar," I said.

"There's not a sign of anyone, Elizabeth. The child's imaginative, that's all."

The doctor spoke. "He didn't imagine the chain."

"He must have found that."

"If he says someone gave it to him, someone did."

The Days went home the next morning. On the drive back from the dock by ourselves we were very quiet. I would miss Norah and her bright, outspoken ways. I turned to tell Thayer so, but I didn't. There were tears in his eyes and on his cheeks, and I was embarrassed for him that I had seen them.

CHAPTER IX

WE HAD SNOW in late October that year. It came swirling in over the lake, melted on our windowpanes, and sifted down among the brown, brittle stalks in the garden. The trees held up gaunt black arms to it, unavailingly, but the pines took it into fat green fingers and held it there. With the color and the screening leaves gone from the landscape, the lake stepped closer to us. At night we could hear it thundering up the beach; the gray swells threw many things up on the sands, but never a sign of Sue Kennedy did it give back, though I knew there were those who watched for it. The water, the wind, the creaking of branches, the sighing of weather strip, and every evening the sweet plaint of the two bells at the Indian church —these were the only sounds I heard for weeks on end, except for a few moments of talk with one of the women from the other house or, in the evening, with Thayer.

Always there was trouble, and it was as if the coming and going of the Days had brought into sharp focus all the hazy difficulties that had been there before. I know that the day after they had left, Thayer quarreled with Effie. He came home with his face as dark as the clouds outside, and he barely touched his dinner.

"I might as well tell you now," he said. "Effie and Anne won't be coming up to the house any more. You'll always be welcome down there, but they can't come up here."

As little affection as I had for his sisters, I felt suddenly bereft. "Why not?"

He was lofty. "Because we think it's better that they don't come."

"Who is 'we'?"

"Effie and Anne and I. Maggie can come if you insist. Or Mrs. Moss or Nathan, if you can't be by yourself a minute."

"I'm by myself a great many minutes."

His mouth was bitter. "Education is supposed to make one resourceful in solitude."

"But it's so unnecessary! Have I done something to offend them? I know I haven't seen much of them this past week, but surely they've made allowances for my having guests."

"Let's say that I've offended them."

"Oh, Thayer, you wouldn't! They're so fond——"

"Damn it, I say that I have! Let it go at that."

So they did not come to our house, and I, kept in my humiliating ignorance, did not go to theirs. The snows deepened in November; Nathan kept a path shoveled between the two houses, and the only one who used it was Maggie, trotting dutifully on her daily visit to me. From her I got the news. Effie had had a bad cold. Anne's nerves seemed to be improving. Thayer never visited his sisters any more.

"What happened between him and Effie, Maggie?"

"I don't know exactly. It must have had something to do with Dr. Day, but I don't know what. I heard Thayer shouting at her the next evening, and she was crying when he left. She hasn't said a decent word to anyone since."

"He hasn't either."

"Has he been mean to you?"

"We seem to quarrel most of the time."

Maggie was cross. "What does he want, I'd like to know? Marries a young girl and expects to keep her under lock and key for the rest of her life while he snarls at her! He tried the same thing before, with Alice. The poor little thing would come to me crying. 'Oh, Maggie,' she'd say, 'I shouldn't have married him. I didn't know him well enough; I should have waited. What shall I do?' Well, I've known Thayer too long not to know what to say to that. 'Leave him,' I told her. 'Leave him this minute! Once he has someone he thinks he can bully, he never lets up. That's the way he is.' But she waited one day too long. Had her clothes all packed when she took sick that night, and after she was dead he just moved them up to the attic. She'd saved him the trouble of having to put her things away, that's all."

"But—but you must be wrong. He cared for her very deeply. The reason he wanted to marry me was that I reminded him of her."

"That's true. He's had to wait all these years for just the right type of girl to come along. Young and pretty and smart and sensitive, that's the way he likes them. It gives him more of a sense of power when he shouts at them or slaps them or locks them in their rooms."

"Maggie, he wouldn't!"

"He did, I tell you! Oh, he was careful in front of his sisters, because they liked her very much. They never knew what was going on. But she told me and showed me a bruise on her shoulder. She couldn't tell his sisters that he had done a thing like that, could she? She made one mistake—she thought she could face him down at the end. I had told her just to slip away, but she had a notion that wouldn't be fair. So she told him she was leaving him. That was on the day she died.

"You're not trying to tell me that Thayer had anything to do with her dying?"

Maggie looked suddenly tired. "I shouldn't be telling you any of this. You're his wife. And I don't really know. She was young to have what she was supposed to have had, and Dr. Day is a friend of Thayer's. No other doctor saw her. If Thayer poisoned her——"

"Poison!" The room was not warm, but I could feel the perspiration break out on my forehead.

"It would have had to be that, wouldn't it?" said Maggie sensibly. "They couldn't have hidden anything else. She took sick right after dinner. That's what started me thinking about it." Then she saw my pallor and was contrite. "You mustn't listen to me when I go on like this, Elizabeth! It's all the guesswork of an old woman who hasn't enough to do and doesn't enjoy her lot in life. All I really know is that Alice and Thayer were not getting along well. All the rest I've told you is pure nonsense!"

"I'm not getting along too well with him either."

"But you mustn't think—— Oh dear! Thayer's changed since then. He's quieted down a lot and he's been much easier to live with. Look how he's handling my little affairs for me, letting me out of all the trouble of worrying about it myself. Ten years ago he wouldn't have done that. Now all I have to do is sign a paper and take the money when it comes in."

"A little bit at a time."

"It's the best he could do."

It was that very evening when, bristling with suspicion and wary as a frightened cat, I found Thayer's brief case lying on the desk in the library and opened it. And after that I knew that Thayer had received the five thousand dollars in a lump sum and was doling it out to Maggie as it suited him. There was no use telling Maggie. She did not have enough nerve to collect, and it would only make her feel worse. But it was then that I decided that I had had enough, that it was dangerous for me to stay, that I would leave as soon and as quietly as I could, that I would go to some strange place where Thayer could never find me and bring me back.

I was not going to make Alice's mistakes. When a man is the grandson of a lunatic and has been proved a liar and a brute, one cannot be too careful in dealing with him. I had arranged a dinner party for Dan Warren and his wife, whom I had not met, the next

Thursday. I would see that through. It would give me time to get ready. Then I would go.

What Thayer knew or sensed, I have no way of knowing. I had tried to put the papers back in the brief case exactly as I had found them. Perhaps I had not succeeded. Anyway, he knew that something had gone wrong. Evening after evening, listening to the November wind howling outside, we would sit by the fireplace, each with eyes fixed steadfastly on a book. Then, sooner or later, I would look up and he would be watching me, quietly, blankly watching.

I tried to be normal about it. I would smile at him. "What are you staring at?" I would say.

"My wife." Even his voice sounded different. It was heavier, duller, than it had been.

"I should have thought you'd seen enough of the creature." Me, gaily.

"I shall never see enough of her till the day I die."

Since we had come home there had been little display of affection between us. Now I could scarcely let him kiss me. I would turn my cheek suddenly at the very last, brace myself as I might. This happened twice. Then he made no effort to touch me again. But his watchfulness doubled. Often, when he walked out into the snowy darkness in the mornings to get into his car, I would find myself leaning against the wooden panels, breathing fast, and listening with all my might for the welcome sound of the motor fading away toward the distant main road. And as I turned back to clear away the breakfast things the fire would leap cheerily in the fireplace, the brass andirons would glow, the rooms would spring into the gaiety I had sensed in them when I first saw them, the gaiety that vanished under the heavy brooding of Thayer's eyes on it. Twelve hours before I had to worry again about his coming home! Twelve lovely long hours!

The nights were the worst of all. Dinner could be borne, and the table-clearing and dishwashing took a welcome hour, while Thayer retired to the library to work. With small talk and careful casualness another hour or two could be patched up presentably. Then came the awful task of turning out the lights and lying down by the side of a man whom I suspected of being half-mad and who must not guess that I thought so. I was firmly resolved not to go to sleep before he did, and it seemed to me he fell asleep a little later every night. Strange to picture two people lying so close in the darkness, one rigidly listening for the first even breaths of the other, and that other surely aware of it. At first I had a hard time staving off sleep, and then it was impossible for me to sleep at all. There were seven nights in a row when I found it absolutely impossible to close my eyes, even after Thayer had fallen into a moaning, restless slumber. Why it was so important for me to stay awake, I don't know. I had the feeling, which I know now is common to insomniacs, that if I closed my eyes I would be defenseless. I would be lost. Terribly frightened as I was, I could not put a finger on exactly what I feared. It had to do with Thayer and the change in him and the fact that his former wife's death had seemed suspicious to at least two people. He could not poison me. I made sure of that. After my talk with Maggie I did not eat or drink anything that I had not prepared myself, and even then I waited until Thayer had taken the first mouthful.

I think, perhaps, that I dreaded most the possibility that he might somehow discover that I meant to run away and take measures to prevent it. In my imagination there was no limit to the severity these measures might take. I fancied him chaining me in the basement or locking me in the little room in the attic or—— Well, the Brandon burying ground was full of tombstones over people who might or might not have died naturally, and the police had been mildly interested in two of them already. But Maggie, with her daily trotting to my door, would have been hard to explain to, and if I disappeared for long, Sergeant Stark, for all his thinking poorly of me, would be shaking the veranda with his heavy black boots and looking through the Brandons' answers to the truth beyond.

And every morning now, after the first glorious relief of Thayer's leaving, I would notice that the rooms were a little different than I had left them the night before. A magazine that had been in the rack would be lying on the pink pouf. The level of the coffee left in the glass Silex would be lower and there might be sugar in the bottom of one of the two cups we had used the night before, although neither Thayer nor I took sugar. Queerly enough, this did not bother me. I was too involved in my own problem to think how horrifying it was that, while I lay sleepless in a room upstairs, someone on the floor below could move quietly as a cat, sit by my fire, read a magazine in the dead of night, finish the coffee. It was worse than that, actually. One morning when I approached my dressing table I found that the nail file had been left out of my manicure kit and that my powder puff had fallen on the floor, and I remembered distinctly that each had been in its proper place when I turned out the lights eight hours before. I had not slept for a moment of that eight hours —that I could swear to—yet someone had entered the room in the dark, had fumbled with the things on the table so quietly that I, two feet away, had not been conscious of it, and had left, all without a sound or a hint of movement. That morning I checked on every door and window on the main floor. They were locked, just as we had left them.

I could mention none of this to Thayer, for fear of provoking him. It might all be part of the great riddle which I was not supposed to try to solve. Evidently someone had a key. I could not believe that Thayer did not know and condone its use. I did not want trouble. My only wish was to keep him quiet until I could leave.

I thought enough of it, though, oddly without fear, to find out what I could. Not from Maggie, because, after her revelation about Alice, she had closed up like a clam on family matters. But when Mrs. Moss came to my door one blowy morning with a chocolate cake, I whisked her inside and had a cup of coffee in her hands before she could protest.

"It's terribly cold out this morning, Mrs. Moss. You're a brave woman to make the trip."

She sat, awkward and uneasy, on the edge of her chair. A faithful, efficient woman, Mrs. Moss, but far from bright. "I'm used to the cold. I've lived around here all my life."

"It seems odd that when they built this second house they didn't make some provision for winter traffic. You'd have thought there would be a tunnel between the two houses, or some connection that would let you get from one to the other without freezing to death."

"I guess they didn't think of it."

"Or maybe there is one that we don't know about, one that's not used any more."

"Oh, I don't think so. I didn't come here until after Miss Effie's husband died and both the houses were already built. But I've never seen anybody go from one to the other except over the road."

I spent part of that day in the cellar, however, tapping on walls and getting cobwebs in my hair to no avail. The cellar was very ordinary. There was a well and pump room with a tank and odd-looking mechanical equipment. There were the high walls, open at the top, that enclosed the soft-water cistern. I climbed up on a chair and peered over the top. Nothing there but the dark water that came in from the gutters and was filtered through tile for all our household purposes save drinking. The furnace and hot-water heater stood in another corner, and the fruit cellar and laundry rooms were exactly what they purported to be. Nothing unusual, nothing sinister. Whoever came in the house came by the front door.

I drove into Petoskey that week to find out what time I could get a train that would eventually lead me to New York. There was a train that left at one o'clock in the morning and reached Detroit in time to catch a New York express. I bought my ticket. I checked two large dry-goods boxes which held as many of my things as I dared take, and the station man looked at me suspiciously as he handed me my tag.

"Any relation to the Brandons up north of Harbor Springs?"

"None," I said. "None at all. I've just been visiting here in town."

"Not an ordinary name."

"No. It isn't."

He let it go at that, and I was glad. Fortunately there were only two more nights before I would be gone. If it were longer, the whole town and Harbor Springs and Brandon Oaks could be stirred by the ripples from this man's curiosity. He watched me all the way out the station door, and I knew that he would ask the next person he saw, "Know of any Brandons visiting here in town? Young woman by that name came in here today acting like she was going to make a quick getaway. Just wondered."

It did not make me feel better to see Sergeant Stark drive by just as I crossed to my car, even though he carefully ignored me.

The Warrens came to dinner the next night. Mrs. Warren was pale and small and gentle, talkative from the long silences that women in that area must endure in the winter.

"We're leaving for Detroit right after Thanksgiving," she said. "This is the latest we've ever stayed here. The doctor thinks it's healthy for me. I don't see how the air can do me much good when I can't go out of the house for fear of freezing to death."

Dan laughed. "She always says that. Actually we take a two-hour walk every morning. I have to drag her out of the house, but by the time we come back she's warm as toast. The next morning she claims it's too cold for her again, and I have to put the pressure on to get her started. She never learns."

"But we do really have to get back. Dan's been away from his business far too long on my account. I know he's itching to get his hands on that factory again."

"I've never said so, my dear."

She smiled shyly at him. "I know you haven't. You're far too nice to me."

Thayer was being urbane and charming. "That would be impossible, Mrs. Warren."

"What about you and Elizabeth?" Dan said. "I suppose you'll be leaving for a while too. Usually take a run down to Florida over the holidays, don't you, Thayer?"

"I can't get away this year. The real-estate business is booming."

"Then perhaps you'll send Elizabeth by herself," said Mrs. Warren. "Winter is so dreary here if you're not used to it. She could stop off on her way and visit with us for a while. We'd love to have her."

"I'm sure she'd like to come," said Thayer, "but I'm a selfish monster. I don't think I can spare her this winter. I was rather hoping that Dan had decided to leave you up here and take the plane back and forth on week ends."

Mrs. Warren stumbled into a faux pas. "We talked about it, and I think I might have considered it if I hadn't had such a scare the night that Miss——" She suddenly realized that Anne was Thayer's sister. There was an awkward silence.

"Yes, we were so sorry about that," Thayer said smoothly. "Anne had no business doing it. We've known the Warrens so long and gotten so in the habit of dropping in on them at odd hours that I don't suppose she thought. I know she was distressed that you had been frightened."

The last night, I kept thinking. Tomorrow night at one o'clock I will be gone. Thayer had planned not to let me out of his sight this winter, but tomorrow I'm going. If I can only keep Thayer as calm as he is now until then! I don't want any scenes, I don't want any trouble; I might say something too honest, and there would be danger in that.

My eyes ached from weariness, but, though I had been without sleep for a long time, I was not sleepy. The evening passed in a hospitable blur from which I did not emerge until Mrs. Warren took my hands at the door.

"You don't look as well as you did, Elizabeth. You must take better care of yourself. Oh, I used to see you walking on the beach and I envied you. You don't look much like the same girl."

Behind Thayer's amber eyes something unpleasant stirred, but he came up and put a careless arm around me. "Elizabeth's nervous," he said. "She hasn't been sleeping well. We'll get her in to see a doctor this week."

"A little nervous indigestion, perhaps," said Mrs. Warren guilelessly, and looked startled when her husband pinched her arm warningly.

Thayer turned to me the minute they had left the porch. "You're not going to have a baby, are you?" he asked harshly.

My knees began to quiver. "No. Nothing like that."

"Then I wish you'd make an honest effort to look better. I can't say I want all our acquaintances talking about your newly poor health."

"I feel all right."

He stared at me thoughtfully. "Do you?" he said finally, and went upstairs.

I took a long time clearing the table and doing the dishes. I wanted to make sure that he would be asleep when I went up. I straightened the whole house, emptying every ash tray, running the hand sweeper, fluffing the pillows.

In our room I undressed in the dark and crept softly into bed. There was no sound of breathing. Thayer was as awake as I was. What was he waiting for? Why didn't he sleep? An hour must have gone by; my hands were wet with nervous perspiration when he finally spoke.

"Are you meeting Stark in town these days?"

I knew that to seem natural I should be indignant and angry. I simply could not manage it.

"No, I'm not."

He didn't say anything more. It must have been three o'clock when I knew that he was at last asleep.

CHAPTER X

THINGS went very much as usual that last morning. At a quarter of seven Thayer was dressed, downstairs, and out in the car for his daily drive to the mailbox for the morning paper. At seven he was back with it, I had breakfast on the table, we were eating to the accompaniment of rustling pages. At seven-thirty he had his coat and hat on and I was walking to the door with him. In the days when we had first been married we had made this little walk arm in arm. Now I lagged a good three paces behind and hoped that my conversation would be friendly enough to hide the unfriendly fact.

Outside the first gray streaks of dawn were showing and snow was driving in on the cold wind from the lake. Thayer slipped on his gauntlets, picked up his brief case.

"Take a long walk today, Elizabeth. You might call on Mrs. Warren, since they are leaving so soon. I'd like her to see you with some color in your face so she'll know we're not abusing you."

I said something, smiled, nodded, closed the door after him, and listened to the wonderful sound of the car crackling and sliding away up the drive. I almost laughed aloud. Almost free now. Only the barrier of the evening to pass. It didn't matter that someone had stacked the glass ash trays neatly, though the night before I had left them separate to dry better. It didn't matter that I had only a hundred dollars to my name or that I was going to a place where I had never been, among people I did not know. It did not bother me that I would have a long, dark walk into Harbor Springs that night, where I might or might not find a taxi to take me on to Petoskey. I did not belong here. Nobody belonged here but the Brandons.

At ten I started for my farewell walk, bundled to the eyes, fur-lined boots tied on firmly. Down the drive toward the lake, eyes half shut against the snow, fingers moving inside of gloves to keep the circulation going. Past the other house, where nothing stirred. Skirting the low stone parapet that I had first seen covered with roses a lifetime ago. Through the woods, now protesting their load of ice and snow. Out into the clearing where the white stones stood,

the gray lake heaving beyond, the snow falling more gently there.
I cried a little. I fully expected that this was the last visit I would
ever make to my mother's grave.

I did not go near the Warrens'. I did not want to see anyone that
day. Miraculous how one can love a place and dislike the people
who live there. I knew I would miss the lake and the trees and the
Indian spire. Under the circumstances I could never come back here.

I did not consider that I was doing a cowardly or underhanded
thing in running away. Alice had taken the brave way, and here I
was standing near her grave.

Sergeant Stark stepped out of the woods to my left, a big, dark
apparition against all that whiteness. He saw that I had been crying, I think, for his manner was friendly again.

"Want to see something?" he said, and motioned me to follow
him.

We went only a little way into the woods, where a little knot of
men clustered around something on the ground. Two of them were
Indians; the other was a police officer. They leaned on shovels and
picks and watched us coming.

"They're both here, Bill," the officer said.

They had found the dogs. I looked at the rough white pelts and
felt that I was going to be sick. The sergeant led me a little distance
away and sat me down on a log.

"They're the Brandon dogs, all right, aren't they?" he said. "I
wasn't sure. The collars are missing."

"How were they killed?"

"Shot through the head. I think right near where they fell. They'd
have been quite a load to drag from a distance. Whoever buried
them didn't do a very good job of it. Shallow and not concealed at
all. One of the Indians got curious and reported it, so we came up
to see."

"Who could have done it?"

"Effie."

"She wouldn't have. She loved them."

"She must have done it. She was the first to know they were gone.
If she hadn't known what had happened to them would she have
given me that story about sending them away to a friend?"

"But why should she kill them? She was sure they'd never touched
the sheep. You were sure too."

"I can't answer for all the sheep that were killed. Remember I saw only one. But from what I can find out from Mr. Lucas, it's possible that the throats of the others were cut too, and that then the dogs savaged them."

"I'm sure the dogs were locked up the time the last sheep was killed."

"Then they were let out on purpose for it. Their teeth marks were all over it."

"Maybe it was the other way around. The dogs found it and mangled it so badly that whoever came along put it out of its misery."

"We thought of that too, but it won't work. The only wound bad enough to inconvenience that sheep seriously was in its throat."

The men were burying the dogs again. The ground was hard, and they sweated in the cold. Sergeant Stark kept his eyes on my face, and I thought how different his watchfulness was from Thayer's, the difference between a friendly, alert studiousness and a brooding, dangerous anger.

"I knew," he said, "that they hadn't been sent anywhere. The station man is a friend of mine, curious as a pup, and he would certainly have told the town if those two big dogs had been shipped from there. He never keeps a secret."

I said nothing, and he finally sighed a little.

"Well, anyway, there's nothing to do about this. It's not our business. No crime to kill your own dogs, and Mr. Lucas was paid for the sheep. Curious, though, and interesting."

He walked back with me as far as the clearing, and when I looked back he was walking around among the gravestones, studying them.

I saw no tracks in the snow other than my own as I went back. Yet that evening Thayer had hardly gotten inside the door when he began.

"Did you send for Stark this morning?"

His eyes were bloodshot, and I could smell liquor on his breath.

"No."

"You saw him, though. You saw him trespassing on our property and you didn't order him off!"

"I didn't know it was your property and I certainly didn't know I could order him off."

"What did he say about the dogs?"

"He said an Indian had reported that something was buried in a shallow grave in the woods, so he came up to see what it was. When he found the dogs he said they were none of his business, and they buried them again."

He set his brief case down and took off his hat and coat. He seemed quieter now.

"I'm glad he's showing some sense. My sister feels badly enough over having to get rid of the dogs without being pried at with silly questions."

I said it before I thought. "Why did she have to get rid of them? They weren't killing the sheep, and she knew it."

"No matter what her private convictions were, she thought, since there had been so much trouble about the dogs, she would dispose of them. It wasn't easy for her."

He was more friendly that evening than he had been for weeks. He ate a good dinner and complimented my cooking. He carried the coffee tray into the living room for me and told me he would help me with the dishes later. Almost I wavered. It was so bitterly cold outside and—this one evening—so warm and peaceful within. The telephone rang just as we sat down with our coffee.

Thayer came back from it and put on his coat. "That was Effie," he said shortly. "Anne's been out of the house since five o'clock and hasn't come back yet. The women have been out looking for her, but they haven't found her. I may not be back for a long while. Lock the doors and go to bed."

I did neither. I ran upstairs to change into my warmest clothes. It was then nine o'clock. I had to allow three hours for the walk to Harbor Springs; the roads were so lonely in winter that I could not count on a passing car to pick me up. Somewhere at Harbor Springs I would find a car to take me in to the station. I had to take the chance that in the four-hour interval between now and when the train left a search for me would not be started in the right direction. I would not go into the station at all. I would wait around some dark corner and get aboard without fanfare.

My fingers were trembling so that I could hardly fasten my wool skirt and jacket, and when I heard a knock on the front door and then footsteps crossing the living room to find me I had a momentary impulse to run into my closet and hide. It was Maggie, ancient black coat and old-fashioned galoshes, who plodded up the stairs to find me. Her nose was red with the cold and she was panting a little.

"We haven't found her yet. I'm about played out," she said, and slumped into the bedroom chair. Then her eyes took in the hasty aspect of the room. "Were you going out? No need for you to freeze to death too."

"I'm leaving, Maggie. I'm taking the one o'clock train from Petoskey."

She sat for a minute taking it in. "I wish I were going with you."

"You can if you want to. Go pack some things and get your money. If I can make it, you can too. There'll be room on the train. We can get your ticket then."

"I—there's not time enough."

But in the end she said she would. It was her big chance, and she could not let it go.

"I couldn't tell you before, Maggie. You might have given the whole thing away."

She was vastly excited. "I'll hurry. I'll meet you at the road, right by the mailbox, in half an hour."

"Don't bring too many things. We may have to walk the whole way."

"Don't worry. I don't have many things to bring."

It was then that we heard the faint stirring in the attic, the light footsteps crossing the floor just over our heads. Maggie looked as though she were going to faint, and I could do nothing but stare out at the hall, waiting. The attic steps swung down gently, and Anne came down, walking slowly. She did not look at us, though we were in the light and only a few feet away from her. Her eyes were glazed; she did not appear to know where she was or where she was going. She went on downstairs, and we heard the front door close softly after her.

Maggie awoke. "I'll run after her and steer her home. There'll be a lot of excitement. I can still slip away."

It made this much difference, though. I stumbled up the slippery drive without daring to turn on my flashlight, holding the gray pottery horse, the last belonging I had not dared to pack lest it should be missed; and the wait by the snow-capped mailbox seemed interminable. Discouraging, too, that not a car passed in the interval, but understandable. The snowplows did not clear this road, and the two icy furrows that cars had cleared for themselves did not invite casual travel.

Maggie came, breathless and apologetic, and we crunched off down the road, keeping in the shadows as much as we could. We turned on our flashlights only where the footing was worst. Otherwise we had the dim and difficult lighting of the starlight shimmering on the ice to guide us. She had not had time to pack a suitcase.

"I can buy new things," she said airily. "I have my thousand dollars pinned inside my dress. They were all rushing around getting Anne to bed, and I couldn't chance it."

"What was she doing in the attic?"

"Sleeping, she says. I think, though, that she had had one of her trances, because she acts worn out and says she has a headache. When I ran after her and took her arm she turned on me and pulled away. 'Dreadful child!' she said in a high, clear voice like her mother's. After that she went willingly enough."

"Do you think she could be losing her mind, Maggie?"

"Well, she's been getting queerer year by year. They all have, for that matter."

It was shortly after that that she sat down in a snowbank and said that she could go no farther.

"You'll have to go on ahead, Elizabeth. My legs are short and they're worn out from this afternoon. I'm not going to be able to make it."

She was still sitting there, in tears, when a lone car came jouncing down the road, and Sergeant Stark put his head out the window.

"Only expected one of you," he said. "Going to Harbor Springs?"

Maggie fell asleep in the back seat as soon as the heater had warmed her a little. I sat bolt upright in front, a little angry that my plans had been so transparent.

"The stationmaster?" I said.

"Sure."

"Why were you interested enough to come? I'm not doing anything wrong."

"You're doing absolutely right. As to why I was interested enough, there are two answers to that. I'll give you the second one. I didn't want you to make a long, dark walk like this alone. It isn't safe. I didn't know you were going to have company. You bought only one ticket."

"She came at the last minute. What's the first answer?"

"I can't tell you that, but you would have heard it if you hadn't married Brandon about two weeks too soon."

I could think of nothing to say to that, and he laughed shortly.

"There's always 'I didn't know you cared,' " he suggested.

Suddenly I was awkward and shy and grateful for Maggie's snoring in the back seat.

"I suppose you don't know quite where you're going yet," he said more briskly. "I want you to send me an address where I can reach you whenever you get settled. You don't have to worry about my giving it away. Just let me know how things are going with you. And if an emergency arises up here, someone should know how to get in touch with you. Legally you'll still be Brandon's wife."

"Unless he divorces me for desertion."

"He won't. Don't count on that. Unless he wants to remarry, which isn't likely."

We slid and skidded through the streets of Harbor Springs and headed out on the Petoskey road. Maggie woke up and began to cry.

"I want to go home," she sniffled. "I'm not brave enough. I don't want to go."

Between us we consoled her. "I think, though," Stark said, "that you'd be better off separately. I can give you the address of a woman in Chicago, Miss Maggie, who'll see that you get on your feet, if you want to go there."

"I don't think I have any feet left," she wailed, but in the end she agreed that it might be better. And when he went on to sketch her probable future as a brisk, well-dressed workingwoman, she grew really cheerful.

"And if I do fail," she said sensibly, "I can always come back. They'd be glad to have me."

"And Thayer still owes you four thousand dollars," I reminded her. "He can't dodge that. You'll be getting it someday, when you decide to let him know where you are."

So it was that Maggie left on a train ahead of mine.

"I'll let Mr. Stark know my address, too," she said, "and he can let each of us know where the other is. I'll write to you, Elizabeth," she shrieked from the train platform as it began to move, "and you write to me. Good-by. Good-by."

There were tears in my eyes as I watched the short, plump figure, frantically waving, bravely clutching the scrap of paper with the address the sergeant had given her, borne away. I cried again when I boarded my own train and looked down at the sergeant.

"Good-by, kid," he said crisply, "and good luck."

It was eight years before I saw either of them again.

I have recorded my first Brandon interlude in detail because the murder that came later is more intelligible against this background. In it are contained the details that the newspapers did not get or, indeed, inquire for, and without it all that followed seems the work of a homicidal maniac, which it was not. Our crime was fully motivated and firmly planned. There were mistakes in its commission, but the very errors misled us; and the mischief and daring and imagination that went into it were superbly camouflaged. They had served the same purpose, more subtly, years before I came to the Oaks; they were still at work on my first and second visits there.

I almost forgot Brandon Oaks during the ensuing eight years. I was busy teaching and working on a doctor's degree and teaching again. Maggie was doing well in Chicago. She had started as a saleslady in the corset department of a big store, and she did so well at it that she was eventually given charge of it. She sent me a snaphot of herself once, and I hardly recognized her. She had lost weight, her hair was done smoothly, and her clothes were quietly smart.

"I'm so glad I came here," she wrote me. "I should have come long ago. I am feeling more and more like a real person instead of a shadow in the corner of the Brandon kitchen. Yesterday I visited the orphanage that took me when I was a baby, to see whether I could remember it at all. I couldn't. If I had not known its name and that it was in this city, I could have passed it every day in ignorance. The matron was very pleasant, and, since she is an older woman too, I think we may become friends. At any rate, she came into the store the day after, and I sold her one of our best corsets. She needs a good one, because her hip measurements . . ."

Thus Maggie. Sergeant—and later Lieutenant—Stark wrote infrequently and with restraint. "There was quite a hullabaloo after you left," he wrote. "I was called in, and I admitted giving the two of you a lift to the station. That didn't hurt anything. It stopped their searching for your bodies, and they could have found out about your ticket to Detroit, anyway. What private investigators Thayer may have on your trail, I can't say. Since you are evidently still using the Brandon name, you ought not be too hard to find. But sit tight. It isn't a crime to run away from a husband, and they can't put you in jail for it."

And later. "Things are very quiet this summer. I saw Thayer in Harbor Springs—he ignored me, naturally—and he looks old. His hair is white and he's too thin. Dr. Day was with him. They visit here quite often, even in the winter."

And again. "I think they know where you are—they must, with you out in the open like that. But I don't think their agencies have located Maggie. Anyway, Anne said something to me yesterday that led me to think they hadn't and that they thought she was with you. I can't account for this. If their boys are any good at all, they should know that you're by yourself."

It was in June 1941 that the letter came from Effie. I had never seen any of her handwriting; I did not look at the postmark; I opened it casually with nothing on my mind but the stack of themes I must correct.

Thayer was dead.

"He died a month ago, of pneumonia," said the letter. "We knew where you were, we have known for a long time, but he did not want us to send for you. We are a proud people, and you left us under circumstances that he found it difficult to forgive. But he willed his house to you, and there are some other legal matters that will need to be straightened up. It seems advisable that you come up here so that matters can be adjusted. You need fear no unpleasantness from Anne or myself. Indeed, we are anxious to buy the house from you. The chances are you will not want to live there permanently yourself, and we should hate to have strangers there."

I dreaded going, but I knew I must. I need not, however, go alone. I sent a hasty wire to Maggie, asking if she could join me there for a month, and, though she was reluctant, she could arrange it.

We met in Detroit, and we were a different pair than when we had separated. I was thinner; I wore my hair up severely; my glasses changed the upper part of my face. Maggie was white-haired now, but it became her; her skin and hair showed care, and her clothes were impeccable. She was excited at the prospect of seeing Brandon Oaks again, but she mourned the fact that she had left Chicago so suddenly that she had not been able to say good-by to any of her friends.

"They won't like it at all," she said, blushing a little. "It was my turn to have the club this week, and I had to cancel that. And I had just met the nicest elderly gentleman who wanted to take me out to dinner. He's a widower. Has one son who's married and lives in California."

"Why, Maggie!"

"Now, Elizabeth, I have no reason to think of him as anything but a chivalrous gentleman who's being kind to a lonesome woman!"

But she laughed self-consciously and bent to peer into the box that held John Silver, my white Persian cat that I was bringing along with me at the risk of his eternal feline hate.

"He'll bother the birds," she said practically.

"He's much too lazy to chase a bird. Anyway, his collar has bells on it."

"Well, Effie won't like it. That's one satisfaction."

I shook her hand soberly. "Maggie, I feel as if I hardly knew you."

We took a taxi from town to Brandon Oaks and laughed to recall the cold night when we had stumbled toward independence.

"To think I almost turned back," she marveled.

She made the driver stop at the mailbox where we left the main road for the driveway. There was a fat letter for her, but it was not from the "elderly gentleman." It was from a Mrs. Page, according to the return address, and Maggie sniffed and tucked it into her purse. But as we wound nearer the lake and the two white houses and the rose-covered garden, some of her new poise slipped away from her, and she huddled down in her corner. I felt a little sick myself. Brandon Oaks was so exactly as we had left it.

CHAPTER XI

EFFIE MET US AT THE DOOR, greeted me with more cordiality than I had expected, and turned a polite, inquiring face on my companion. Her eyes were failing her and she wore thick glasses.

"You've brought someone with you," she said. "Then you will want to stay in this house, of course. Anne and I had thought you might be lonesome, and I was thinking of asking you down to stay with us."

"This is Miss Mitchell," I said.

"Hello, Effie," said Maggie. She sailed into the house under Effie's dumfounded nose and threw herself nonchalantly into a chair. "I'm dying for a cigarette. Have one, Ef?"

I had never before heard Effie Brandon addressed as Ef, and the effect was startling. Effie reached out a trembling hand and accepted a cigarette and a light from the blithe Maggie.

"It's—it's been a long time, Maggie," she said. "How have you been and what have you been doing?"

Maggie told her, emphasizing her importance to the store, dwelling on the large numbers of good friends she had made, hinting at a large and stylish wardrobe, doing herself complete justice.

"You've no idea how many people you can meet in a big store," she finished, "or how a woman will love you like a sister if you can sell her the girdle she needs. You look as though you'd be better off with a new one yourself, Effie. Put on a little weight since I last saw you."

"I'm afraid Anne and I have both gained," Effie said stiffly. "We're not as young and active as we used to be."

She was even less pleased when she saw John Silver emerge from his long confinement, feathery tail waving, white ruff abristle, green eyes bored.

"I hope you plan to keep that cat in the house, Elizabeth. You know how many birds we have around here and how many of them come to bathe at the pool in the garden."

"He's a house cat. He prefers being indoors. And I don't think he would exert himself to catch anything."

John threw himself against Effie's ankles in an unprecedented ecstasy, and she bent down to pet him. "Well," she said grudgingly, "maybe he'll be all right."

She unbent, then, and told us all the news. Dan Warren had come back and opened his house the week before. "Mrs. Warren died two years ago, you know." Dr. Day and his wife and son had taken a cottage two miles away for the summer. There were new summer boarders at the Lucas farm. We would find our refrigerator and cupboards stocked with food—"Enough to see you through lunch, anyway"—but she and Anne would like to have us for dinner that night.

"I have the papers down there," she said, "and we can get things straightened out. I've asked Dan Warren, too, and the Days may drop in later."

Maggie brightened. "A party! Do we dress, Effie?"

"It won't be formal. I'm wearing a long dress, though—black, naturally."

I had been looking around the living room. It was precisely as when I had left it, colorful, gay, dimmed only a little by the passage of the years. The pink velvet pouf still sat in front of the fireplace with the two big chairs flanking it. There was the drum table where Thayer had always put the coffee tray. There was the group of chairs in the bay window, just as they had been that cold afternoon when Anne and Maggie and I had had tea. The piano was closed, but there was music on its rack. Through the open windows came the perfume of a thousand roses on the warm wind from the lake. At any minute I had been expecting to see Thayer come into the room with his long, lithe stride, his aquiline face amiable, his amber eyes friendly as they had been the first months I knew him. Now Effie and her black dinner dress reminded me.

"I'm so terribly sorry, Effie."

"Perhaps we should have notified you sooner, but there seemed to be no reason for disturbing you. He had had a bad cold for a month, and he refused to take care of it. Then, suddenly, it was more than a cold. We called Dr. Raymond from Petoskey, but it was too late. He was delirious for two days, and then he died."

"I can't pretend that our marriage was a fortunate one, but I am sorry that I did not see him again."

"Mrs. Moss suggested that we send for you, but Thayer was quite vehement about it. Of course his temperature was already very high. Perhaps he did not know what he was saying."

When she got up to go she did an astounding thing. She took Maggie's hand and smiled at her. "I think I'm very glad to see you, Maggie," she said simply.

Maggie's knees barely held her up until the screen door closed. She fell back into her chair again and stared at me. "Now what do you make of that!" she exclaimed.

"What I make of it is that we're going to have a better summer than I had thought."

I could not wait to unpack. I wanted to take my old familiar walk, down past the garden, through the woods, out to the cemetery, and from there down the cliff and on to the Indian village on the beach. All but once I had stopped just out of sight of the village and turned and gone home. Perhaps today I would go on and see the church again, and perhaps by this time the villagers would not be so shy and I would not have to feel myself unwelcome and strange.

"I see someone has taken Alice's picture down," said Maggie. "It was there when you left, wasn't it? I wonder if Thayer took it down afterward or whether his sisters thought it would be more tactful for you not to inherit a house with a first wife's picture looking at you."

"I didn't mind the picture. It was pretty. I'm rather sorry it's gone."

Maggie—the new, smart, tailor-made Maggie—was abruptly shy. "I've been trying to tell you, Elizabeth, that I'm a very different person now than when I was here before. It's thinking of Alice that makes me feel most guilty. I remember how silly I was to tell you that I thought she had been poisoned. You mustn't hold that against me. I was ill then, sick with years of resentment for what I considered unfair treatment from the Brandons. Anything I could do or say to bother them, I did. Now I can see that I should have been blaming myself, that if I had had any initiative or self-respect, I would have been independent long ago. But simply because I was lazy and limp and weak-spined, I allowed myself to be treated like a poor relation, and I deserved it. I'm to blame, not they."

"That's very generous of you, Maggie."

She took out a prim white handkerchief and dabbed at her eyes. "Tell the truth and shame the devil," she said, "and I guess I need my lunch. I'm starved."

We went into the kitchen, found cold ham and potato salad in the refrigerator, made coffee and buttered bread. Maggie had lost none of the appetite that had formerly been a source of amusement to the Brandons. She ate largely of everything, while I sipped a token cup of coffee and longed to be outdoors. I escaped at the first decent moment, leaving Maggie still sipping and about to open the letter from Mrs. Page.

I raced down the sandy drive, John Silver playing feline tag at my heels. Such a panorama of blue and white and silver! Such a wonderful day to have come back to such a beautiful place! What an imaginative, nervous little fool I had been, years before, to have sensed death and tragedy and decay in this superb setting!

It was my last moment of unmitigated gaiety. Anne and Mr. Warren were standing by the garden parapet, and, while they spoke to me hospitably, I could not help but sense that there was a certain reserve in their manner, a guardedness that would increase and grow and spread until it took in almost everyone I met.

"You never came for that visit you promised us," Dan Warren said.

"I wanted to, but I had to keep my nose pretty close to the grindstone. I was so sorry to hear of Mrs. Warren's death."

"Yes. It wasn't sudden. We had been expecting it for years. Cancer. She was a brave woman. Kept up right to the minute she died."

Anne interrupted. "Effie says Maggie is with you and that she didn't recognize her at first."

"She's been in Chicago. I thought she might enjoy coming along with me, and I found she could arrange it."

Dan was watching me. "You and she were always great pals. I suppose you have no secrets from each other."

"You could hardly say that. When I was here before we had little time to get together, and I haven't seen her since we—left."

Their patronizing airs were annoying, and I had a childish impulse to disturb them. I turned to Anne. "I never did find out how you came to be having a nap in my attic the day I left."

I had succeeded. She flushed and bit her lip. "I had gone up there to look for something. I—I hadn't been sleeping well, and the bed looked inviting."

"That dusty old mattress? You must have been sleepy!"

Dan came to her rescue. He was smiling as falsely and pleasantly as I was, but there was viciousness behind it. "And we never found out just why you ran away as you did. Surely it must have been a temptation to leave a note. All women leave notes."

"You would know better about that than I. As to why I left, it was because I had reason to think that my husband was going to kill me."

Anne burst out indignantly, "Thayer? How absurd!" But she threw an imploring look at Dan when she said it.

He broke in smoothly. "Thayer was under a great strain at the time, and you were very young. You misconstrued his attitude, of course."

"I don't see why 'of course.' There are men who kill their wives. The papers are full of them."

He smiled. "I see I shall have to secure a medical statement of the cause of my wife's death."

I had forgotten that, and the enormity of my behavior overwhelmed me. "I'm dreadfully sorry, Mr. Warren. I didn't mean that personally. Please believe that."

He laughed; the conversation became more polite. I was glad to escape. Johnny and I pelted through the woods and brought up sharply in the clearing. There was a new stone there, beside Alice's. The legend on it was stern and restrained: "Thayer Brandon—Born 1889, Died 1941." Try as I would, I could feel no real tie between myself and the body under that stone. It was seeing Mother's grave again that made me cry.

Then John and I were off again, both of us careening with the drunkenness of the sun and the air. I took off my glasses and let my hair blow. Down the rocks I scrambled, painfully grasping at boughs and twigs, skinning my knees on that descent that had always seemed more natural to me than the rustic stairs at Brandon Oaks. John leaped precariously from rock to rock, his surprise at human awkwardness apparent, his own balance meticulous and accurate, his eyes shining at the revelation that there was a better life than was possible in a two-room apartment.

I had my walk, felt guilty when I got back to the house at having stayed away so long, and felt guiltier still when I found the cases not yet unpacked and Maggie in bed, her face a pale green.

"I ate too much lunch," she moaned. "Potato salad never did agree with me."

"What can I get you, Maggie?"

"Nothing. I've taken everything I could lay my hands on, and I've already given back the lunch. I think I'll be all right."

When the time came to go down to the other house for dinner, she still looked white and strained but she insisted on going. I helped her dress, and, while she was limp, she was thoughtful.

"I don't think I should have come back here," she said. "I think I was better off where I was."

"You'll feel better in the morning."

To which she said nothing.

The dinner was not hilarious. Dan and I and Effie did all the talking; Maggie slumped in her chair and played with the silver, and Anne watched Maggie as a mouse watches a cat. Afterward Effie led the two of us into the library and we sat down around a desk covered with papers.

"It makes it simpler now that you're here, Maggie," she said. "Thayer had four thousand dollars of yours, and it's been drawing interest. Also he had the deeds to your other properties, and I can return those to you now."

She showed me the will which said that I was to have the house and that his sisters were to have everything else.

"I hope you think that's fair," she said. "As a matter of fact, that house and the things in it was all that belonged absolutely to him. The rest we held jointly."

"It seems perfectly fair to me. Legally, I daresay, he might have found ways to exclude me entirely. I wouldn't have blamed him."

I pinched Maggie's arm comfortingly as we walked out to the porch where Dan Warren and Anne were entertaining the Days. "Feeling better, Maggie?"

"I can't say that I do."

She perked up a bit for the benefit of the Days, however, and Dr. Day was impressed.

"Just goes to show you," he said, "what a change of scenery will do for a person. I wouldn't have known you, Maggie. Feeling on top of the world these days, I bet."

"I was, until this afternoon."

"And what great change," he said jokingly, "took place this afternoon?"

"I ate lunch."

The words fell like small, round pebbles into the silence on the dark porch. A cold draft swept my ankles, and I was clutching the arms of my chair, just as I had in the old days.

"And it didn't agree with you? Well, the weather's pretty warm and you've had a long trip. You'll be good as new tomorrow."

"Will I?" she said.

Another silence followed that, and Norah Day crashed into it.

"You girls will all have to come up to our house soon," she said. "Mrs. Deever has come for a visit. You remember, Elizabeth, she's the old nurse that took care of Thayer and Anne and Effie and Maggie when they were little. She's very old and frail now, but we thought she might enjoy a month here. Wonderful for Michael, too. He minds her when he won't pay any attention to me."

"I don't think I ever liked Mrs. Deever much," Anne said. "She wasn't fair."

Almost I could feel Effie reach out to warn her sister. "I don't know, Anne. She did her best. After all, we weren't an easy group to get along with."

Maggie rose abruptly and said that she would have to get back to her bed. "Don't come, Elizabeth. I'll be all right, really. I just need to lie down, that's all. Lovely dinner, Effie. Thanks so much."

Dan walked up the drive with her, despite her protests, and when he came back he was smiling. "Same old Maggie, really," he said. "Fussy and full of corners. Only now she has self-confidence with it and she isn't afraid to tell you what's on her mind. The way she goes on, you'd think that food had been poisoned!"

"You have to admire the way she's pulled herself up by her own bootstraps," Dr. Day said pontifically. "I didn't think her capable of it. Shows you the enormous reserve of strength latent in the human spirit."

Nathan came up to the door to say that he had turned the visitors' cars so they could head right out the drive, and he grinned a welcome to me.

"How are you, Miss Elizabeth?"

"Fine, Nathan. And you?"

"Can't complain. The station wagon—that's yours now—I have it all polished up and ready to go whenever you want it."

"Thank you, Nathan. I'll let you know."

He touched the brim of his old straw hat and turned to amble off to his rooms over the barn. Effie called after him to stop by at the kitchen, Mrs. Moss had something for him, and then we were drinking our coffee again in silence. There was desultory talk about the war in Europe, and Norah made the mistake of saying that war made only rich men happy.

"I don't see why," said Effie stiffly, "when a man manages, through his own skill and intelligence, to gather together a few more dollars than his neighbors have, he should be the butt for all the venomous things poorer people choose to say about him."

"I didn't mean——"

"My father was one of the richest men in the country, and, I daresay, if he had lived a few years longer he might have made a profit out of the First World War. It would have been a legitimate profit. He would have had something to sell that somebody else wanted to buy, and he would have been smart enough to get hold of it first, that's all. But, as the whole world knows, my father was not mean, nor was he a moneygrubber. I don't know how much of his fortune he spent on charities. We never knew the extent of his generosities. He made millions and he gave them away."

"I know," said Norah, "that Mr. Brandon had the reputation of being a Christian gentleman and lived a life above reproach. Even the newspapers had to admit that, and if they could have found a flaw in him, they would have. But can't you see, Effie, that giving a man charity isn't the same thing as giving him a chance to earn it in the first place? Now your father——"

John Silver leaped suddenly up on the step outside and meowed plaintively in the moonlight.

"Maggie must have let him out," I said. "I'd better take him home. He hasn't been here long enough to know his way around, and I'd hate to lose him."

It made a good excuse to break away. I found Maggie in bed, tossing restlessly.

"I brought the cat back," I said. "We'd better not let him out by himself for a while yet."

"I didn't let him out. He was asleep in his basket in the dining room when I came up."

"Then there's a screen loose somewhere."

But there wasn't. Every door was tight, every window faultless.

"You must have been mistaken, Maggie. He slips out so fast you must have missed him. He got out when you came home."

She was sure he hadn't, and there was no use arguing with her.

"Would you like a cold compress for your head?"

She said that she would and added, "But don't run any more water than you have to. Something's gone wrong with all the drains. We'll have to call some men in tomorrow."

Like any city dweller, I was outraged at this glaring inefficiency in country plumbing.

"What do you suppose is the matter with the darned things?"

"It's an old system and it hasn't been touched for years. I'll bet they have to dig a whole new drain field."

As I cold-creamed my face in lieu of washing it, I reflected that if the summer was to be spent watching men dig trenches on the lawn to the tune of six hundred dollars, the price Maggie had quoted me from experience, I might put the house on the market right away and cut my stay short.

CHAPTER XII

IT WAS EARLY in the morning of the second day of digging my new drain field that the men discovered Sue Kennedy's bones and notified the sheriff of our county. The first I knew that anything was wrong was when he tapped on my door and introduced himself as an officer of the law and the man with him as the county coroner. It could not have been more than eight o'clock in the morning; I had just taken a tray up to Maggie and was having my own toast and coffee in the bay window. The two of them walked in, forbidding, reserved, and suspicious, and though I was still in ignorance, my hand began to tremble so that I could not lift my cup. I asked what was wrong, but they ignored that.

"How long have you lived here, Mrs. Brandon?"

"I came two days ago."

"Why?"

"My husband died three months ago. I was asked to come to get the estate settled."

"You lived here before?"

"I lived here for six months in 1933. I have not been back since then. My husband stayed on here until his death."

"Alone?"

"Yes. His two sisters live in the other house."

"During the time you have lived here have you ever heard of anyone who was missing under suspicious circumstances?"

"No, I—— There was a little girl who was thought to have drowned. They didn't find her body, as far as I know."

The sheriff turned to the coroner. "That's right. I forgot about that, Doc, but it's down in the old records. I wasn't in office then. I think Lieutenant Stark tried to help the county out on that one."

"He was the one who looked for her," I said. "Her name was

Sue Kennedy. She and her parents had been staying at the Lucas place."

"How old was the child?" asked the doctor.

"Seven, I think."

He nodded to the sheriff. "That's about right. I can tell you better after the autopsy."

They told me then what the workmen had found and offered to take me out to see the spot.

"Do I have to? I'd rather not."

Which made them look more suspicious than ever.

The inquest was held at Petoskey the following Tuesday and lasted two days. I am indebted to the good offices of the law-enforcement agencies of Emmet County for permission to reprint here certain of the statements that were given in evidence. I quote first from Effie's.

I never saw Sue Kennedy alive or dead. I remember when the accident happened. I call it an accident because I am accustomed to thinking that she had drowned. My sister-in-law saw her from a distance on the beach the day she died. I know that Mr. Stark came to our house to ask if we had any information about her and we could not help him. It was an unfortunate time because my sister-in-law's mother had just died and she was staying with us. "How do you account for the fact that the child's body was found buried in the long stretch of lawn that separates the two houses?" I cannot account for it. "Where do you keep your gardening tools?" The smaller ones are kept in the areaway by the grade door. The larger ones are kept in the barn. "A spade or shovel, then, would be kept in the barn?" Yes. Nathan does all the heavy digging for us. "Are any digging tools kept at the other house?" Not to my knowledge. If my brother needed one he went to the barn for it. "Your nearest neighbors are half a mile away, are they not?" Yes. "Then it seems likely that the child's grave was dug with one of your own garden tools, does it not?" I have no opinion about that. It is a matter for the police to decide. "Do you recall an injury to your sister's hand the same evening the little girl was missed?" No, I—— Yes, it seems to me that she did cut her hand. I cannot say with what. She simply told me about it. "It was not serious enough to require a bandage?" I think not. "Yet we have evidence that blood was found in her bathroom in greater quantities than one might expect from a minor injury." If she had been badly hurt I would have known it. "Did you see the cut?" I don't remember. "We have been told that bits of the dead child's hair ribbon were found in the Indian church and on your lawn. Did you find any such bits of ribbon?" I did not.

I did not know that any had been found. "You owned dogs at that time. Do you believe they would be capable of attacking a child?" No, I do not. They were gentle, well-bred animals. Besides, at that time, they were being kept close at home. Mr. Lucas thought they were killing his sheep. I did not think they were. "Did you at any time examine any of the dead sheep?" Yes. "What did you think had been the cause of their death?" I thought that dogs had been after them. I did not think my dogs had. "Lieutenant Stark thought at the time that someone had cut the throats of the sheep and then urged the dogs upon the bodies. Were the throats of the ones you saw cut?" I can't say. The throats were badly mangled. It was distasteful to look at them. I can't see what the sheep have to do with the little girl. "Only that if there was a random killer at large, he might not have been too particular about what he killed. I understand that you are careful about locking your house." During the day all the doors are open, unless someone chooses to lock the door to his own room. At night we lock the outside doors, too. "And the doors to the individual bedrooms are kept locked at night, are they not?" Yes. It is a habit of ours. "It is not because you are afraid?" Afraid—of what? "I don't know, Miss Brandon. I submit to you that such a locking of doors usually indicates fear of something." I have never been afraid of anything in my life. "Do you recall having been down to the beach the day Sue Kennedy disappeared?" Anne and I took a walk down there after dark. We had not been out of the house much that day and we had a guest staying with us. "Was your brother with you?" No, he had gone back to his own house. I did not see him again that evening. "You and your sister met no one on this walk?" We did not. "You heard nothing suspicious?" There was a storm. It was hard to hear anything. "Do you usually walk out in a storm, Miss Brandon?" I have walked out in all kinds of weather. "Where did this walk take you?" We went out the front door, across the front yard to the steps, and went down to the beach. We walked back and forth there for a while watching the waves come pounding in. "Your sister had not hurt her hand at that time?" No, I believe that happened after we got back to the house. I did not know of it until the next morning. She said she was cutting herself a piece of bread and the knife slipped. "Is your sister in the habit of eating after dinner?" If she is hungry, she eats. Our meals had been on an irregular schedule that day. "Did you, at any time that night, look out your windows at the back lawn?" I did not. My room is at the front of the house. We rarely use the back lawn. It is, really, the front yard of the other house, and we considered it as such. "Can the other house be seen from your back windows?" Glimpses of it. It is a long way away, and there are trees. We could not tell from our house what was going on at the other. Nor could we see much of the yard. The trees would block us there too. "Is the barn kept locked?" The place where the tools are kept is locked. I believe the main floor is usually open. Nathan can lock the door to the second floor if he wishes. "You cannot, then, explain how a spade or shovel of yours could have been used to dig the grave?" I cannot.

There was more, much more, for they took her over the same ground again and again, but she remained obdurate. Anne substantiated the story, but when it came to the injury to her hand she wavered. She said at first that she could not remember, then that she had scraped it on a stone, and finally that she had cut it with a knife. The sight of blood always upset her, and the pain had made her cry. By morning the wound had closed and she had not needed a bandage.

By this time Mr. and Mrs. Kennedy had been summoned from Detroit and put through the harrowing ordeal of identifying the scraps of clothing that remained. They had another child, a little boy, with them, and it was pitiful to see the way Mrs. Kennedy clutched him to her when she was walking on the street in broad daylight. She was not going to risk losing another child while she wept over the tragic resurrection of the first one.

Nathan added a note of mystery to the record:

I remember the little girl. I saw her once down on the beach with her mother. I did not see her on the day she was lost, though after Stark come up and told us she was missing I took a turn around the woods and the beach. Miss Effie, Miss Anne, and Miss Maggie, they didn't realize. To them it was just that a kid was out late, and they kept sitting on the porch and talking. There was a storm coming up, and when I got back from looking around, they told me the garage doors had been banging. The garage is part of the barn, and I live on the top floor. I thought I had padlocked those doors, but sure enough they were banging away in the wind. So I thought maybe the little girl had managed to get in somehow, and I gave the place a good going over. She wasn't in the barn, and there were no signs she ever had been. We get lots of trespassers at the Oaks. They park their cars out of sight on the drive and try to sneak down to the lake. Well, I thought and I still think that one of them sex maniacs was driving around up here and came trespassing and saw the little girl on the beach and killed her. Then he had to hang around somewhere till it got dark for a chance to bury her. "Why would he have had to bury her? Why wouldn't he just have driven on?" Because then there'd be an investigation right away and he might get caught. He had to hide the body to keep the police off his tail. "And what, in your opinion, did he dig the grave with?" I didn't get a good look at the grave. He might have scooped it up with his hands. "She was buried too deeply for that, and in a place where the soil is not light and sandy. A spade or shovel would have had to be used." No spade or shovel was missing from our place. I'd have noticed. No, I didn't see any strange man around the place that day. That doesn't say he mightn't have been there. Looks to me like a man's job. "Tell us about the bit of ribbon you found." There's nothing to tell. I was raking leaves, oh, a month or so later it was, and along by the garden wall I see this piece of blue ribbon. It's just a scrap, and I don't figure it amounts to anything, so I just rake it up with the leaves, and when I set fire to them it goes too. Young Mrs. Brandon called my attention to it. "Could it have been lying where it was for a long time without your noticing it?" Well, I suppose it could. But it didn't look faded or worn out. I don't think it had been there long. "Then, according to your theory, the sex maniac who had killed her had kept her hair ribbon and stayed around the vicinity just to cut it up in little pieces and drop them around where they could be found?" All right, you're so funny! Let me tell you about the next morning. It had cleared up by then, and I went down to the beach to have another look around, real early. Well, there was a place near where our steps come down that looked like an army had been scuffling down there. And the funny part is there were no footprints on either side of the scuffle. Somebody had taken a broom and swept 'em away, neat and clean. You couldn't tell a thing what had happened, except that whoever did it probably came up our steps, because you can't sweep footmarks off too long a stretch of beach. "Did you advise Lieutenant Stark of this at the time?" He could see for himself, couldn't he? He was around all day. "Lieutenant Stark says he saw no marks of the kind on the beach at any time." The feller's blind then. They were right there.

Asked to further describe the marks he had seen, he was vague. It just looked as though people had been milling around, and the sand had blown around in the night till you couldn't tell what was what. He had sat up late that night reading, but because of the noise of the storm he had heard nothing.

Maggie had, by this time, recovered some of her zest for living. She agonized over which dress she should wear to the proceedings, and when she sat down in the wooden chair in front of the coroner she was obviously delighted with her own importance. She made everyone sit up a little straighter by saying that she thought she had seen the burying taking place.

My room was at the back of the house and looked over the lawn where the body was found. I had gone to bed early that night, feeling ill. At that time I was given to stomach trouble and many nights went to bed earlier than the rest of the family. I have had a recurrence recently, which is why I could not come in yesterday when you wanted me. I am quite well today, thank you. I had been up and down a great deal that night, and it must have been about midnight when I was sitting on the edge of my bed watching the storm and beginning to feel a little better. The wind was blowing hard, and, spasmodically, I could hear voices. They were distorted by distance, and I could not tell who was speaking. I know only that there must have been more than one person on the grounds that night. I went closer to the window, wondering who could be out on such a night and what they could be doing. Mr. Stark had come by earlier in the evening to tell us that the little girl was missing, but I didn't associate her with this. In fact, I have not thought of any of this since that night, or connected it up in any way. When I got to the window I saw the light. It was far back, toward Thayer's house, and it either was not being held steadily or the person in whose hand it was moved around a great deal. At any rate, I knew that more than one person was out there in the dark and doing something that necessitated the use of a flashlight. Presently the light went out; I stopped watching and fell asleep. I had taken a great many anacin tablets and they make me sleepy. If I had been myself, I might have thrown on a robe and gone out to investigate. "You did not mention this to anyone in the morning?" No. I have not mentioned it to anyone. By the next day I had almost forgotten it. "Could you distinguish the voices at all?" No. The wind was blowing so. They seemed quite high and faint by the time I heard them. "Could they have been women's voices?" They could have been. I cannot say. "Have you at any time seen a piece of ribbon like this in the house or on the grounds?" No, I have not. "Would it be possible for anyone coming up from the beach by the steps to have seen what was going on behind the house?" I don't think so. The wings of the first house would bar their vision. "Have you ever heard any conversation between the Misses Brandon that would lead you to think they knew what had happened to the little girl?" No. We did not speak about it, to my recollection, except to say how terrible it was. "Did you go out to the back yard the next morning to try to verify what you had seen?" By that time it seemed like a dream to me. I did not go out. But the spot must have been covered carefully, or I would have noticed it from my window in the daytime.

The newspapers were on to us by then. "Body Of Child Missing For Eight Years Found On Brandon Estate," "Homicidal Maniac Still At Large In State," "Sheriff Opines Same Hand That Killed

Sheep Slew Child." And when Mrs. Moss admitted that she had lost a knife some months before Sue Kennedy's disappearance, the press, with many cautious "allegedlys" and "it-would-appears" and "seeminglys," ventured the opinion that the murderer would be found not too far from Brandon Oaks.

Effie kept her head high, but Anne was stricken. She was so dazed that her testimony was almost incoherent, though they were very patient with her. They had an idea that the blood on her hand might have come from the body of the child.

I don't know how I hurt my hand. I must have scraped it on a stone. No, I remember. Effie went straight upstairs, but I stopped in the kitchen. I was hungry and I wanted to make myself a sandwich. As I was cutting the bread the knife slipped and I cut myself. It was not a bad cut, but it bled a great deal. I wrapped my handkerchief around it. When I got upstairs it had stopped bleeding, but I let the cold water run on it and I rinsed out the handkerchief. I mentioned it to Effie in the morning. No one else knew. I did not need a bandage for it. It never gave me any trouble. "Mrs. Moss did not find anything out of place in the kitchen the next morning. It seemed just as she had left it." I was careful to put everything back. It is a large house and we are accustomed to making as little extra work for each other as we can. "You washed the knife, then, and put it away?" Yes. "And you ate your sandwich?" Yes. "What kind of sandwich was it?" A cheese sandwich. "You remember that very clearly, do you?" Yes. "You can remember after eight years the particular kind of sandwich you had on a certain night? Can you tell us what you had for dinner a month ago today?"

It was then that she began to cry, and they had to let her go for the time being. They got her back the next morning to ask her what dress she had worn that night.

I think I was wearing a green seersucker house dress. I remember that because when Elizabeth came she was wearing one of the same material. Hers was made differently and was more of a street dress. I did not undress after dinner. I was fully dressed when Effie knocked on my door and asked me to go walking. "Had you been alone in your room all that time?" Yes. "You had not left it, say to go out to the barn?" I had not left it. "Yet when Mrs. Brandon—she was not Mrs. Brandon then, of course— knocked at the intervening door, you opened it only a few inches and kept hidden behind it. Would that not be unusual if you had been fully dressed?" I know that I was fully dressed. "When you hurt your hand, was the dress stained?" I don't think there was any blood on it. There were grass stains, however, from a previous wearing. "Can you tell us what became of that dress?" I wore it out and then discarded it. "You had it for quite a while after this particular day?" I wore it the next summer. "Mrs. Moss does not recollect ever seeing you in it again." She is mistaken. I could not wear it for a good dress, because it was stained. I wore it in the mornings to do my work. "What becomes of your dresses when you are through with them?" I cut off any buttons or trim I want to save and throw the dress in the wastebasket. It is then burned with the papers. "Who burns the papers at your house?" Anyone who wants to. Sometimes Mrs. Moss, sometimes my sister, sometimes myself. We have an iron basket outside and we burn them in that. "Did your late brother, Thayer, know that you had hurt your hand?" I think not. "I put it to you, Miss Brandon, that it would have been impossible for the body to have been buried in the spot where it was, especially by people who were using a light, without your brother becoming conscious of it from his bedroom in the other house." He slept heavily. If he suspected that anything was wrong, he did not say so to me.

And then Effie Brandon, the second afternoon of the inquest, dressed herself in her best white silk, tucked her silver hair under a white straw sailor, smoothed white chamois gloves over her garden-stained hands, and went to ask a special audience with Lieutenant Stark at the state police post. She had to wait two hours, but she sat there firmly while the teletype rattled and officers and cars came and went. It was an unheard-of thing for her to do, and the things she had to say were even more incredible.

She began by saying that the conversation must be confidential.

"What I have to say is not fact," she said. "It is merely guesswork. But since I fear that my sister may be in jeopardy, I must say it. I think, Lieutenant Stark, that my brother buried Sue Kennedy."

"What makes you think so?"

"The process of elimination, for one thing. If Anne or I did not, he must have."

"There's still Nathan, or Mrs. Moss, or Miss Maggie."

"Neither Nathan nor Mrs. Moss would have any reason to do it. As for Maggie, she was locked in her room that night. I turned the key and took it myself. I didn't want her intruding on our guest, and I knew that she would be the minute our backs were turned."

"Let's suppose a story, Mr. Stark. Let's suppose the little girl was drowned, accidentally. And that her body was found by someone— Thayer—on our beach. The little girl was dead; there was no helping her. We have had so much undesirable publicity during our lives, Mr. Stark. Doesn't it seem logical to you that his first impulse would have been to get rid of the body, to arrange it so that there would be no further investigation that concerned us, no headlines to annoy us, no gaping curiosity seekers come to plague us?"

"Why did he have to dispose of the body so that no one could find it? Why couldn't he have carried it a mile or so down the beach? That would have been wrong too, but not nearly so wrong as the other."

"Perhaps he thought that there would have been signs in the sand, that everyone would know just what had happened, and that would have made things worse than they were in the first place. He would never have harmed the child in any way, but she was already dead——"

"You know that for a fact?"

"No, of course not. I'm just telling you the only way it could have happened. I came to you rather than to the sheriff because I feel that we know you better, that you might get these ideas to him without mentioning where they came from, so that an innocent woman will not suffer. It was wrong of Thayer, dreadfully wrong. I am not condoning that. Nor is it easy for me to blame my dead brother for a thing like this. Perhaps he himself regretted it after it was done, but by then it was too late to come forward with the truth."

"To be frank with you, Miss Effie, I can't see the fear of publicity as a strong enough motive for the chances he took. If the lake throws a drowned person up on your property, you are in no way responsible, nor will anyone say that you are. As it was, Miss Maggie saw the burial, and if she could have she might have run down to see what was going on, and the whole thing would have been out as easily as that."

"You mean that story about the lights? Perhaps she really saw them as she says, but, if she did, they were not what she thinks they were. I am quite sure that she could not have seen the spot from her window in any case. No one has come to the house to test it."

"The view would be different than it was eight years ago. Trees grow fast."

"She's lying about the voices then. There were no voices."

"How do you know that? I must warn you again, Miss Effie——"

"If Thayer did it, he was alone. There would have been no one for him to speak to. Maggie says that she saw lights 'moving.' Why would they be moving? If you were digging a hole at night you'd put a lantern on the side of it and let it stay there so you could see what you were doing."

"Carrying the body there and getting the tools ready would have entailed motion."

"Thayer wouldn't have needed a light for that. We all know every inch of that place, even in the dark. We ought to. We've lived there long enough."

He says he read her a lecture then on the insignificance of personal wishes and preferences as opposed to the law of the state. "I told her it was dangerous for her to say as much as she had said," he told me, "and that, for her own safety, I would not dare to breathe a word of it to the sheriff."

"There's only one thing," he said to her. "You're so far out in the county that the sheriff may ask us to take charge of any further investigation. That's what they did before, which was why I was around pestering you. And if I am in charge, I'll bear what you've said in mind. That's the best I can do for you, Miss Effie."

The next morning the coroner gave his full report. There were no marks of injury that could be determined. The skull was in a good state of preservation and showed no signs of damage or injury. The girl might have died of drowning, of strangulation, or of stabbing, though in the latter case the knife must have penetrated perfectly, since there were no marks on the skeletal structure to indicate its passage. Shooting was less probable; there was no bullet and no signs that one had been in what was left of the body.

The jury, after due deliberation, returned the verdict of "Death by unknown causes." This, and a request from the sheriff, put the whole thing in the hands of Lieutenant Stark for further investigation, and instead of the burden of guilt being placed on any one person, we were all conscious of bearing part of it.

CHAPTER XIII

By the end of that week my new drain field had been dug and filled in—the scars on my lawn would be months in healing—and old Nathan had taken to posting himself near the intersection of the main road and our driveway to keep the curious out. That was the last summer in the heyday of the vacationer; Petoskey and Harbor Springs were swarming with leisurely transients, and they all shared the common impulse to come out and look at the scene of the excitement. Lieutenant Stark said that you could not call it a murder.

"Unless somebody confesses," he said, "we're going to be in the soup a long time on this thing. We've been eight years just finding a body. It may be we can prove who buried her, but, short of somebody telling us, we're never going to discover how she died."

"If Thayer did it, you'll not be able to prove anything now."

"If Thayer did it, his sisters knew about it too. Don't let Miss Effie mislead you. She knows everything we want to know, but she's not telling. The main reason I think he had nothing to do with it is that she said he had."

"Nathan knows more about it than anyone. He saw those marks on the beach in the morning."

"I was down there fairly early myself that day. I saw nothing unusual. He's been attached to the family for a long time. I don't know how much faith can be placed in his evidence."

"He wouldn't lie."

"Well, somebody's lying, and you can take your choice which one."

He himself suspected Anne, though he was not open about it. One afternoon he cornered Dr. Day on my porch and gave that stately gentleman a bad half hour.

"You studied psychology in Vienna, Doctor. What is your opinion of the mental status of the Brandon family?"

"Mr. Brandon and his wife were very intelligent people. It is not surprising that their children are mentally superior types."

"Isn't it the person with superior mental capacity, which implies sensitivity and imagination, who is most apt to lose balance? I don't see many big, healthy, stupid fellows in our state institutions."

"Naturally you have to have a mind before you can lose it. I have no statistics on the matter."

"How do you account for the fact that these three Brandons, all of whom possessed good minds, had fine educations and enough money left them so they could live in comfort—these three superior people, then, hid themselves up in this comparatively lonely place and lived in absolute seclusion from the rest of the world?"

"I think the reason was an emotional one. They were tired of living in a glass bowl for the rest of the world to stare at. They wanted to live as other people did, privately and in peace. There was only one way to achieve that, and that was to remove themselves from the common ken."

"Grant that they wanted privacy and peace. How much of it have they achieved in all these years of trying for it? Miss Effie's husband commits suicide; her child is born and dies prematurely; Thayer's first wife dies suddenly, his second runs away from him in fear of her life; Miss Anne's engagement to Dan Warren is broken off abruptly; she goes in for spiritualistic trances; their dogs are accused of killing sheep, and now the body of a child is found buried on their property. That's a great deal of commotion to be stirred up by three people who want only peace and privacy."

"They have not been fortunate, that's true. I think, however, that you might find that much excitement in the lives of three ordinary people and not find it a cause for comment. In the case of the Brandons, I think that public interest has magnified the events."

"I'll ask you a perfectly plain question, Doctor. Have you ever thought that any one of these Brandons might have become mentally unhinged? Not insane, perhaps, but not normal by a long shot either."

"I have not. There are neurasthenic symptoms, but nothing psychopathic."

"Let me put it another way then. Which of the three would you say could be most easily upset emotionally?"

"That is merely a question of temperament. I would say that Anne was less firm and resourceful than Effie or Thayer."

The lieutenant sighed. "You're a tough man to talk to, Doctor. That isn't what I wanted, but I guess it will have to do."

After Dr. Day had left, I ventured my opinion.

"I think he was right. I've revised my opinion of Thayer. He wasn't insane. He was furiously angry about something he didn't want known, and he took it out on whatever was closest to him."

He was busily writing in a small notebook. "I know there's a nigger in the woodpile somewhere. We'll have to rout him out. When we find him we'll have the answers to a great many things."

I now possess copies of all the evidence about the Brandons that Lieutenant Stark collected that summer. It is an amazingly bulky manuscript, proving the efficiency of the state police, not only in our state but in several others, covering a space of time of eighty years, taking the reader to the very root of the trouble of which Sue Kennedy's burial was the merest offshoot.

"I went back so far," Lieutenant Stark says, "because the only place that no one had started before was the beginning. I found out that Thayer's grandfather had died in a home for the insane, and I wanted to make sure of every member of the family from then on. I wanted medical reports on every death and I wanted eyewitnesses from each funeral. I didn't want any dead men walking in and mussing up the investigation. Resurrections aren't in my line."

At the beginning I think he held the notion that, concealed in one of the two houses, there might be someone of whom we had no previous knowledge, someone of whom only the Brandons knew, someone who ate and slept and walked out at night so secretly that for twenty years no outsider had seen anything unusual.

"James Brandon had died, all right," he said, "a hundred years ago. He had been an inventor, and somebody bilked him out of his rights. It was easy, back in those days, because patents and royalties were hard to nail down. He wasn't a poor man. When he went to Sunny Hill Home he left his wife and son well provided for. William Brandon never had to scratch for a living, and he built what he had to one of the greatest fortunes in the world, for a while. He married Anne Thayer back in 1884, and Effie was born the year after."

He showed me a letter from one of his friends who was on the Florida state police force. The letter said that its writer had contracted a bad sinus infection from the dust of the old archives that Stark had driven him to.

"However," said the letter, "William and Anne Brandon did die as the results of a motoring accident while living at their home in St. Petersburg."

He had enclosed copies of the death certificates and a cutting from an old newspaper which told of the cremation. "The ashes will be returned to northern Michigan and buried there on the estate of Brandon Oaks. Mr. Brandon was nationally known for the rigorous, clean life he led, setting a fine example for our young men by neither drinking nor smoking, and for the many Christian charities he helped generously to sustain."

The station man in Petoskey remembered the occasion of the elder Brandons' funeral, and though he had been thirty years younger then, he was already possessed of the tremendous curiosity about people and their personal affairs that I had encountered.

He said, for Stark's little notebook: "I was there, and so was the whole town, when the train pulled in and the three Brandon kids— well, Effie was darned near thirty then, so's I don't know you could call them kids—got off. We expected to see a couple of big white urns, because we had heard they were going to bury the ashes that very day, and old Reverend McAllister was going out with them to the Oaks for the service. They must have had them with 'em, but we couldn't see 'em. And they pushed right through the crowd so fast that nobody hardly had time to speak their sympathy. Well, I knew as well as anybody that the funeral was to be private. But I had an afternoon off, so I hitched up my horse and buggy and went riding out that way. I was hanging around the edge of the woods there, so I saw the whole thing. Just the Brandons and that girl that lived with 'em—Maggie something—and the reverend. And after it was all over and they had gone away, I went over and looked in the graves. They wasn't covered yet, you understand. I guess Nathan was to do that. Anyway, there was an urn in each of them with a little ground thrown in when the minister said 'dust to dust.' So I guess you might say I had been to the funeral and that I know for a fact the two of 'em are buried there. They were the second ones. There was one marker ahead of them. Mrs. Brandon's sister had been buried there—oh, it must have been twenty years before."

The information concerning Margaret Thayer was scanty and entirely from hearsay. People had heard their fathers and grand-fathers say that she certainly was a good-looker and that she could ride a horse as good as any woman born. She had come up to the house at the Oaks when it was first built, and at first people thought that she was the fabulous Mrs. Brandon. But it turned out that she had come on ahead to get the place ready for them. She was a great hand for keeping herself *to* herself, and she had spent a great many months of each following year there with an Indian woman to help her, while her sister and brother-in-law were traveling elsewhere. The Indians had liked her and she had liked them and given them a stained-glass window to prove it.

Mr. Brown, the undertaker, was particularly helpful, since he had inherited his father's business and the stories of old deaths that went with it. "Old Doc Murphy—he's been dead for twenty years—was the one who used to go out there. He said she had tuberculosis. She was only twenty-two when she died of it, and Dad had charge of the funeral. He said that she was one of the most beautiful women he had ever seen, and he and Mother used to wonder why she went out to that godforsaken house and stayed there, summer and winter, a year at a time, but I suppose it was for her health. The Brandons were a young couple then, and he had just made his first hundred thousand or so, I guess. She died all alone up here, and they came up for the funeral and went right back South again. Mr. Brandon came up the minute he heard she was dead, but Mrs. Brandon didn't get here until three days later. Just in time for the services. It was her sister, but she didn't seem as grieved as he did. Margaret Thayer died, though, and was honestly buried, I can tell you that much!"

He himself had taken charge of the funeral of Thayer's first wife. "She was a handsome woman too. I don't know that she ever consulted a doctor in this town, but if she did, I'll bet that it was Dr. Avery. He was the best here, even twenty years ago."

And, by some wonderful chance, that was exactly what Alice had done, and Dr. Avery recalled it very well because he had not been called in for her brief final illness.

"She came to me saying that she had been troubled with indigestion. That wasn't too far out of the ordinary. She told me that she had had colitis a year or so ago. Then, too, she had been married only a short time, and I can't tell you how many women have nervous indigestion the first year they're married. I prescribed a diet and some mild medicine. Dr. Day told me after her death that when she had been in Detroit some months before he had made extensive tests and discovered the ulcer. She wasn't told, although he had warned her to be careful of what she ate."

"Have you heard of similar cases?"

"Oh yes. Not many of them are as sudden, nor do they usually occur in so young a person. But it's possible. Possible."

"Is there a poison which might give the same symptoms?"

"Poison. Good lord! I don't know a great deal about poisons, but I'd say arsenic would come the closest. Small doses would give her the stomach trouble, and a good big one would kill her. But Day was right there. He wouldn't have given the death certificate if he had had any doubts at all."

Mrs. Moss, who had nursed her during the last hour or two of her life, had little to add. "The first thing I knew was when Thayer came running down to the house to get me out of bed and tell me to come up. The others were there. They had been invited to dinner that night and they had had it. Shortly after the meal Alice became violently ill. They had put her to bed, and Dr. Day had done what he could. By the time I got up there, there was nothing for me to do but sit by her bed and watch her. She was unconscious most of the time I was there."

"What was the effect on the other members of the family?"

"The girls and Miss Maggie were just sick about it, and Thayer was wild. Naturally he would be, with him being married just such a short time and all. I guess Dr. Day had as hard a time dealing with Miss Effie as he had had trying to save Alice. He was shut up in the library with her until almost morning, and every time I went by the door I could hear her talking and crying like a madwoman. And Miss Maggie comes down the next morning and says to Thayer, 'I don't think Alice died of what the doctor says she did,' she says. 'I think there should be another examination.' Well, Mr. Thayer turned on her like a tiger. 'And what do you think she died of, Maggie?' he said, and if I'd been her I'd have kept my mouth shut, the way he said it. But she was feeling brave that morning, braver than I've ever seen her before or since, and she says, 'I think she was poisoned.' I saw what was coming before she did, and I ran forward to stop it, but I was too late. He swung his fist and hit her in the face, and she dropped to the floor like a limp rag. He didn't even look down at her, just walked away. And Miss Effie came to me afterward and said that Thayer was overwrought, he hadn't meant it, and she hoped I would forget the whole thing."

"I thought then of trying to get an order to have her grave re-opened," Lieutenant Stark says now, "but there were three reasons why I didn't. In the first place, I don't think I could have gotten the order on the evidence I had. In the second place, she had been dead more than twenty years and it was problematical how much we would find that would be helpful to us. And in the third place, I didn't want anyone else to know what line of reasoning I was following. They thought I was worrying about Sue Kennedy. Why stir them up about Alice? The best thing for me to do was to go on the assumption that she had been poisoned and see what I could turn up. The man who knew everything I wanted to know was Dr. Day, and he was the one I didn't dare ask. If he had covered up for one of the Brandons by issuing a false certificate, he ,wasn't going to help expose himself now."

At the time that all this information was being assembled I knew little or nothing about it. The lieutenant came and went, the sun shone, the birds sang; life was as ordinary as possible under the circumstances. I would forget for hours at a time that anything had gone wrong, that Effie and Anne had locked themselves up in their house to emerge only in the early evening to look after the garden, that Dan Warren did not come to visit either of the houses any more, and that all of us were objects of comment when we chose to walk abroad.

Maggie had recovered her health and her good spirits, but she mourned the fact that she had left Chicago. "I shouldn't have come with you, Elizabeth. I should have stayed right where I was. I asked Lieutenant Stark when we would be allowed to leave, and he grinned and said he'd let me know. I've written to the girls and told them I didn't know when I'd be back, and they were—well, annoyed."

"Not so annoyed that they don't write to you every day of your life. I notice that you're willing to miss your lunch just to be out on the road to catch the mailman when he comes by."

Of us all, she was the only one who did not mind going into town to be stared at. She would invent a small errand, dress herself in her best, and spend the afternoon presumably shopping, but actually walking the streets busily, watching out of the corner of her eye to catch the amazed recognition of some passer-by.

It was on one of these occasions that I asked Mrs. Deever in for tea at Lieutenant Stark's request. I had to explain to Norah that he did not want anyone else present, and she smiled and shook her head.

"It isn't being excluded from the invitation that bothers me," she said. "It's what Mike will say. He's been tired of the poor old dear for weeks now and keeps hoping she'll go home. Yet he's given me strict orders to keep an eye on her and not to let her leave the house without me. What am I going to do about that?"

"You can pretend to be coming to tea with her and then stay outside and drive around until we get through."

"Well, I'll do it. But I'll drive around for just an hour, and I'll expect a large tea when I get back."

Mrs. Deever was frail and old, but her voice had an unusual vigor, and she must have been at one time a woman of great strength. Now the skin hung loose on the big bones, her eyes had sunk to mere slits, and she had great difficulty in walking. She said she was eighty-five years old and expected to live till she was a hundred.

"I'm sure you will," Lieutenant Stark said, "and it's great good luck for me that you are alive and in this particular spot right now. I want you to tell me all you can remember about the Brandons."

She wheezed and rattled, and I was alarmed until I saw that she was only laughing. "That'll be about all I know, young man. I was with them for fifteen years."

She began, however, and I was fascinated. Sixty years slipped away, and she was a young woman again, employed in a rich house, living and traveling in luxury as the establishment moved with the whim of its head. Effie and Anne and Thayer became babies and then willful children; great dinner parties and balls came to life with the last ruffle in place; Maggie was a backward urchin peering over the banisters at the good times that went on below, and Mr. Brandon's booming laugh resounded again.

"Perhaps it's my fault that the children weren't better behaved," she said. "Effie was five and Anne was four and Thayer not a year old when Maggie came to live with us. It was her coming that made the trouble. The children saw how their mother treated her—mean in a sly way whenever she could be without Mr. Brandon seeing it— and maybe they imitated her. They would all be good as gold for a month at a time, and then they'd break out again. They'd smash Maggie's toys, or tear her room to pieces, or hide all her shoes, or refuse to eat at the same table with her. Once I came across Anne trying to cut Maggie's hand with a penknife. I wasn't allowed to punish them much, but I gave her a spanking that day, I'll warrant!"

"How did you get along with Mrs. Brandon?"

"Well enough. Mostly she didn't pay any attention to me or the children either. She wasn't what I'd call an affectionate woman, or if she did like you she might change her mind about it at a minute's notice. She couldn't stand anything to be helpless or dependent on her. Take her own sister, for instance. Margaret was three years younger, and she didn't have another relative in the world. When Anne married it wouldn't have been proper in those days for Margaret to go on by herself or do anything except come to live with her sister. And at first it was all right. Then Mrs. Brandon, right after Anne was born, began to be spiteful. I don't know how many times I've heard her shouting at her, and all Margaret would do was cry. She was a pretty girl, prettier than Mrs. Brandon, some said, but she wasn't healthy. It finally got to where the two of them couldn't be in the same house without trouble, even though Margaret tried her hardest to efface herself and please her sister."

"That's why she came up here so much the last few years she lived?"

"Yes. And Mrs. Brandon didn't want her to be allowed to do even that much. Wanted her to get clean off the face of the earth, I reckon. But some time before, when Margaret had a chance to make a good marriage, Mrs. Brandon wouldn't hear of it. Said there was no hurry, that she needed Margaret with her, and that the man wasn't good enough anyway. So Margaret turned him down."

"How were the children affected by all this quarreling?"

"Lord bless you, they were too young to notice. Effie was three and little Anne was two and Thayer wasn't born yet when she left. The two of them never lived under the same roof after that, and Mrs. Brandon didn't see her sister again until she was dead."

"Then there's always been trouble in the family?"

"All the years I was there, there was. It came, I think, from Mrs. Brandon not having enough to do and being so confoundedly jealous of her husband. He didn't dare hold the babies for more than a minute before it was, 'Nurse, take them away; it's feeding time,' or, 'Mr. Brandon will get all wet.' Mr. Brandon was a good man or he wouldn't have stood for it. He couldn't even tell his sister-in-law that she had on a pretty dress without there being a flare-up afterward. Oh, not *to* him, you can bet that! She was always nice as pie to him. But anyone he ever gave a kind word to was her enemy, and the rest of us knew it."

"Which of the children do you think resembled their mother most when they were grown?"

"Why, Thayer, I guess. He had that same highhanded way about him, though as a child he wasn't as naughty as his sisters."

"And you say that at times Mrs. Brandon was quite beside herself?"

The little dark eyes snapped at him. "I say, Lieutenant, that there were times when Mrs. Brandon was crazy as a loon!"

Lieutenant Stark said only one more thing that was significant. "After Margaret came up here to live, were any of the Brandon babies sent up from time to time for her to take care of?"

"Never. Mrs. Brandon would have had a fit."

"From the Indians I've had evidence that years ago there was a baby with her for a short while. It's all hearsay, of course, and vague. I got it from the daughter of the woman who used to work for Margaret, and she's not a talkative girl."

"It wasn't one of the Brandon babies. I can vouch for that."

Norah came in then and we had tea.

CHAPTER XIV

ABOUT THAYER'S DEATH, at least, there was no question at all. Two Petoskey physicians knew that he had died of pneumonia and that, by the time they had been summoned, he had been beyond medical aid. If they had been called sooner, they might have saved him. Pneumonia wasn't the dread and fatal disease that it had been. But, as they understood it, the patient had concealed the severity of his condition from his sisters and had seemed not unwilling to die. One of the doctors told me that he had grown very frail in the year before his death.

"I knew him slightly," he said. "Used to pass the time of day with him when I'd see him on the street. At first he was polite and short with me. Later he seemed glad of the chance to talk to me, to anybody. That was when I told him that I thought he was doing too much, not taking proper care of himself. He laughed and said that, on the contrary, he didn't have enough to do, that he took far too good care of himself. And it's true that he wasn't nervous and jumpy, the way he had been. He was past that, burned out, spent, ready to go under with the first thing that came along. Which he did."

I would have liked to hear more about Thayer, but I did not dare ask his sisters. In his sunny, quiet house the memory of him grew greener, and I could not remember him as the tense, threatening man whom I had feared, but as a man who had been driven past endurance by a secret trouble and who should have inspired pity rather than contempt. I was not so proud now of having run away all those years ago. I was beginning to think that I should have stuck to my guns and seen the thing through, that I should not have left him to an intolerable loneliness, to a proud, empty existence. All this made me apologetic and shy, so that I could not risk storming the barricade to get in to see Effie and Anne and condole with them in neighborly fashion. Maggie had gone down and had been turned away by Mrs. Moss.

So I watched the other house furtively. It could not be seen at all from our porch, but if one walked a hundred yards to one side and pretended to be looking at the trees or the birds or the cat, a good view of one wing of the other house could be obtained. The windows were kept closed and the shades were pulled. The porch was always deserted when I passed it on my walks. But, as I have said, in the early dusk the two women would emerge as far as the garden, and before dark they would be back in their house again with every door locked tight. Mrs. Moss went with Nathan in the station wagon to do all the shopping, and Maggie often went with them. Day after day the sun shone on acres of trees and grass and flowers, the lake lazed on the white beach, and no one but myself would be abroad in all that enticing weather.

I learned from Lieutenant Stark that Dan Warren no longer saw Anne, that the Days were staying close to their own cottage, and that Mrs. Deever had left.

"The good doctor had a word to say to me about underhanded methods in police work," he told me. "He claims that I was taking undue advantage of the garrulity of the aged, and he took the precaution of packing old Mrs. Deever off in a hurry so it couldn't happen again. As if I didn't know where I could find her if I wanted her."

In spite of the quietness of our lives and the innocent monotony of our days, the police were watching the place. The lieutenant favored us with a weekly visit, but between times I would encounter men I had not seen before walking on the beach or strolling through the woods or once, even, sitting on our back steps in the shade and cursing softly at the heat. They were all in uniform, and, though they were not obvious about it, they were keeping close tabs on us.

Not close enough. It was on the evening of June twenty-sixth that Maggie, having made a very successful caramel pudding, announced her intention of going down to the other house with it.

"They can't do more than send me away again."

"It's after ten o'clock, Maggie, and dark as pitch. You'd better wait till morning."

"I'd never get in then. They'd just pretend to be not at home. Right now they have lights on down there. I was just out to look, and they can't very well send me away."

She was shivering with the excitement of her daring, however, as I helped her into her light jacket, tucked the pudding under one arm, and put the flashlight in her hand. I heard the screen door bang after her, and I settled back to my work of combing John Silver, a process that took concentration and vigor.

It seemed to me that scarcely a minute had gone by—though the police established it later as nearer five—that I heard her running back on the gravel of the drive, tearing the screen door open, stumbling into the room where I was.

"Call the police," she gasped. "Dan Warren's lying in the garden and he's hurt!"

She whirled back into the blackness outside and I ran to the telephone, stepping on the cat in my haste and leaping into the air at his sudden howl of protest. My conversation with Lieutenant Stark was guarded, for we are on a rural line, and in ten other houses, including Effie's, there was a chance that someone might be listening in.

"You'd better come right away. There's been trouble."

"Who?"

"Dan Warren."

"We'll be right there. Hang up. I have to call the sheriff."

All of that took perhaps a minute, and my search for a second flashlight took three minutes more. Then I was running down the drive in the windy, stirring night, slipping on the loose stones, coming sharply to my knees once, caring nothing for all the noise I was making. The sight of the other house brought me up short. Not a light showed from any window. Big and dark and quiet it loomed beside me, the recessed grade door full of shadows that made me wish I had come down more quietly or that I had not come down at all. Where was Maggie? Why had she not given the alarm to this house, and why weren't there lights and an excited group in the garden, and was Dan Warren still lying out in the dark helpless and in pain?

"Maggie!" I whispered as loud as I could. "Maggie!"

Not a sound, not a sigh came back. I thanked God that I had not turned on my flashlight, preferring to follow the dim white glimmering of our road rather than outrun a brighter but too localized illumination. I did not turn it on now. I stepped silently onto the grass strip and followed the wall around to its entrance. In the middle of the garden the birdbath showed white, and I groped my way to it and stood silent, wondering, listening, with the wind pulling at my hair and making a rushing sound in my ears and my knees shaking with the prospect of stepping on a dead man in this intense blackness.

Off to my right a woman sobbed, caught her breath, sobbed again. I moved gently that way, stooping once to disengage a rose thorn from my skirt, then freezing to the deeper shadow of a tall bush. It was Anne who was crying, crying as she had the night she washed blood from her hands in the room next to mine.

"Dearest," she was saying, and "all my fault," and "I told you," and "never, never, never." The words jumbled and the wind pushed them by me too quickly to hear.

It was twenty minutes later that the police car came rushing down our drive, lights full on, and I moved at last and ran like a madwoman to signal it to stop. They found Dan Warren, bleeding from a wound in his throat, lying unconscious with his head on Anne's lap. Her skirt was soaked with his blood; she lifted a white, placid face to the fireflies of light that now danced over the garden and told us that he was dead.

He was not, however. The knife had not struck high enough. It had caught on the collarbone and sliced downward, not deeply enough to be mortal. The police bundled him into the car, and one of them drove him off to a doctor. Lieutenant Stark roused the house, and we led Anne in to the porch where Effie stood, clutching a voluminous robe closer around her. Anne dropped in a chair, stroking her terribly stained skirt gently, while we explained the little that we knew, and Effie watched the flashlights of the men who were still searching the garden sweep in wider and wider circles. Suddenly Anne threw back her head to look her sister full in the face with a tragic intensity and a defiance that made her the stronger of the two for that moment.

"I'm going to marry Dan," she said. "I don't care what you say or do, Effie. I'm going to marry him, and you can't stop us. Nothing's going to stand in my way this time, do you hear? Nothing!"

She began to cry hysterically then, and they led her off to bed.

The men outside had found no trace of the attacker. The knife that had stabbed Dan Warren was not in the garden. But they did find Maggie, crumpled in a heap on the little porch off the grade door, with a huge lump rising on the side of her head and her flashlight, with blood on it, lying beside her. One of the men had tripped over the caramel pudding that she had set down carefully on the step and had fallen right across her.

She sat up in her bed the next morning and informed me that several of her ribs had been broken and that she blamed the state police for it. "It was bad enough," she said, "to have my head smashed in, but when a two-hundred-pounder sits down on your stomach, something's got to give!" She looked rakish and piratical with her bandaged head and her cigarette, and she covered reams of letter paper with descriptions of her plight. "I've actually," she said, "heard this place referred to as a health resort! It doesn't seem to be healthy for me!" As a matter of fact, her injury, while uncomfortable, did not keep her once from her morning trip to the mailbox for her voluminous mail.

Once again there were questions and answers, and I copy them from the lieutenant's notebook. Maggie was not enlightening. "About ten o'clock I decided to take my caramel pudding down to the other house. I knew they were home because I stepped out and saw their lights. That must have been about a quarter of ten. I walked out on the lawn far enough to one side to see their lights. It was then dark. I had no flashlight with me. I came back to the house, and Elizabeth found me a light and I started off. As I came to the garden wall I heard a groan. Well, I was scared to death, and I might have run if I had not known other people were close by in a lighted house. I found Mr. Warren lying near the birdbath in the middle of the garden."

"You are certain of his position?"

"Yes. At first I thought that somehow he might have struck his head against it. Then I saw that his shirt was all bloody at the neck. He was groaning, but he wasn't conscious. So I ran back to tell Elizabeth to telephone the police."

"The other house was nearer. Why didn't you go there?"

"I didn't think of it. It's been so long since I've been in it. Then, too, I didn't want to run into Anne and have to tell her about it right out like that. Anyway, I told Elizabeth to call the police and I ran back down the drive. I think I would have gone back to the garden to see if there was anything I could do for Mr. Warren, but I saw that all the lights were out in the house now, and I stopped being brave. I had put the pudding and the flashlight down on the back step when I ran back the first time. Now I went up on the little porch to pound on the door and get someone out to help me. I think I had just raised my hand to knock when something hit me on the head and I felt myself falling. The next thing I knew that policeman was sitting on my stomach."

"You heard no one come up behind you?"

"I didn't hear a sound. Perhaps I would have, but I was excited, of course. They tell me that I was struck down with my own flashlight. I don't know whether that was still on the step at that time. I recall stepping over the pudding dish. The flashlight may have been there. I didn't notice it."

"When you first saw Mr. Warren was there a knife lying beside him?"

"There may have been. I did not look for one."

Once more it was Anne who was pounded with questions that bristled with suspicion, but this time she stood it better. "I had an appointment to meet Dan in the garden at ten o'clock. He could not come to the house because my sister did not approve of it. I have been meeting him there several nights a week for some time. It was almost ten when my sister decided to go to bed. I went upstairs too, and waited until she had turned off her light. Then I went back downstairs again and out into the garden. I took no light with me. I heard him groaning as soon as I reached the garden gate, and I stumbled around until I found him. He was lying near the wall to the right of the garden. I sat down beside him and took his head in my lap. He stopped groaning, and I thought he was dead. I did not hear Elizabeth enter the garden. There was a high wind, and I was too overcome to pay much attention. I saw no knife beside him. There is no knife missing from the house as far as I know. There was one missing eight years ago. We never found it."

"Your house belongs as much to you as to your sister. Why couldn't Mr. Warren see you there?"

"He could have, if I had wanted to force the issue. My sister has always had my best interests in mind. Even though I did not agree with her in this case, I saw no reason to openly displease her."

"There was blood on your hands from Mr. Warren's wound?"

"Yes. I tried to see how badly he had been hurt."

"You did not see Miss Mitchell in the driveway or at the side door that night?"

"No."

"The hand that held the flashlight that struck her had blood on it."

"Whoever stabbed Mr. Warren might have had blood on his hands."

"That's doubtful. The knife did not reach a main artery. There would have been no sudden spurt of blood."

"I have told you it was not I who struck her."

"Suppose I were to tell you that your fingerprints were on that flashlight."

"I would say that that was an untruth."

She had them there, for whoever had used the light as a weapon had mopped at it hastily with something, not enough to remove all the traces of blood, but enough to effectually destroy any clear prints that might be on it. Still they were morally sure that Anne had used it.

"You did not knock Miss Maggie down?"

"I did not."

"You did not stab Mr. Warren?"

"I would be the last one in the world to do that. I have been in love with him for years. I intend to marry him as soon as he is well."

They had to let it go at that. Lieutenant Stark had hoped that she would confess to having attacked Maggie.

"It would let her out of the attempt on Warren," he said. "I don't think for a minute that the same person did both. Whoever did the stabbing high-tailed it away from there, you can bet on that. Or if he did hang around, he still had the knife, didn't he? Why use something else to put Miss Maggie out of the way?"

"Anne's in her fifties. I don't think she'd have been strong enough to use either one."

"It doesn't take much strength to wield a knife. And, as far as that goes, you're the only person here or nearabouts who isn't in her fifties. Ergo, you must be our criminal."

"I'm not," I assured him seriously.

He laughed. "I know it. You're not the killing type. Too much ancient Greek background. 'Moderation in all things.' If a person was disagreeable to you, you'd try to reason him out of it first. Then, if logic failed, you'd remove yourself from his vicinity. Never, never would you remove him from yours. You're mental, primarily, not emotional."

"I have emotions, too. The reason that I'm mental, primarily, if I am, is because that, physically, I'm a coward."

"Most educated people are. They've learned the superiority of the mind over the flesh and they don't trust the latter. You're not the kind to hold a grudge, either. You'd either do something to retaliate or you'd forget about it. You wouldn't clutter up your mind with a lot of dead wood you weren't ever going to be able to build something with."

"I can't afford to. I need all my mental faculties for my job."

"Nobody can afford to, really. But there are a lot of people, especially women, who don't need to keep their heads clear and workable. So they store all kinds of odds and ends in their mental attic without classifying them or discarding the mothy ones, and finally their heads are so full of junk that they can't think straight any more, they can only feel. And one fine day an especially potent emotional spark sets off the whole rubbish pile and the whole thing goes up in smoke. Then you have a nervous breakdown, or maybe a crime, or maybe a suicide."

"I'm not neurotic enough for any of that."

"You will be. Cooped up with a bunch of giggling girls the whole year and then spending your vacations with a bunch of old women. Hardly the natural life."

"It isn't exactly the life I would have chosen had I been a free agent."

"Yes, it is. People kid themselves. Everybody's a free agent to some extent. Nobody has to live a life he doesn't like. There's always something to be done about it, if he really wants to do it."

"You're ignoring the fact that his previous life may have so conditioned him that he's not able to do anything about it."

"That doesn't hold in your case. It didn't even hold with Miss Maggie. You'd have sworn, wouldn't you, that she had dallied too long, that it would be impossible for her to pull herself up by her own bootstraps? I thought that. When I gave her that address and put her on the train, I expected her back within three days. She fooled me. And now that she has come back and doesn't have her job to tie to, she's deteriorating into a fussy little old lady with a desire for the limelight. As soon as I can let any of you go, I'm going to see that she gets back to Chicago so fast that her head'll swim!"

"She wants to go. There's an elderly widower back there she's scared to death she'll lose."

He looked pleased. "A boy friend for Miss Maggie? Good for her!"

"And good for Anne?"

"About marrying Mr. Warren, you mean? Yes, I think so. I don't know why she's put it off so long. Sisterly disapproval isn't usually as big an obstacle as that, especially when it's spasmodic. First he can come courting, then he can't. Then, all of a sudden, he can again. Then, equally suddenly he's barred. Effie can't make up her mind about him, it would appear."

He had asked Effie about that after we had put Anne to bed the night of the attacks on Maggie and Mr. Warren.

"Did you know your sister was meeting him in the garden at night?"

"I had no idea of it. She had promised me she would not see him."

"Why had you asked for such a promise?"

"It's not that I have anything against Dan. I was married to his brother, and the two of them were a great deal alike. Personally I am fond of him. Both times when I asked him to refrain from seeing Anne it was that I thought she was becoming too fond of him."

"All the more reason for your letting him come to the house, I'd say."

She twisted her hands painfully, but even the bulky robe could not rob her of her dignity. "There is insanity in our family, Mr. Stark."

"That did not keep you from marrying."

"I should not have married. Anne knows what a grave mistake that was. She saw how Thayer's marriages turned out. I am trying to spare her the tragedy we suffered."

"Dr. Day must have told you that the chief danger in marrying would be the transmission of undesirable characteristics. That danger is past in this case."

"There are other reasons. I do not care to give them."

"I put it to you, Miss Effie, that if you suspect your sister of a recurring homicidal mania, it is your duty to her and to the state to say so."

"I would not consider it my duty. I am proud of the name we bear. It has been dragged in the mud enough these last thirty years."

"Have you reflected that, in such a case, you yourself will not be safe from bodily injury or death?"

"I am not afraid to die."

"And you do not consider that this violence may be turned against other innocent people?"

"I do not think it will be."

"Dan Warren suffered from it. It is by the merest stroke of fortune that he is still alive."

"He would have been safe had he taken my advice."

"You cannot expect anyone to take your advice unless you are willing to reveal the reasons behind it. I have been charitable and easy so far, Miss Effie, because I have had very little direct evidence to go on and I am anxious not to make a mistake. But you are forcing me to stern measures that will bring more publicity than your confiding in me ever would. I'll put the question direct. Do you consider your sister subject to periods of insanity?"

"In my opinion Anne is perfectly sane."

Lieutenant Stark muttered to himself the whole way back to my door. "That doesn't make any sense," he kept saying. "It doesn't make any damned sense at all."

"Do you think she was telling the truth?"

"Not all of it. Did you notice what she was wearing under that kimono? She was fully dressed. Either she had been out or she was just going. I'll make more out of that after I get a chance to talk to Warren."

But Dan Warren, lying in a private room in a Petoskey hospital, was uninformative.

"Lord, I don't know what hit me," he said cheerfully. "I was waiting for Anne by the birdbath. Sure, I felt foolish. If I'd acted like a man I'd have walked right up to the door for her, no matter what the two of them said. I don't like this skulking around corners. Well, I was standing there watching the lights in the house and waiting for them to go off. There was a hell of a wind blowing, and I didn't hear anything strange. The first thing I know, something jumps at me, full in the chest, and I don't even have sense enough to grab at it. I just fell down, and then I found I didn't have strength enough to get up again. I was worried about the people in the house. If something wild was loose, they'd better be warned of it. So I tried to creep closer, where they might be able to hear me call. I didn't make it, I guess, though I don't remember when I stopped. I was right here when I woke up."

"When did Miss Effie ask you to stop calling at the house?"

"Right after the inquest on the body you found."

"Did she give any reason?"

"Not a very good one. Some bosh about Anne being too old to be silly and that she and Anne could never be separated. Well, they *are* going to be separated! As soon as I get well I'm going to marry Anne and take her as far away from here as I can get. If Effie wants to come along, she can, and if she wants to stay here, that's her own business!"

"In your opinion, Mr. Warren, why did your brother Robert commit suicide?"

"There was trouble between him and his wife. They had taken to quarreling. She was pregnant at the time, and not responsible, maybe, for all the things she said. He didn't tell me what it was about."

"In spite of the lights in the house it was dark in the garden?"

"Black as pitch."

"So your assailant could have been Miss Effie or Miss Anne and you would not have recognized them?"

"It wasn't either of them."

"You can't know that."

"I do know it."

"That garden lay in a peculiar light. It was too dark for you to see who attacked you, but it was light enough so you could see it wasn't one of the Brandon girls."

The patient smiled. "That's exactly the way it was, Lieutenant."

It was no wonder that Bill Stark grew more profane as the week went on.

CHAPTER XV

I CALLED AT THE HOSPITAL with flowers for Dan Warren and was politely turned away. The police had left orders that no one was to be allowed to see him. The small, tired woman at the desk tried to be pleasant about it.

"I'm certain, of course, that he did not mean it for you, Mrs. Brandon. But those are our orders, and I have no authority to change them."

"It's not because he's too ill to see anyone?"

"Good heavens, no! He'll be up and around in a week, and there isn't a nurse on his floor but'll be glad of it. The way he carried on when he found out he wasn't to have visitors! Swore he'd leave the hospital that very day, and he did try it. Fortunately Miss Brown, one of our prettiest nurses, was on duty, and she was able to persuade him. He's taking it out in phone calls now. We leave a phone right beside his bed all the time. It's the only way you can live with the man!"

I had a rather difficult invalid on my own hands. Maggie's concussion had been slight, but Dr. Avery did not want her to get on her feet permanently yet.

"Give it another week," he said. "You're not as young as you used to be, and there's no use taking chances."

She felt better when I told her of Mr. Warren's plight and said she wished we had an upstairs phone.

"Whom would you call, Maggie?"

"I wouldn't have to call anybody. I could just listen in. With as many people as we have on our line, that'd be company enough for anybody!"

The other house was barricaded tight again, and the gardening hours had changed. They now fell in the early part of the afternoon, and after five o'clock there was never a sign of movement on the lawn, though sometimes old Nathan came out in the early evening to finish his morning stint. He was past most hard work now, and I wondered what the Brandon girls would do when his strength failed him entirely. He had told me once, long ago, that he wouldn't have to worry, Mr. Brandon had seen to it that he would be taken care of for life.

I tried various schemes to be invited in. I made a point of passing the house at the hours when they had been wont to sit on the porch, but they did not sit there now. And once, when they were in the garden and I started down the drive for a walk, they both went into the house before I could reach them. I should have been offended, but instead I was sorry. What could they do in that house for twenty-two hours out of the twenty-four! Sometimes I would hear Mrs. Moss rattling pans in the kitchen, but there was not another sound that would indicate human habitation.

Effie telephoned me on the night of July second. It was nearly midnight, and she apologized for the hour.

"I knew you were in the habit of reading late," she said, "and I took a chance you'd still be up."

"I was just going to turn out my lights."

"I won't keep you. I wanted to ask if you had decided what you were going to do about your house. Have you put it up for sale?"

"I've done nothing about it. There's been so much excitement."

"Will you give us first chance at it? We are willing to give you twenty thousand dollars for it. I believe that is a fair price, considering its age."

"It's a very good price. As soon as I am allowed to think of leaving, I shall let you know."

There was a pause. "The police are keeping you there, then?"

"Yes. I hope it doesn't last too long. Maggie is supposed to be back at her job in another two weeks, and I must go back East the beginning of August."

There was a note of relief in her voice. "I'm sure Lieutenant Stark would not refuse you if you asked him."

"I may have to ask him."

She thanked me and said good night, but just before I hung up she said something else. "If anything should happen up there—anything unpleasant—don't hesitate to call me at any time of the day or night. I've—I've worried about you."

"That's good of you, but I don't think———"

"Remember. At any time of the day or night. I pray that you may be able to get to the phone!"

There was a click, the connection was severed, and I was left staring at the black instrument. Then I had to smile. Effie wanted us gone and was trying to scare us out! As if we wouldn't have gone long ago if we could.

To tell the truth, my life was lonelier now than it had ever been. Maggie was a semi-invalid and slept a good deal. No one had come near me for a long time except the lieutenant, and his visits were brisk and businesslike. So when I found young Trooper James Caldwell sleeping gently on my front steps early the next morning, I was glad to ask him in for the first of a series of breakfasts. He was embarrassed, but he was hungry. He moved after me into the kitchen, long and lanky, the big pistol in his black holster slapping a little at his hip, his shy smile incongruous with his official paraphernalia. He ate like a harvest hand and explained carefully that the Army wouldn't have him because a horse had smashed his one foot when he was a youngster.

"It doesn't bother me any more. If it did, I couldn't be holding down this detail. Me and two other fellows—we've been patrolling these grounds every night for weeks, and believe me, it's lots of territory!"

"Necessitating a short rest now and then?"

He blushed. "Aw, now, Mrs. Brandon, you mustn't think I was taking it easy all night. The sun was beginning to come up when I sat down there. The other two guys were somewhere in the woods or down on the beach and I thought I'd wait for 'em to come by and pick me up. We leave our car parked in the shrubbery out by the main road and we drive back to the post in time for breakfast. They must of missed me this morning or else thought it was cute to leave me here. I guess they're a little sore because they figure I've got the easiest part of the job. Since Monday the lieutenant told me I was to stick close to your house and not let it out of sight, so I don't have to do as much walking as they do."

I was surprised. "I should think it would be the other house you'd be told to watch!"

"Well, I swing around there too. But the two times I've bumped into him, it's been near here."

"Bumped into whom?"

He crunched his toast reflectively. "The prowler. The murderer. Whoever it is we're trying to get our hands on. I can't tell you more than that because we haven't got him, see?"

"You mean to tell me——"

"Oh, yes'm. I thought maybe you knew. I can't tell you who it is, because they're always covered up. The first time I'm just rounding the corner by your back porch and I plump right into somebody standing there. I'm about to say 'Pardon me' from force of habit when they turn and start to run like blazes and me after 'em. They could never have beat me, but they knew the place better than I did. I got just one good look at the thing when it turned at the top of the steps to the beach and looked back. It didn't have a face."

I set my cup down painstakingly. "I don't think I——"

"That's a manner of speaking, of course. It had a face, all right. You put something black over your head and cut holes in it for eyes and you'll be plenty hard to see on a dark night. Well, the next time I run into it, it's in the drive. And darned if it don't take a swipe at me with something it has in its hands. Something good and heavy. I duck just in time and the thing melts away. I don't even know where it's gone. But I tell Stark and he says stick close to this house. Which is what I'm doing."

Something black out in the blacker night, and young Trooper Caldwell all that stood between it and us! I looked at him with new respect and I pressed food upon him in even larger quantities. We were old friends by the time he left for town in the station wagon with Nathan.

After that my nights were more exciting. I would be sitting in my living room reading, keeping a wary eye on John Silver's ears for a warning of sounds that I could not hear. John would sit, dozing placidly; the night would be quiet, not a pebble moving on the driveway, not a footfall whispering on the grass. Suddenly from just outside my porch would come a loud "Hist!", John would leap straight up in the air and come down bristling, and I would make a dying run to make sure the screen door was fast. There would be no one there, but I would know that Jim Caldwell had passed by and sought to reassure me.

Maggie's first glimpse of him was not auspicious. She had joined me in my nightly vigil in the living room with her embroidery hoops and a collection of linen that looked suspiciously like the beginnings of a trousseau. When I looked up from my book she was sitting motionless, needle suspended in air, her terrified eyes fixed on a side window. Trooper Caldwell's nose was flattened against the pane. When he caught my eye he grinned and made a circle with his first two fingers, a gesture which he told me later meant "on the beam."

Half an hour after he had vanished and I had explained, Maggie was still trembling. "Oh my!" she kept saying. "Oh my!"

At one of our breakfasts later in the week, he told me that the Days had left.

"And Norah didn't come to say good-by! I've been meaning to drive up and see her, but with Maggie——"

"I think they'll be back," he said. "There's something queer about it."

He puffed at a pipe that seemed too mature for his pink, young face and told me about it. He had been on our grounds the night before, and he saw Dr. Day's car come down the drive and, after the two other troopers had stopped it to examine credentials, draw up in front of the other house.

"The older woman—Miss Effie, is it?—came to let him in, and I thought I'd stay around to see what happened. The windows were all closed, so I couldn't hear what they said, but I could see very well. They were quarreling—quite violently, to judge from their gestures and facial expressions. Miss Effie was asking for something, and he kept refusing. She almost went on her knees to him at the last, but it was no use. He stamped out of the house and drove away, and she sat there for a long time before she turned out the lights. I walked up to the Day cottage as soon as it was light this morning, and they were gone. The doctor's clothes are still hanging in the closet, though, so they may be back."

So the Days had gone, Dan Warren was still in the hospital, Lieutenant Stark sat at his desk in town tabulating the information that was slowly gathering by mail and telephone, we sat tight within our police cordon at night, and the calendar told me that the first few days of July had slipped by without my noticing that June had gone. Maggie had had news of the death of her friend, Mrs. Page, and sniffled because she couldn't go to the funeral.

"Even if they'd let me," she said, "I couldn't get there in time. She wasn't a young woman, and when you get to be my age you don't expect your friends to last forever, but I met her when I first went to Chicago and I shall miss her when I go back."

She did not say *"if* I go back," for which I was grateful. I went down to the basement and did a wash and hung it out to dry feeling that we were being sporting about our uncomfortable situation. Unfortunately, when I brought the clothes back in I left the line strung up, and Lieutenant Stark walked into it that night when he came to check his patrol. I can only say that this was unintentional on my part and that I had other things to think about.

For it was while I was folding the dry clothes that I noticed Nathan carrying boxes and barrels out of the other house, and I walked down brazenly to see what was going on. I was wearing a sun suit made up of three scarves, and he kept his eyes averted as we talked.

"Just house cleaning, Miss Elizabeth," he said. "The girls haven't had anything else to do, I guess, so they've got at this early. We usually don't get to it until later in the fall."

"What are you going to do with it, Nathan?"

"Take it down on the beach and burn it. It's too big a pile to burn near the house."

I wanted to go back to my house and telephone the police, but I wanted worse to know what was in those boxes. They were so carefully nailed shut that there was no guessing at the contents. I picked out a big one that was resting precariously between two rocks and upset it. The top split open, and Nathan and I both scrambled to set it right. He didn't seem annoyed, and it was my impression that he was curious too.

"It's toys, Nathan!"

He retrieved a rattle and a small wooden horse on a string. "All kid stuff," he said. "There's some baby clothes here too."

I shook one of the small yellowed dresses out of its creases. It wasn't the kind babies wear nowadays. It was yards long and hand-made and lace-trimmed.

"It seems a shame to burn this kind of thing. They're heirlooms."

He closed the box and dragged it into the main heap. "They told me to burn 'em. I've got to do it."

Fast as I hurried to the telephone, it was twenty minutes before the lieutenant and some of his men got there, and by that time the boxes were a smoldering heap of ashes on the beach. They went directly down to the beach to talk to Nathan.

"What was in those boxes, Nathan?"

"Old stuff from the attic. I don't rightly know what. I just heaped 'em up and started 'em going."

"You didn't dump them out?"

"Nope. Burnt 'em just as they came."

I have the rest of the story from Trooper Caldwell, who tagged along faithfully during the whole procedure. Lieutenant Stark went to the house and showed his search warrant to Effie when she answered the door.

"I don't understand, Lieutenant."

"If you're going to turn the whole house inside out, I want to have a look at it first."

They began with the basement and worked up through to the attic. Mrs. Moss gave them a piece of her mind for mussing up her kitchen as she was trying to get dinner, and Anne was lying down in her room looking so wretched and pale that they contented themselves with the most cursory of searches. Elsewhere they were thorough, and Effie walked along with them and watched them grimly.

They found only three things that interested them. One was a shiny new ax propped up in a corner of the basement.

"I haven't had time to give it to Nathan to put in the tool shed. He needed a new one."

"When was this bought?"

"Last week. In Petoskey."

"Who bought it?"

"Nathan and Mrs. Moss drove in with my shopping list. They brought this back with the other things that were on it."

"And Nathan left it here instead of taking it on down to the barn with him?"

"I daresay he forgot it."

But one of the officers went out to talk to Nathan, and he told a different story.

"Sure, I bought the ax. No, I didn't especially need a new one. My old one's still plenty good. Miss Effie wanted it for something up to the house. I didn't forget it. She told me to leave it there."

They confronted her with this, and she lost not an iota of her poise. "Nathan is old and he is forgetful. When he has had time to think it over he will tell you just what I have."

"Or when you have time to get to him to tell him what to say. Just what is Nathan's connection with your family, Miss Brandon?"

"He was hired by my father to take care of this place forty-odd years ago. He was left a pension in my father's will for good and faithful service."

They did not find the rusty old knife they were looking for, and there was no trace of it in the ashes on the beach.

"What was in the boxes that Nathan burned today?"

"We cleaned out the attic yesterday. There were old clothes and some of the playthings we had as children."

"And papers?"

"There were some papers. And some old books. Nothing important. Most of them had belonged to my aunt Margaret. She lived in this house the last three years of her life."

"It seems strange that after having kept her things out of sentiment for so many years you should suddenly destroy them."

Her voice was tight with anger. "I never had any sentiment for my aunt Margaret. She was a horrible woman. I should have thrown her things out long ago."

"She was only twenty-two when she died and she had been ill a long time before that. She couldn't have been too bad. She didn't have time to be."

"I was only five when she died, but I remember her quite clearly. She quarreled constantly with my mother, who provided her with a better home than she had ever known before. She was a black, heartless ingrate!"

"Lots of sisters don't get along. There may have been some faults on the other side too."

She turned white at that, but she held her tongue.

It took them a long time to go through the attic. There were more boxes and crates and trunks there, and they opened each one methodically. At the bottom of one of them they came across the letters, dozens of them, tied together with heavy green cord.

"Those are family letters. I have saved them for the time when a proper biographer wishes to write the story of my father's life."

"I will have to look at them, Miss Brandon. I would like to take them with me to my office, but, if you insist, I can do it here. It will take me a couple of days."

"I consider it an unwarranted invasion of privacy, but I daresay I can't stop you. I shall ask you to be careful with them, however. There are some letters there that I value a great deal."

"I shall be very careful."

One of the men brought up a jar of white crystals.

"This was in a steel box all by itself, chief. There's no label on it."

"The label came off some time ago," Effie said. "It contains arsenic. It's very old. I don't know where it came from or what it was used for. You may take it along if you wish."

Caldwell says that he was sorry for the poor old lady. She had been beaten to her knees; she was ready to agree to anything if these intruders would only leave. They did, but not before the lieutenant had walked to the back attic window and discovered the binoculars on the floor. The window topped the trees, furnished a good view of my house, and had been newly washed. It was obvious that our movements were a source of interest to somebody, but no comment was made.

CHAPTER XVI

THE LETTERS had been edited carefully before the police ever got them. Someone had gone through them and inked out the lines which might be too illuminating, inked them out so thoroughly that no manner of test could bring the hidden words to light again. But it had been a mistake to preserve the letters, even in their censored form, for Lieutenant Stark read them and sent a wire to the police in another state. It took them a week to track down the information he wanted, and after that it was plain sailing. Except that he blames himself for the dreadful crime that was committed while he waited.

"I should have gone through the house sooner," he said. "I was being tender with them, and I should have been tough. I thought, you see, that I could let everybody sit tight and solve the thing by going quietly around to a forgotten back door. Then Effie started cleaning house, and that worried me. I knew I wasn't going to get my evidence easily, at best it would be tenuous and slight, and she might be throwing some of it away. So I had to come out into the open and tip my hand."

"I don't see what else you could have done."

"It was damned bad luck that the woman had died, or I'd have had my case completed in time. Just three days too late, imagine!

And there were two other leads which would have told me what I needed to know if I had followed them earlier. Right under my nose the whole time!"

I have since secured copies of the letters, and, though they are most interesting, I cannot see how he deduced as much as he did from them.

First, in order of time, was a group of letters which had been written by the elder Mrs. Brandon to her sister Margaret. They may have been left in the house after Margaret's death, and one of the girls had found and preserved them. Mistakenly, for such letters should never be written, much less kept. Mrs. Deever had told me that Mrs. Brandon hated her sister, but hate is a quantitative word and its meaning ranges from a strong dislike to a frenzied desire to destroy, mutilate, and kill. The latter was Mrs. Brandon's kind of hate, and though the dainty note paper was dry and yellow and the writing a smooth, even, decorative one, the half century that had passed over the words could not dull the intense emotion they could invoke, the savage rage with which they were freighted.

"I hope you are conducting yourself well," one letter said, "though I have little confidence that you will. We value Nathan, he is indispensable to us, and I trust you will not let his youth tempt you. If you must have a man, try to find one in the town, one with whom we have no acquaintance or connection. We love the Oaks and we plan on returning to it many times. It would be unfortunate if some scandal in which you were involved would make it uncomfortable for us to take residence there again."

And, "I think you will find a doctor up there who will diagnose your case and prescribe for you. You have never had any regard for your health, and the life you have led has not been calculated to improve matters. If you wish to travel somewhere to consult a specialist, by all means do so. It is more spectacular than trying to improve one's self by quiet and sensible regimen, and your profession must have brought you a great deal of money by this time."

Early in 1890, the year of Margaret's death, the letters took on an even more vicious tone. "We are planning to come up to the Oaks in June, and you will have to make other arrangements for living quarters. Where you will go is entirely your own affair, and I have no suggestions to make. Our house here will be undergoing a complete redecorating, and the Beeches is always closed up for the summer, with not even a servant staff to look after it. I cannot consult William, for I have promised him not to mention my family affairs to him. He is heartily sick of the whole weary business and feels that he has been taken advantage of. Since you have chosen your own station in life, we have no right or reason to interfere in protecting you from the hardships it may bring you."

And, later, "Your letter was very touching, I have no doubt, but it had little effect on me. You ask me to recall our girlhood and our long friendly relation. I cannot. It seems to me now that I never had a sister and that the child I used to play with at the old house is dead. We have had a letter from your Dr. Avery, written, I suppose, at your instigation. He paints a very pessimistic picture of your condition of health and says that you should not be living alone. It's no use, Meg, no use at all. You will never get back under the same roof with me, and you need not waste any future time trying it. I asked Dr. Day his opinion, and he hemmed and hawed in the way all medical men do when they are confronted with a decision offered by one of their colleagues. I fear the poor man is getting old, for he was inclined to intercede for you. Then I recalled that you had always been exceptionally friendly with him, putting on your best dress when he came and disposing yourself in some conspicuous place where he might see you. His wife spoke to me once about what she considered was your overfriendly manner toward him. I can place no confidence in his opinion either, and, if you find yourself alone, you must take your own measures of remedy. I know all too well what they will be."

The last one was brief. "Your letter to William came yesterday, and he turned it over to me with an expression of distaste. You are indeed foolish if you hope to get around us by tragic words and pleading. Thayer is a year old now, and the doctor has said the journey north will not hurt him. We have given you a home for some six years, and I do not think it too much to ask that you make your own arrangements from now on and vacate the Oaks for us at once."

In all the time I had spent at Brandon Oaks I had not seen a trace of Robert Warren or heard his name mentioned more than once or twice. In the case of Alice, it was different. Things had been pointed out as "belonging to Alice," and Alice "had done things so-and-so." Her tastes and talents had occasionally come up for discussion, her picture had been on the wall of her house, and the clothes she had worn were packed in its attic. Robert Warren had come and gone and left no sign of his presence. Until now. Here was a group of— not letters, strictly—notes, written on casual scraps of paper. They had not been put in the mail. They had been left for Effie to find, and some of her answers were still clipped to them. There had been periods of time, evidently, when they had not spoken to each other, and this was their way of communication. I believe that many of them had not been preserved, lost perhaps, or torn up. There were no dates on them, but Effie had married him in 1915 and he had died in 1917. The chances were that these had been written the last year of his life.

"I hate doing this, my darling," he had written, "but it is the only hope I have of bringing you to your senses. I cannot live with you or speak to you until this dreadful wrong has been righted. It is more of a wrong to you, my dear, than to anyone else. You would be happier if the cloud were dissipated. I must force you to make a choice between your pride and the great affection we have for each other."

And her answer: "I cannot do what you ask, Robert. Really, I cannot. I never meant that you should find out, but you were too clever. If I promise not to speak of it, not to think or dream of it, not to waste my life on hating it, will that be enough? It should not affect our happiness; we can keep it at a distance from us; it must not spoil the first precious thing I have found in my life."

Perhaps he came back for a while, but it did not last. "I am not at all uncomfortable. The barn is weather-tight and the hay is dry. I feel safer out here than I do in the house. I will give you another month to make up your mind. If you cannot by then see this thing in its true light, I will have to take measures of my own."

And she: "I cannot see why you make such a stir about it. In reality I am harming no one but myself. If I am willing to put up with it, I cannot see why the rest of the world should not. You must not believe everything you are told, you know. You don't have to. You know the truth. If by 'measures' you mean going to the newspapers, I solemnly swear that if you do I will kill myself. I cannot face that sort of thing again, and they would tear us to tatters."

"Dearest," he wrote, "this is all absurd. I would be ashamed to have outsiders know that it is going on. They know it in the other house, I'm sure of that. They have their own ways of finding out.

Someone came into the barn last night and I awoke and sat up, but I could see nothing. I didn't want to call out to them and give the whole ridiculous show away. If it was the person I think, neither of us is safe any longer. Do you really think that one can deal off-handedly with a mind that has gone mad? That, by ignoring lunacy, however mild, one can cure it? I am glad that Nathan is sleeping on the first floor. He will be very helpful if trouble does arise. But can you imagine his face when I enter, not from the up-stairs, where he imagines me, but from the barn? It will be humiliating enough, in all conscience."

Effie had stopped dealing with his direct plea. She went off on a tangent. "You must keep your notes from being so explicit. I had to destroy the last two almost before I had read them. Remember that our private note box may not be a complete secret, and these things must not fall into the wrong hands. Thayer is leaving for New York tomorrow, and they will think it queer if we do not both come up to dine there tonight. Stop this silliness, Robert, and come home!"

And again he must have gone back to her and played his role as loving and contented husband, for by the time he wrote again the paper, the writing, the spirit, all had undergone a drastic change. "This is the last time, Effie. There has been too much dawdling, too much putting off. This time I am in dead earnest. They need soldiers now, and though I am married and past the age classifications they most want, I think they will take me. I cannot stay here, that much is plain. But I have no heart for the Army, or indeed for anything, until our personal trouble is cleared up. You say you love me. I ask you now to prove it. Once I thought that I could take matters into my own hands and solve the thing myself, but I have come to see that I cannot do that. It means too much to you; you would hate me forever; the whole thing is balanced too delicately, too precariously to be undertaken by anyone but your-self. And if you will not do it for my sake, think of the baby. In a few months he will be here, another mortal to undergo the strain and the torture and the monstrous teasing, awful because it pretends to be innocent. Will you subject him to that, as I have been subjected to it?"

Effie again refused to meet the issue. She was pregnant now and perhaps subject to the self-pity and emotional strain that sometimes goes with the state. "If you do not come back at once you need not come back at all. We have handled our affairs and managed our troubles for a long time without interference. You are making things worse for me at the very time when they should be made easier. Have you thought how much I am at the mercy of circumstance? A bad fright, or a fall, or any of a thousand things and my life and the child's would be in danger. You could protect us from this, but instead you prefer to sulk over what you consider a principle. I have never taken orders from anyone and I do not propose to do so now. If you give me no consideration now, then you never will, and it is well that we look the truth squarely in the face and decide that we are better off apart."

The last piece of paper was torn and crumpled and blurred, though patient hands had smoothed it and made it whole again. "My dear wife," it said, "I see now that there was never any hope of changing you, that you are determined the situation shall remain as it is, that you get a certain arrogant pleasure from it. Much as I love you, I cannot stay to watch it. I think perhaps that my mind has been affected by my long and futile brooding. I cannot live with you and I cannot imagine life without you. So I can think of only one solution, and it is a cowardly one. Whatever I own is yours and the baby's. If my going brings you to your senses, I shall feel that my death has benefited the child more than anything else I could have done for him. Try to think kindly of me. I cannot go on this way."

A quiet man, Robert Warren, and a determined one. He had left this final note at their secret place and walked into the barn for the last time. Effie must have found it after she knew he was dead.

There was the letter from Thayer that told his sisters that Alice Norris had consented to marrying him and that he expected them to come to New York for the wedding. Alice had written in a round schoolgirl hand to say that their honeymoon trip was being lovely, that she hoped all the things she had ordered had come, and that she knew what a nuisance it must be to them to unpack it all. "I am so anxious to meet you all," she said. "We were sorry you couldn't come to the wedding. But as soon as we get settled—or I should say as soon as you settle us, for you have all the hard part to do, I am imposing on you so badly—Dad and Mother will come out for a week or so and we can have our family party then. I am such an inexperienced little goose that I shall have to have help with the housework and cooking. Is there a girl in the neighborhood who would be available? I thought that maybe your funny little Maggie might come to stay with us and give me a hand, but Thayer won't listen to it. He says she's a snooper and a busybody and he has had to put up with her as long as he can remember. If no one else can be found, I shall try to persuade him."

Another one, under the letterhead of a large hotel in Quebec, said: "The most dreadful thing has happened here, and we are leaving at once. A woman has been murdered, and by her husband! Their name was Oliver, and they had been here for a month. Mrs. Oliver was not in good health and spent most of her time on the veranda in a deck chair with a robe over her knees. She was a pretty, frail little woman. I had spoken to her several times, and she had told me what a great deal of trouble she was having finding things to eat that agreed with her. The trouble had been going on for a year, she said, but before that she had been the healthiest thing imaginable. Well, she died suddenly last night, and the doctors here are very thorough. They took some samples from her supper tray and had them analyzed, and this morning we hear that she was poisoned with arsenic! It seems that she had money and her husband was anxious to get his hands on it. Anyway, there is not a doubt in the world but what he is guilty. Thayer shocked me by saying that the woman was a fool not to be suspicious, that the man was a fool not to know that the best place to poison a person was at home where suspicion would not arise so quickly as in a place where people don't know you. He does not mean this, of course. He is simply trying to talk me out of the gloom this has brought on me."

Evidently they had come home from the trip then, and Alice had been ill. In her last letter, dated several months later from her home in New York, she said: "The week's change has done me good, but I am anxious to get back to Thayer and my lovely house. The doctor here says I must be careful of what I eat and that I will be all right. Mother insists that I stay longer, but I am homesick and will be back as I planned."

Poor Alice, that was her last trip home, and her mother never saw her alive again.

The last group of letters was from Dr. Day. They were brief and cryptic, telling when he would come, when he would leave, how much time he could spare. There were sentences like: "Everything is all right, I tell you. Insanity is out of the question." And: "You are pushing the matter dangerously far. I told you long ago that you were not behaving fairly. After all, we had no proof and no time to verify our suspicions. We did what we had to do, and a pretty thing will come of it if it is ever discovered." And, further: "I have no notion what you are driving at. I never have had. It would have been better had you let me in on the ground floor. I will say, however, that a perfectly normal mind can be pushed too far, that insanity is acquired far faster than it is inherited, and that no mind is safe from it if environment be too unbearable."

The police had searched the other house on the fifth of July. The morning of July sixth was sunny and perfect. Maggie was well and strong again, and, defiantly, I suggested that we go swimming. I had seen Nathan and Mrs. Moss drive away to town; the other house looked blind and forbidding. I was bored with walking.

Maggie was tempted. "I haven't gone swimming here since I was a little girl," she said. "Do you think we'd dare?"

"I don't know who could stop us. This house is mine, and some rights to the beach must go with it. I brought a bathing suit and I intend to swim!"

She had not brought one, but we contrived something out of my three silk scarves that was sketchy but not unbecoming. She giggled when she looked at herself in the mirror.

"Really," she said, "for a woman in her fifties, I don't look bad at all. It's a good thing I lost all that weight. Though the first man who invents a bathing suit with a built-in girdle is going to make a fortune!"

There was no back way to the beach. We put on robes and walked down the drive, carefully ignoring the other house. The lake was glorious. I splashed and wallowed for two hours, while Maggie waded daintily and sunned herself on a rock. Mr. Lucas came by and was complimentary.

"Some kid!" he told her. "Say, if you'd dye your hair I know a night club where you could get a job in the chorus."

Maggie wriggled with pleasure and then remembered the insecurity of her costume. "I don't dare breathe," she confided. "This business is held together by three knots and two pins."

"I'll stick around."

He did not, however. He waved to me and started off down the beach. He turned again to signal me. "One of your friends up there watching you," he called. "Maybe they want to see you."

"Who?"

"Looked like Miss Anne. Just saw her face peeping over the edge."

But when Maggie and I came up the steps later, there was no sign of anyone.

The unwonted exercise had made us both sleepy. We ate lunch and retired to our respective rooms. I slept until three o'clock and had to wake Maggie.

"Let's have something to eat, Maggie. I'm starved!"

She did not bother to dress. She zippered a cotton house coat on over her nightdress and came on down to the kitchen. I made sandwiches, and when John Silver meowed at the screen she let him in.

"He's hurt himself, Elizabeth. Look!"

One of his front paws had blood on it, and she got a damp cloth and sponged at it.

"A thorn, maybe," I said.

"No, it doesn't seem to be. I can't see anything wrong with it at all."

I picked him up and looked at the paw. The blood was gone now, and there was no sign of an abrasion.

"That's funny. Could he have been killing something?"

"A mouse, maybe."

"Or worse yet, a bird, maybe."

Maggie ate her sandwiches and sat down to her interminable letter writing. I took a book and went out on the porch. From where I sat I could see Maggie scribbling busily for the next hour. Then the telephone rang four times, which meant that the call was for the other house. It rang again and again.

"Shall I answer it, Elizabeth? That's the way we used to do. If one house didn't answer, the other one took the message."

"Better let it ring. I don't think our status is on that friendly a basis."

The phone was quiet. Fifteen minutes later it started again. After the first signal it was answered, for it did not ring again.

"I guess they woke up," said Maggie, and went upstairs to dress.

Twenty minutes later Lieutenant Stark drove up and yelled at me.

"Is your receiver off the hook?"

"No, I don't think so."

"Go and see."

I went dutifully and came back with a good report.

"It isn't. Nothing's wrong with the line. Somebody rang the other house a little while ago. They couldn't have done that if a receiver had been off."

"That was me ringing the other house, and I can't get them! The first time, nobody answered. The second time, after one ring, somebody lifted a receiver off and went away and left it. Now I can't get them at all."

"They're the ones who must have broken the connection, then. Nobody else could."

He grinned. "I know it. I just hate to see anybody comfortable while I'm out driving around in all this heat."

"As a taxpayer, I think I should report you."

"You haven't had time to pay any taxes yet."

"That's all that saves you."

Thus we jested and laughed while the red stream from the open front door of the other house dried on the planks of the porch where John's paws had left little cat tracks, and the screen door, left ajar, admitted flies that settled with an approving hum.

It was five minutes after five when the lieutenant left my front door. It was eight minutes after five when he mounted the steps of the other porch and followed the red line into the living room. There, just inside the door, lay Effie Brandon, her head laid open with three strokes of an ax. Beside her, at a distance of some feet, lay Anne, unconscious but unharmed. The new ax he had seen in the cellar the day before was there too, but it looked new no longer.

CHAPTER XVII

WITHIN AN HOUR our grounds swarmed with people, policemen, the sheriff, the coroner, and what seemed to be the entire population of Harbor Springs and Petoskey. Dan Warren fought his way out of his hospital room and, with a pair of trousers pulled on over his hospital gown and slippers on his bare feet, tried to get in to see

Anne. She was still unconscious, however, suffering from shock. Mrs. Moss had been appointed temporary nurse, and a trooper sat on a needlepoint chair outside her door. Dan went back to the hospital to collect his belongings and go to his own house.

Then, by plane, bus, and train, newspapermen began to stream into the area, from Detroit, from New York, from the big news-collecting organizations. The police tried to keep them out, but they were young and active and shrewd. They lurked in the shrubbery and took the back paths through the woods. Having gained a vantage point, they pounced upon the first person not in uniform who went by. Their armament consisted of cameras, pencils, notebooks, and a steady fire of pertinent questions. No one was safe from them, for even with the war in full swing the Brandon name meant something and this was a spectacular crime.

Maggie and I had been running back and forth between the two houses, taking food for Nathan and Mrs. Moss and being helpful in any way we could. The gentlemen of the press stopped that in a hurry.

"What's your name, miss?"

"Really, I don't care to——"

"You must be young Mrs. Brandon. Why did you leave your husband?"

"My husband is dead."

"Yeah, I know. But before that you left him. Why?"

"You're not supposed to——"

"Is it true that Lieutenant Stark has a case on you and that you've been working with him on this thing? Are you engaged to him?"

"No."

"Too bad. He looks like a pretty good guy and it would have made a swell story. What about the body they dug up on your front lawn?"

And by that time a trooper would appear and march the inquisitor away, his cheerful impertinence not at all dimmed by the indignity of his retreat.

A man was stationed at our front door to keep all but officialdom out. It did not do much good. I came into the kitchen that evening to find Maggie serving coffee to a tired young man who said he had been on a hiking tour of Michigan and had almost fallen

dead of exhaustion on the highway. Then he had seen our driveway and thought that human aid might be near.

"Poor soul," said Maggie to me. "He's walked thirty miles today,
and when he tried to get a drink of water at a farm they set the
dogs on him!"

"If he had walked more than two blocks in those shoes he'd be
crippled for life."

At which the young man rose and reached for his hat. "You
can't be killed for trying," he said genially.

"You have a nerve——" I began hotly, but the screen door had
closed after him, and Maggie was almost in tears.

"He wasn't a poor young man, Maggie. He was a reporter."

She was less gullible after that, though if one of them had come to
the door with a camera in his hand he might very well have gotten
in. Maggie could not resist having her picture taken.

Effie Brandon's body left the Oaks for the last time on a litter in
an ambulance. I was in the driveway when they lifted the covered
stretcher through the doors. All I could see of her was one hand
which hung down over the edge of the sheet, and because it was
blue-veined and a little wrinkled and the garden calluses showing,
it made me want to cry. She was brought back for burial three days
later in the cemetery that overlooked the lake.

Meanwhile there had been an inquest, but it was simply a for-
mality. Anne's fingerprints had been found on the ax. On the morning of July ninth she was arrested for the murder of her sister and
taken into the jail at Petoskey. The trial was hastily set for the latter
part of the month, and Geoffrey Lord, a prominent attorney from
New York, arrived to act for her. I believe Dan Warren had sent
for him.

I was allowed to visit her in the jail, and two things surprised
me. The first was that she was in a small, comfortable room that
would not have looked like a cell at all save for the bars on the windows. There was a comfortable-looking bed, an armchair, a chest of
drawers, a rug on the floor, and flowers everywhere. The second
thing was that Anne, though she looked every one of her fifty-five
years, was not particularly distressed by her predicament.

"Everyone's been so kind," she told me, indicating the flowers.
"It has been such a long time since I've been with people that I'd
forgotten how kind they were. I've had a great many visitors."

"Are you under medical supervision here? Are you feeling better?"

"I am very well. Naturally my sister's death was a great shock to me. I can see how they had no choice but to bring me here, though I'm sure that just a little further investigation and they'll let me go. I can't expect them to know that I am incapable of such a dreadful act. They will have to find it out for themselves."

I told her that Geoffrey Lord had arrived the night before to handle the case for her.

"It's very kind of him. We knew the Lords in the old days. But it won't be necessary, really. They're sure to discover the criminal before the trial."

I could not say that they thought they had discovered the criminal. If she could stay here contentedly under that illusion, it would be cruel to rob her of it.

"Do you know who did it, Anne?"

She looked at the floor a long time. "I think I do. I'm not sure, of course. Effie and Thayer kept so many things from me, and I did what they told me. They were stronger than I, and they kept me in ignorance so that I would be protected. I shall make no accusations, however. I might make a mistake and do someone a great wrong. The police will find out the truth."

"And if they don't?"

"They will."

Such complaisance troubled me, but it made Dan Warren furious and alarmed Mr. Lord. They had spoken to her at the jail that afternoon, and they came to my house in the evening. I don't know why, for they hardly addressed Maggie or myself. They conferred with each other and drank our coffee and smoked our cigarettes absent-mindedly. They had been down to the other house so that Mr. Lord could get the lay of the land. When they came out they could see my lights and drifted to them almost unconsciously, I suppose.

"You can see she doesn't appreciate her danger," Dan said. "She's a child, always has been. A warmhearted, dreamy, tender kind of a child. Did what she was told and asked no questions. She's always been protected, and she thinks she still is."

Mr. Lord had white hair, friendly blue eyes, and a firm chin. "They can prove a good motive, Dan. Her sister had forbidden her to see you, for one thing. Then the estate has grown. She's in line to inherit almost fifty thousand dollars if she wants to sell out."

"Those wouldn't be motives for Anne. The first one she thought she could talk her sister out of. The second she wouldn't give a damn about. She's never cared about money."

"It's difficult to convince the general public—from which the jury is chosen—that there's anyone in the world who doesn't give a damn about that much money!"

Dan brooded. "There's no death penalty in this state, that's one good thing. The worst that can happen to her is that she'd have to serve part of her sentence while I ferreted out the real murderer."

"We must try to avoid that. In the first place, it would leave her a marked woman. People always read the trials and the verdicts, and that's what they remember. If you're adjudged innocent later on and let out, they don't read about it. The courts declared you guilty once, and that's what they keep fixed in their minds. In the second place, she's rather frail. Her health isn't going to take too much."

Dan groaned. "Listen, we've got to think and think fast. Anne didn't do this thing. Let's start from there. So someone else did. And with what motive? The fifty thousand dollars, maybe. Who gets that money after Anne?"

"It is Anne's as long as she lives. If she were to die, it would be disposed of in accordance with her will. If she left no will, it would go to the nearest of kin."

"She hasn't a relative in the world."

"Oh yes, she has." Mr. Lord smiled at me. "She has a sister-in-law whose very excellent coffee we are drinking at this moment."

They did not discuss the case after that. Dan watched me thoughtfully while he drank his coffee, and they left as unexpectedly as they had come.

Lieutenant Stark was unhappy, and he grew unhappier as the date of the trial drew nearer.

"Hell, I don't know what's the matter with me!" he exploded. We were walking on the beach that afternoon, and I remember that he kicked hard at the sand, hit his toe on a concealed rock, and had to sit down for some time. "It's all as plain as the nose on your face. Effie and Anne were the only two people in the house. Anne says she was lying down in her room from twelve o'clock on. The coroner says Effie was killed between two and three. Anne didn't hear anything. She thought Effie was downstairs sewing with all the doors locked. She says that Effie wouldn't have let anybody into the house, except maybe you. But she's cutting her own throat there. Because if anyone did come in, he came through the screen door on the porch, and it had to be unhooked for him. There isn't a sign anywhere of surreptitious entry.

"Well, Anne came downstairs two or three times during the afternoon, but she didn't even glance toward the living room. She went to the kitchen to get fresh ice for the ice bag she was keeping on her head. Once she says she called to Effie but got no answer, and she figured Effie had gone out to the garden.

"The phone rang shortly after four, and Anne didn't answer, because she thought her sister was downstairs. She heard it go on ringing and then stop just as she was getting ready to get out of bed and go to it. She lay back down, but when the ringing started again fifteen minutes later, she did go down. From the table in the hall where the telephone is you can see the front door, and she glanced that way just as she picked up the receiver. She saw her sister on the floor, put the receiver down without saying a word, and walked into the living room. Then she saw the ax—stumbled over it, in fact—and picked it up, like she was walking in her sleep. She says she doesn't remember another thing until she was in her own bed with Mrs. Moss hovering over her."

"I believe her."

"That's what bothers me. I'd like to believe her, God knows, but look at it the other way. She was mad at Effie because of Dan. Maybe she even thought that Effie had stabbed him that night in the garden. She must have seen that her sister was dressed to go out that night and it made her wonder. Let's say the two of them have an argument in the living room. The ax is propped up in a corner of the porch outside, ready to give to Nathan when he drives up. They get angry at each other, and Anne thinks she'll show her sister how serious she is about this thing. She steps out to the porch, gets the ax, and comes back with it. Maybe Effie doesn't bluff. She tries for the ax, and Anne hits her with it two or three times before she knows what she's doing.

"Now what shall she do? It's no good to run away. We'll find her, and her attempt to escape will be as good as an admission of guilt. She's too smart for that. She puts the ax down by the body and goes upstairs where she can remove every trace of blood from her person. No one knows what she was wearing that day, but we can't find that anything is missing. We've checked your wardrobe and Maggie's, and they're intact too. But somewhere out there, there ought to be a dress missing, and she's the one who had the best chance to dispose of it."

"Have you looked at all the old things in the attic?"

"Mrs. Moss and I have ransacked that attic and yours, and nothing's been disturbed. There aren't even footprints in the dust up there, except what we made ourselves."

"She might have come down with no clothes on at all."

"I don't believe it. Not Anne. Too Victorian. Even to avoid bloodstains and a murder charge, I can't imagine her coming downstairs in the nude."

"I can't either. And I don't think she did. I'm just trying to help you theorize."

"Well, there are a lot of holes in it, any way you look at it. Boiled down, though, it's this. Anne had the opportunity, Anne had the motive, Anne had the weapon. That adds up, doesn't it? And I can believe it until I talk to her. It's that innocence of hers, that 'I have faith in the police and justice' line that throws me."

"And there isn't a sign that someone else might have done it?"

"The screen door was open. That looks as if someone had gone out after Effie was dead. But Anne could have unhooked it to make it look that way. There's sand on the living-room floor. There's sand on every living-room floor for miles around here. That doesn't tell us anything. Whoever killed her must have been very tall or Effie was sitting down at the time. That's ambiguous."

"Why was she struck so many times?"

"Wanted to make sure she was dead, likely. Any one of the blows would have caused immediate death. But whoever did it got blood on him, that I'd tie to. There were splatters of it on the floor and the walls. There were splatters on him too, you can bet. Yet I can't find a trace of it anywhere but in that room!"

Two nights later, however, as Jim Caldwell was patrolling the beach, he came upon a small fire burning briskly. He stamped it out in a hurry and called Stark. A dress had been burned, no doubt of it, though the fabric was ashes and unidentifiable. Some buttons were left, a plain white kind that had been serviceable rather than ornamental. But Mrs. Moss still maintained stoutly that the only dresses that were missing from Miss Anne's closet were the ones she had with her in town.

"You saw the dress she had on that day," she scolded, "when you found the poor dear lying senseless by the body of her sister. There was no blood on that. What other dress are you looking for?"

"It's conceivable that she changed the dress in which she did the murder, hid it somewhere, and came down again in a fresh one."

"You mean she had time to pick out the dress she wanted to faint in? For that was a real faint, Mr. Stark, make no mistake about that. I've seen too many of them not to know."

"Somebody burned a dress on the beach last night."

"You can't blame Miss Anne for that, locked up the way she is. I suppose you're thinking that Nathan or I did it to help her out. Well, we didn't. And if I may say so, Mr. Stark, there are two other ladies not so far from here that might be having the wish to get rid of a dress or so. You have your own reasons for not pestering them, I daresay!"

Before such venom the startled lieutenant could only beat a retreat.

He had traced the purchase of the arsenic found in the attic, however, and it had been a job. Many of the pharmacies had changed hands and new ones had sprung up and old ones gone out of business in the last twenty years. Fortunately the poison had been bought at one that kept careful records which were still extant. No one could remember who had bought the stuff, but some forgotten clerk had written "Brandon Oaks" on the dusty old page dated "March, 1921." Alice had died in the fall of that year.

Lieutenant Stark said that didn't help much now. "We don't have to beat around the bush hunting for old speculative murders," he said. "We have a nice modern one looking us right in the face. If they'd have been able to put a name on the person who bought the arsenic, it might have been a different story. I was going on the theory that all the troubles the Brandons had had up here were the manifestations of one person. Ergo, that person poisoned Alice, killed sheep, buried a child, stabbed Warren, and took a swipe at Maggie. And murdered Effie, if you want to push it that far. Only we have the person we think killed Effie, and we don't have to worry about the rest any more."

I knew that he did worry, though, in spite of all his rationalizing. The state's case was strong, but no stronger than the case against Lizzie Borden had been years before, and she had gotten off scot free. The newspapers had pointed out the similarities between her case and Anne's: the same choice of weapons; the same empty house; the same tension between members of the family, this time directed against a sister instead of a father and mother; the same lack of bloodstains on the clothing and person of the supposed murderer; the same burning of an anonymous dress. The differences they did not stress, and they were significant; the weapon in Miss Borden's case had not been proved as found, and here the ax had been left in plain sight; Miss Borden had had a careful alibi, and Anne offered none; and Miss Borden had made a determined fight for her life, while Anne sat listless and indifferent in her room at the jail.

Geoffrey Lord was worried too. He was planning his defense carefully and he did not overlook a single trick. For his own information he had summoned a New York psychiatrist to examine his client. This was not generally known nor was the fact given to the press. Mr. Lord took the doctor in as a plain medical man, and the ruse was not discovered. His report was that Anne Brandon was sane. She had led a repressed, abnormal life and she had made some queer compensations for it, but basically she was in normal mental health. A plea of insanity would be out of the question.

The press had a good many columns to devote to the inefficiency of the police all that week. Here was a place where three murderous attacks had already been made. The police had the grounds and the two houses under surveillance at night. Yet in broad daylight they had permitted this latest tragedy to occur. The papers inferred that had the merest reporter been living within a radius of forty miles, such a thing could not have happened, so alert and superior were their people to those employed by the state for police work.

"Monday morning quarterbacking," said Lieutenant Stark. "They wouldn't have thought any more than we that anybody'd have the nerve to try a thing like that in the middle of the afternoon. Especially after I'd warned Miss Effie to keep everyone out of the house except the people who belonged there and not to budge outside unless she was in plain sight of somebody else. We'd have had to put one of our men inside the house to prevent this, and Miss Effie would have seen us in hell before she'd have allowed us to do that! Also I'd like to point out to the press that we have a limited staff and can't go out and hire more whenever we feel like it. We have quite a chunk of the state to look after. As it was, some of my men were working twenty-four hours a day!"

Meanwhile Anne had made an astounding revelation to her attorney. He had been with her for hours that week, and it was the very day before the opening of her trial that she opened up in a calm fashion.

"I have been thinking it over," she said, "and I can see no reason why I should not tell the truth about two things. They will not help you, Mr. Lord. I am afraid that, instead, they will distress you, but if the police are to work successfully they must be in possession of certain other facts."

The two things she had to tell him were that she had helped bury the body of Sue Kennedy and that she herself had made the attack on Maggie!

"I didn't understand just why we had to bury the child," she said calmly. "Effie had found her dead on the beach. Someone—not ourselves—had buried her carelessly in the sand, and her clothes were still wringing wet. Well, you can see how it would have looked for us. The child had been missing and we find her—not washed up, but buried by human hands—on our beach. If we had come forward with that, suspicion would have been directed against us, naturally. No one would have believed that we had found her as we said.

"Effie had discovered her early in the evening of the very day Elizabeth first came to us. She covered her with sand again and waited until late that night. She did not want Thayer to know about it, so I had to help her. Effie said that there was nothing to do but bury her again, but in a different place. So we carried the poor little thing up the steps in the dark—it wasn't easy—and took her around to the back. We used no light, so whatever Maggie saw, it was not us.

"Effie brought a shovel from the barn and we dug the grave. I was on my knees scraping loose dirt from the hole, and Effie brought the shovel down on my arm in the dark. It was painful, but I wrapped my handkerchief around it and we finished the job. I said a short prayer for the poor child and we went back to the house. I wore a long-sleeved dress the next day, and no one noticed that I had been hurt.

"I am sorry that I struck Maggie, but I thought she was the person who had hurt Dan. I went out to the garden and found him lying there. I was afraid to move, but I heard footsteps on the gravel and then someone moving on our side porch. It was so dark that I couldn't see, but I was terrified that this was a murderer and he intended to do away with all of us! I moved very quietly that way. I didn't realize that I had no weapon until my foot struck the flashlight on the steps. I picked it up and brought it down as hard as I could. She let out a sigh and dropped down at my feet. I knew then who it was, and I should have rapped at the door myself and called for help, but I didn't think of that. I only wanted to get back to Dan. I thought he was dead or dying, and I knew I couldn't have hurt Maggie much. So I went back to the garden and stayed there until the police came."

She looked at him with the pleased smile of a child who has just told an interesting story, and she saw no enormity in her words.

"Good God!" said the lawyer. "Miss Brandon, do you realize that you've committed perjury and worse? That if any of this comes out in the trial your word will not be worth the breath it's spoken with? That the jury and the police will judge you guilty of any crime you want to name on this basis alone?"

"I have done wrong, Mr. Lord, and I am willing to suffer for it. I did not kill my sister, and I am not willing to finish my life under that stigma."

Mr. Lord was an honest man, though his last words of advice to her did not sound so. "For the love of heaven," he said to her, "don't let any of this out in court! I intended to put you on the stand in your own defense, and I think I will have to. The prosecution are not apt to bring up much of this, and if they do, dodge it any way you can. You're too far in the soup to be meticulous now. Answer the questions put to you as briefly and concisely as you can. And forget that you've told me any of this. I'll try to forget it too!"

But he did not forget it.

CHAPTER XVIII

I CANNOT REPRODUCE HERE all of the trial. It dragged on for three of the warmest days of the year. The courtroom was filled with waving palm-leaf fans, secured temporarily from one of the churches. A majority of the audience was elderly, older people being the only ones who can find the leisure for long summer vacations and attendance at murder trials. And when Anne walked in and sat down, pale and cool in a sheer dress, her big dark eyes shy, her dark hair with its white streaks piled high on her head, her whole manner more suggestive of the tea table than the witness stand, there was a murmur of approval from the courtroom. She was so obviously one of their own kind.

The district attorney made a powerfully effective opening speech, part of which I quote:

"We will show, gentlemen of the jury, that this woman had openly defied her sister in announcing her intention to marry. Once before she had been on the verge of marrying this same man. Her sister forbade him the house, and eventually he married another woman. He and his wife spent some of each year in their home which borders, though distantly, on Brandon Oaks, and, mark you, the defendant still continued to see him. She never met the man's wife. She did not want to meet her. But she did want to see the man, even to the extent of waylaying him on his walks and lurking outside his house to await his return to it. Mrs. Warren complained to the police of it once, but the situation did not better itself.

"I tell you this to show you how much the defendant cared for this man, how sorely the frustration wrought by her sister had affected her, how desperately she must have regretted allowing herself to be influenced.

"For the chance offers itself again. The man's wife died, and eventually he comes back to live near Brandon Oaks. Again he visits the defendant, again he offers marriage, and again the older sister seeks, for reasons of her own, to come between the two. The defendant is older now and more assured. When Effie Brandon forbids her to see the man, Anne Brandon meets him secretly. One night he is murderously attacked while waiting for her, and we will show you that she suspected her sister of this attack. Now there is no gainsaying her. She announces frankly that she will marry the man as soon as he has recovered from his wound.

"The sisters are quarreling now, and there are days when, alone except for a housekeeper, they do not speak at all. There is an ax in the house by this time, a bright new ax, ordered and bought on a flimsy pretext. There was an adequate ax in the Brandon tool shed. We will show that Effie Brandon kept this ax in the house as a weapon of defense should she need it. For Effie Brandon was afraid, ladies and gentlemen. We have ample evidence to prove that.

"On the afternoon of July ninth, the two women are alone in the house. The gardener and housekeeper have been sent into town with a list of errands to perform. They will not be back until six o'clock. Before they leave, Effie Brandon makes a peculiar request of the housekeeper and the ax is brought up from the basement and propped up in a corner of the front porch.

"Let me give you a picture of the front part of the house that will show you the strategic placement of this ax. The front door of the house opens directly into the living room. Since the porch is a screened one, the main front door of the house is left always open in the summer. On that afternoon Effie Brandon hooked the screen door of that porch after Mrs. Moss and went back into the living room to sew. From where she sat it was only a step through the open door to the corner where the ax was. The defendant is lying down upstairs. Lately she has spent much of her time in her room.

"On her own admission the defendant comes downstairs several times that afternoon, but as to the actual, horrible happenings in the house between those hours of noon and five o'clock we will have to depend upon mute evidence and our own reason.

"At a few minutes after five Lieutenant Stark comes to the house, having been unable to establish contact by telephone. He finds Effie Brandon lying on the floor of the living room just inside the front door. The screen door has been unhooked, although there is no sign that it has been forced or that anyone has had passage through it. There is blood on the floors of the porch and the room, blood on the walls, blood on the ax. But there is no blood at all on the defendant, who is lying some six feet away from her sister, presumably in a state of unconsciousness.

"We will show, gentlemen, that the defendant requested another person, later on, to destroy a dress for her without unwrapping it. That the curiosity of this person led them to open the package. That there they found a bloodstained dress, wrinkled and old, evidently pulled from some rag bag. That the person had qualms about its destruction, but, because of an old association, carried out the instructions and burned the dress on the beach. And that then this person returned to a consciousness of civic duty and offered us this information as late as yesterday.

"The defendant had the opportunity to commit this crime. She had the motive. Her fingerprints and no others have been found on the handle of the ax. Her clothing had been bloodstained, which fact she attempted to hide."

Brick by brick he constructed the house of guilt, and, hard as Geoffrey Lord fought back, the jury was not impressed.

Mrs. Moss came to the stand to tell about Effie's request that the ax be brought from the cellar and left on the front porch. She kept worried, imploring eyes fixed on Anne, and once when Anne smiled at her she picked up her handkerchief and mopped at her eyes. The district attorney led her through the ordeal gently.

"And what did you say when Miss Effie asked you to bring the ax upstairs?"

"I said that Nathan was waiting and that we were in a hurry to get started. I asked her why I couldn't put the ax in the station wagon right then, so that when Nathan unloaded later on he would find it and put it in its proper place."

"And what did she say to that?"

"She said that she preferred to give it to him when we came home, that there was no use leaving it in the station wagon while we ran all over town. She said it might be stolen."

"Has anything ever been stolen from the car under similar circumstances?"

"Not that I know of."

"And can the car be locked up?"

"Yes, easily."

"Did you point out either of these facts to her?"

"No. I didn't think it mattered. We were anxious to get started. Nathan wanted to see an afternoon movie and he wanted to be on time for it."

"Then when you reached Petoskey you separated?"

"Yes. We had divided up the errands, but his wouldn't take him long. He was going to the show while I finished mine. We planned to meet at five o'clock."

"Was this your usual procedure on shopping days?"

"Yes. Only sometimes I went to the movies instead of him, and sometimes we both went together."

"Now to go back. How long had the ax been in the house?"

"For almost a week."

"It had been in the cellar all that time?"

"Yes."

"Had it ever been disturbed?"

"It always seemed to be in the same place."

"During the previous month, what would you say had been the feeling between the two sisters?"

"They quarreled over Mr. Warren."

"And you overheard these quarrels?"

"I heard Miss Effie say that such a thing was ridiculous at their age, that nothing but trouble would come of it, that she was only trying to do Miss Anne a favor by keeping her from doing it. Miss Anne said there was no use, her mind was made up."

"Did you hear the defendant make threats against her sister?"

"No, she didn't threaten her. Once she said, 'I'm not a child. You can't treat me this way. It's time I stood up for my right to live.' Mostly she just went to her room and cried."

"And in your opinion was Miss Effie afraid of her?"

"I couldn't say that. She was afraid of something, had been for years. All the doors were always kept locked at night. In the daytimes the front and back doors were left open, but the upstairs rooms were kept locked. She was being extra careful lately and kept the outside doors locked in the daytimes too, and all the shades pulled down."

"You did not think such excessive locking of doors unusual enough to comment on?"

"It wasn't very handy, but it wasn't my place to say anything."

"You have acted as a practical nurse from time to time, Mrs. Moss?"

"Yes."

"You took care of the defendant while she was presumably suffering from shock occasioned by her sister's death?"

"Yes."

"She was not delirious at any time?"

"No. She just laid there quiet. She didn't want anything to eat, and she slept most of the time."

Geoffrey Lord was more brisk with her.

"Now, Mrs. Moss, is it not a fact that Miss Effie bought the new ax because she was afraid they would be hard to get later on when the one she had might be worn out?"

"That's what she said."

"And that it is quite possible that she was keeping the ax, not from any sense of fear, but simply because she kept forgetting to have it put away properly?"

"Yes. She's been absent-minded lately."

"Did Miss Anne know the ax was in the house?"

"I don't know. She never went to the cellar."

"In any case, you never heard her make a reference to it?"

"No."

"And when you left that afternoon, Miss Anne was upstairs and had no reason to know where the ax was then, even had she known of its existence in the first place?"

"That's right."

"These discussions that you overheard between the two women—would you designate them as quarrels?"

"I'd call them a difference of opinion. Miss Anne and Miss Effie, they're ladies. They don't scream and throw themselves around."

"Miss Anne, then, is not of a violent temperament?"

"She's one of the quietest people I ever knew."

"And as to the locked doors. The only change in those was that now the outside doors were kept locked in the daytime also. Would that not indicate to you that the danger Miss Effie feared came from the outside?"

The district attorney sprang to his feet, but Mr. Lord had made his point, delicate as it was.

I was amazed to find that Maggie was the nebulous person who had burned the dress. She was not happy on the stand, and I knew that she feared recriminations from me when she got home. She told how she had found a package wrapped in brown paper in the mailbox and had been surprised to find a note pinned to it addressed to herself. The note had said: "Maggie, for the sake of our childhood together, burn this without opening it and say nothing to anyone. You are the only one I can trust and I shall not forget your kindness." It had been signed simply "Anne."

"This package had not come through the mail?"

"No. It had no postmark on it. It looked as though someone had left it there."

"Surely that was a long chance to take. How could they be sure it would reach you before anyone else got hold of it?"

"Everybody knew that I always met the mailman. It was kind of a joke."

"What did you do with the package?"

"I went back to the house and got some matches. Then I went down to the beach. If the wrapping hadn't come loose, maybe I wouldn't have looked inside. But I saw a corner of a dress and it made me curious, so I opened it. It was an old wash dress and it had brown stains on it from top to bottom. That scared me. I stuffed the paper under it and set fire to it. It was almost burned up when I heard someone coming along the beach and ran back to the house."

"You did not mention this to the police?"

"No, but it worried me. I wanted to tell Elizabeth—that's Mrs. Brandon—but I knew she wouldn't have approved. It got so I couldn't sleep at night for thinking about it, so I came to you and told you."

"The note was burned with the package?"

"Yes."

"Was it in the defendant's handwriting?"

Maggie brightened. "I couldn't say. I've never seen any of her handwriting to notice. It probably wasn't. I never thought of that!"

The district attorney could not have been more surprised if his pet puppy had turned into a dinosaur before his eyes.

"You can't say a thing like that, Miss Mitchell!"

"Well, anybody could have left the thing there and written the note. Miss Anne was in jail. She couldn't have put it there."

"She could have asked someone to do it for her."

"If there was anyone she had trusted to that extent, she wouldn't have had to ask me to burn it!"

The courtroom broke into sound; Geoffrey Lord leaned back and

laughed; the judge rapped and told Maggie severely that the stand
was no place for theorizing, that she was there to answer questions
and not propound new ones. But the jury was amused, and though
Maggie had been the instrument of this deadly bit of evidence, she
had done something to counteract its effect. Not enough, I thought
as I looked at the head juryman. Though he was smiling tolerantly,
he looked like too calm and logical a man to have missed the deadly
facts.

There was a medical wrangle over shock and its various physical
reactions. The state was trying to prove that Anne's unconsciousness
could have been feigned. The doctors were tactful and not inclined
to commit themselves definitely. Unconsciousness, of course, could
be feigned, but if the coroner had found the defendant's heartbeat
and pulse slow and faint, the chances were that it had been genuine. He had so found it.

"But isn't it possible that, in the period of lying there, her pulse
and heart rate might have subsided from inactivity?"

"Well . . ."

"It is possible?"

"It could be possible."

The district attorney threw in a sentence pointed directly at the
jury. "And even were the shock quite genuine, it would be impossible
to say whether it was caused by her discovering her sister's tragic
state or having caused it. Isn't that true?"

"Naturally."

The bloodstained ax was produced, the fingerprints on it verified
by experts.

"There are other fingerprints on the ax?"

"Yes, a good many. They belong to Mrs. Moss, to Effie Brandon,
and to the man who sold the ax a week ago. We have taken prints
of them all."

I had not seen Dr. Day in the courtroom, and I gasped when he
was called to the stand. He was wearing a white suit, and his black
beard was neatly trimmed. He sat down deliberately and folded his
immaculate square hands.

"You are an old friend of the Brandons', Dr. Day?"

"We grew up as neighbors. My father was their family physician."

"During your stay here this summer you were often at Brandon
Oaks?"

"We went for dinner occasionally. Sometimes they visited us."

"You were called down to the house late in the evening of the day when Dan Warren was stabbed?"

"I was. It was eleven o'clock or thereabouts. I had just come in from a drive, and my wife gave me the message."

"Why were you called?"

"Miss Effie wanted me to talk to her sister to try to calm her. She was very upset over what had happened."

"And did you calm her?"

"I didn't get a chance to speak to her. She was asleep when I got there. She had a habit of falling asleep at the slightest excitement or unpleasantness. Instead I spoke to Miss Effie. I told her that I thought she was foolish to try to dominate her sister's life, that everyone had a right to make his own mistakes."

"You are a psychiatrist, Dr. Day?"

"No, primarily I am a surgeon. I have studied psychology abroad, however, and have been interested in it. I have written several books on the subject which are used as texts in some of the colleges."

"The defense would have us believe that there is, or was, loose in the neighborhood, a lunatic who attacked and stabbed and killed for the joy of it. Have you met such a person?"

"To my knowledge, no. I have seen no sign of an unbalanced mind in anyone I have been in intimate association with. There are people I don't know very well, of course. Mr. Warren, Nathan, Mrs. Moss, and Elizabeth Brandon, I cannot vouch for. They seem very normal people, however."

Geoffrey Lord seized on him.

"You are willing to stake your professional reputation, then, Doctor, on the fact that Miss Anne Brandon is sane?"

"We are speaking of sanity in a very general sense. Avoiding all technicalities, I would say that I consider her as normal, and that, were she to have a temporary departure from the norm, it would not take a violent form. Of course the human mind is an unpredictable thing. You will have to take what I have said as a mere opinion."

"This hideous murder, would you call it the action of a sane person?"

"I am sorry to say that it could be. It would have to be the work of one who had an exceptionally strong motive. If the desire for the death of an enemy is strong enough, the method of killing is unimportant."

Which was not what Mr. Lord had bargained for.

Dan Warren was an unhandy witness. He was inclined to shout and storm and make insolent remarks about the stupidity of anyone who could believe a woman like Anne Brandon guilty of this thing. All in all, he probably did her more harm than good.

So the witnesses came and went: experts, doctors, we from the Oaks, the police, townspeople. And the case against Anne grew and grew until Mr. Lord, taking a last long chance, put her on the witness stand and asked her to tell the story of her attack on Maggie. The courtroom grew very quiet as her voice went faintly on.

"Perfectly natural," said Mr. Lord, "that you should have done what you did, knowing that there was a dangerous person in the vicinity. Will you tell us how it happened that your fingerprints were not found on the flashlight afterward?"

"I had read about fingerprints. I was careful to wipe them off."

And though her lawyer pounded away at the fact that, since she had been careful to avoid fingerprints once, it was foolish to suppose that she had deliberately left them on the ax, I was afraid that the jury was more impressed with the idea that this woman had been capable of one criminal attack and thus could not be the fine gentlewoman the witnesses of the defense had drawn her.

"Did you at any time suspect your sister of the stabbing of Dan Warren?"

"No. What Nathan heard me say was that it was strange that she should have a robe on over all her clothes and that it was fortunate she had not been outside. I meant, of course, that she might have been hurt, not that she might have hurt someone else."

She had not sent the dress to Maggie or caused it to be sent.

"We have a rag bag. Everyone has, I suppose. I cannot say whether the dress was one of mine or not. But I sent no dress to be destroyed."

And later. "Your sister's eyesight was not particularly good?"

"She had glasses but she did not wear them. Her sight had failed a great deal in the last few years."

"If someone had come to the door of the porch, would she have been able to tell who it was from the living room?"

"No, she would have had to go out to the porch, and even then she might have had to speak to them before she recognized them."

"She might, in other words, let someone in whom she had not really intended to let in?"

"Yes. I think that is what happened."

The district attorney took up the same theme but with a different motif. "Would your sister have been likely to admit to the house anyone whom she did not know?"

"She might have thought she knew them."

"That is not an answer to my question. Would she have admitted a stranger?"

"No."

"Why were the individual bedrooms locked at night?"

"We were in a lonely location and practically without protection. We felt it a safeguard. I was not careful about it, and Effie often scolded me about it."

It was early that same evening that the jury filed out for what was to be twenty hours of deliberation, and we went home to await the verdict. That night, too, Lieutenant Stark received a telegram and knew at last who the killer was.

CHAPTER XIX

IT WAS ELEVEN O'CLOCK in the morning when he walked into my house and asked for Maggie.

"She's down getting the mail," I said. "It's a wonder you didn't see her on your way in."

"She'll be disappointed. The postman has just been by, and your box is as bare as the palm of my hand."

"The elderly widower must be slipping."

But when Maggie came in she was waving, triumphantly, a fat letter.

"I'm going back to Chicago on the first train," she said. "That is, I'll wait until we hear about Anne. You don't think they'll convict her, do you, Mr. Stark?"

He was looking at her with a strange gentleness. "No, I don't think they'll convict her," he said. "They don't know it yet, but some new evidence has just shown up."

She clasped her hands joyfully. "Oh, how wonderful! And how wonderful for Mr. Warren!"

I didn't say anything. I didn't like what was happening.

"You were very good in court," he told her. "You certainly threw the district attorney off his stride. He thought you were a state's witness until you turned on him."

"I had to tell the truth."

"Why?"

Her mouth fell open a little. "What a peculiar question, Mr. Stark."

He reached over and picked the letter from her hand. "Unusual handwriting for a man, isn't it?"

She colored and said nothing.

"Funny how it came all the way from Chicago without a postmark," he went on.

She burst into tears. "It doesn't matter now, Mr. Stark. It was Effie I wanted to impress, and she's gone now. I don't mind Elizabeth knowing."

The lieutenant turned to meet the question on my face. "There is no elderly widower," he said. "Maggie made him up. She's been writing these letters to herself. That's why she had to meet the mailman every day. So no one else would know. That mailman has a good memory, by the way. He says Miss Mitchell has had only two letters since she's been here. Who were they from, Maggie?"

"One was from Mrs. Page, a friend of mine. The other was from a friend of hers telling me she had died of a gall-bladder infection." She sat on the edge of a chair, her eyes pink with weeping, her small hands clenched.

"Mrs. Page was the matron of the Bayville Orphanage in Chicago?"

"I guess she was. I knew she was the head of some place like that."

"Come now, Maggie, you knew who she was. You met her for the first time when you went to visit the orphanage."

She did not answer. She kept turning her handkerchief around in her hands and looking at it.

"And after you came to know her better you told her that you wanted to know who your parents had been. Maybe she was reluctant, but you persuaded her. She had trouble finding out, even in the position she was in, didn't she?"

Maggie's voice was dull and low. "It took her six months. The records had all been hidden. I didn't know until the first day I came up here. She had just found out and she wrote it to me."

"That is why you were ill?"

"Yes. I had never suspected. It was a dreadful shock to me."

"You'd better tell me all about it. I'll want to see the sun suit you were wearing the morning of the day Miss Effie was killed. The jig's up, Maggie."

"I thought so when you walked in."

I felt as though the whole world were falling down around my ears, but she was quite calm. She talked for a long time, and he wrote it all down in his notebook.

"There's a lot of it I'm not sure of. You must remember that I've known the truth for only a month and I haven't had much time to figure out just how it must have been. Mr. Brandon adopted me when I was almost three years old. He knew who I was, of course— the records that were hidden showed that, and Mrs. Brandon must have guessed. She was a high-spirited woman, ordinarily not unkind, but she was possessive. She must have known that her husband and her sister had become more friendly than they should have. That's why the sister had to leave the house and come up here to live. I believe that I was born in this house with no one but an old Indian woman in attendance. I am the daughter of William Brandon and Margaret Thayer, and my real name was Margaret Brandon. They changed it to Marjorie Mitchell on the adoption papers.

"I am sure that Mr. Brandon showed my mother every kindness. He had the reputation of being a moral and upright man, and he must have deplored his one temporary weakness as much as anyone could. I think he gave my mother money and promised her that I would be taken care of. Somehow I was transferred from here to the orphanage without anyone knowing. And Mr. Brandon got me out again as soon as he could and took me into his own home.

"I don't believe his wife knew for certain that I was his child and Margaret's. If she had had proof, she would not have had me in the house. But she did have her suspicions, and she could not be good to me. I can remember even now the aching resentment I felt then.

I was not pretty, an ugly duckling born of two swans, and I lacked assurance and felt that nothing I could ever do would be right. The Brandon children were good children. They would have been nice to me, but I would not have it. I dared not be insolent to their mother, but I could take my anger out on them. I was clever, you see, cleverer than they, and I could do things that would make it look as though they had done them. Once I smashed all my toys, and when Mrs. Deever discovered it I cried and would not answer. She inferred that it must have been one of the other children, and they were punished for not admitting the truth. And once I gave one of them a knife and ran into it on purpose so that it looked as if a childish attempt had been made on my life. I deviled them this way for years, and naturally they grew to hate me. But I was a good, quiet little thing as far as grownups were concerned, and they were inclined to believe me rather than the other children.

"When we grew up it was not much different. I enjoyed wearing poorer clothes than they and slumping down in corners so that outsiders would click their tongues and pity me. It made the Brandons look bad, and I wanted that. Not for Mr. Brandon. He was always good to me. As long as he was alive he insisted that I live with them. Mrs. Brandon was all for letting me go when I was of age, but he wouldn't hear of it. I was twenty-six when they were killed in the accident.

"I don't know when Effie discovered who I really was, but I am sure she knew shortly after that. Perhaps there was something in the diary and letters her mother left. I do not know. I only know that if she had confided in me then, I would have been the happiest person under the sun. Keep remembering that I did not know who I was—I never knew until a month ago. But had she told me all those years ago, I would have thanked her and gone about my business and let them alone. Knowing that I was really a Brandon would have given me confidence enough to make everything all right. I would have felt that I was like other people, and I might even have grown to feel cordial toward my half brothers and sisters. After all, they had never done me any harm. It had all been the other way around.

"I was surprised when Effie insisted that I stay on with them. I knew, of course, that I had shared in the will, and I also knew that the Brandon fortune had gone. The children were not obligated in any way to keep me on, and I have wondered since why they did.

I think Effie was afraid to let me go, afraid that somehow I might find out the truth about my birth and make it public. A thing like that would have sullied her father's reputation, and that had become too great an American myth for her to want to see it spoiled. She was dreadfully proud of her father and proud of belonging to the family.

"Anyway, she insisted that I come up here and live with the rest of them, and I did. I was having too much fun making their lives miserable to want it interfered with. Only now I was doing serious things, things that I since have been ashamed of, things that made me a criminal. I don't think you know how it is to be an idle, useless woman in a house where you don't belong. Dr. Day tried to straighten me out. I don't know how much he knew, but he warned me. I remember that he said once, 'You have a better than average mind, Maggie. If you concentrate on hate, you will make more of a success at it than most people. If you concentrate on making something of yourself, you'll be better at that than most. Don't choose the wrong thing to concentrate on!' But I did just that. Feeling myself ugly and unwanted, I had to make my presence known in the world somehow.

"The Brandons were terrified of me, though they tried not to show it. Somewhere about this time Effie must have told Thayer the truth, but Anne never knew. I'm positive of that. All Effie could do was keep the doors locked and keep her eye on me every minute.

"Then Effie married and the rest of us went to live in the other house. She worried about marrying. She didn't know what I might do to that, but she was in love with Robert Warren and she took the chance.

"I can't tell you how eaten I was with jealousy of her. I saw her as a rich girl who had always had everything, while I had the crumbs from the table. I told myself that she kept me on, not because she thought it was the fair thing to do, but because she wanted to make a drudge of me. That wasn't true either—I had never done as much work as they—but I made myself believe it, and my rage and hate grew. Now she was married happily to a fine man, a good, sensitive, kind man, and I could not bear it.

"I think that somewhere during the first year he found out from her who I really was. I recall that his manner to me changed from an offhanded courtesy to a sort of sympathetic, pitying attitude. I did not know what the reason for the change could be, but I welcomed it because it made him malleable and easy to convince. I let him force out of me a whole long list of imaginary wrongs that Effie and the rest had done to me, and he believed them all. I know he quarreled with her. I think now that he was trying to make her tell me who I was and let me do whatever I chose. But she was frightened more than ever. If I had gone to the trouble to turn her husband against her, thinking I was a waif and a stray, what might I not have done with this new knowledge? Might I not have published it to the whole world and turned her father's precious name into dust? Or contested the will and gotten more of a share?

"Whatever her reasons, she would not give in, and he believed that he had married a hard, vicious woman who persisted in preying on the helpless. And in the depths of that disillusionment, he hanged himself.

"That was more than I had bargained for, but it made the next step easier. Thayer married, and on their wedding trip Alice wrote a letter telling about a woman whose husband had poisoned her with arsenic. I didn't want to see Thayer happy either, but you must believe I had no intention of killing her. I wanted to make her think she was being poisoned, so that she would leave him and he would be miserable. So I bought some arsenic, and every chance I got, I put some in her food. But long before she got suspicious I gave her too much by mistake, at a dinner we had at their house one night, and she died suddenly. Dr. Day was there at the time, and that was all that saved them and myself from the suspicion of murder. He issued a false death certificate, and that knowledge has been hanging over him ever since. He did not want to do it. Effie had to beg him on her knees. Perhaps she told him then that I was her half sister and that it would be as bad for me to be tried as it would for any of the rest of them. I remember he said to me, 'I think you're sane, Maggie, but I'm damned if I wouldn't have you put away! An asylum or jail is the place for you.' I pretended not to know what he was talking about. Thayer struck me that day, but otherwise they pretended that Alice's death had been natural, as Dr. Day had had to say it was. They had to act that way to protect themselves.

"By now I was puzzled. I had not meant to commit a crime, but the Brandons knew that I was guilty. Still they pretended that everything was all right; still they kept me on. I could not understand it. I never understood it until that letter came from Mrs. Page.

"I was more careful now. Effie wouldn't let Anne marry Dan Warren because she was afraid that the next thing I might do would uncover all the things that had gone before. I think Anne would have been safe, though. I was alarmed at the lengths to which I had gone. For many years I did nothing more strenuous than be provokingly dull and stupid and abused. I stayed in my own room at night and did not bother climbing out my window and going to Thayer's house and upsetting it for him. I had a key to it. No matter how many times they changed the locks I always had a key.

"It was I who found Sue Kennedy on the beach, late in the afternoon of the day she was lost. She had drowned, and the water had washed her body in between two big rocks. Perhaps she had been climbing on the rocks and fallen down and had not been able to get up. I wouldn't have hurt her had she been alive, you must believe that. I never wanted to hurt anyone but Effie and Anne and Thayer.

"I saw the best chance to be bothersome that I had had in a long time. I brought the body into shore and buried it on the beach in an inconspicuous place. It would be hard for them to explain its presence there when the police found it. You can imagine how surprised I was when it was not found and when, upon going to the spot, I found it was no longer there! It wasn't until the body showed up in the drain field that I knew what must have happened, and then I made up that story of having seen the lights during the night.

"Elizabeth married Thayer, then, and I liked Elizabeth. She was the first person I had ever met that seemed to enjoy being with me. I have liked her to this day. She was puzzled, too, by the locked doors and the instructions they gave her about being carefully dressed always and not going swimming. That was because I had declared myself disgusted with swimming and beach wear, saying that it was only an excuse for women to show themselves off, and I had made vague threats about the things that might happen to anyone I saw doing it. It was all part of the mean teasing I had kept up from childhood, but they took it seriously now. I think they liked Elizabeth, but they were afraid to show it. They were afraid to show a liking for anyone, for fear I might injure that person. Thayer, even, thought awhile before he married her. She was safe as could be, but they had no way of knowing that. I used to go to her house at night, just to be there, and smoke and read. Effie didn't object to my smoking, but I told other people that she did. It was all part of my being abused.

"But I could tell Elizabeth lies that would influence her against her husband and his sisters, and I did. The sheep killing had made her nervous to start with. I had found one sheep dead at the foot of the cliff, and the dogs were with me and they jumped on it. When I saw how annoyed Effie was about it, I kept it up. I think I killed only three sheep in all. They were so gentle, I hated to do it so badly that I could not keep it up. But what with that and with what I told her, she decided to leave. I never meant to go with her. I simply wanted to make sure that she got away. If Lieutenant Stark hadn't picked us up in his car, I never would have reached the station. I had planned to be too tired and turn back.

"But I couldn't get out of it very well then, so I left on the train they put me on, planning that I would take the very earliest one back. The city fascinated me, though. It was a long time since I'd seen a city. I thought I'd look up the woman whose address the lieutenant had given me just for fun. The upshot of that was that I found a job and got settled and loved every minute of it.

"It was just as Dr. Day had said. If I wanted to turn my mind to being a success, I could manage it. Those eight years were the loveliest of my life. I wish I had never been curious enough to hunt up the orphanage and meet Mrs. Page. I wish I had not come back here when Elizabeth asked me to. But I knew I had improved and changed, and I could not resist the opportunity of showing off. I just intended to stay a month and go back. I wouldn't have bothered them any more ever. I felt like a different woman from the one who had done all those terrible things to them. I was a different woman. I had better things to think about.

"Effie sensed that with her first look at me. She was ready to be friends. But after I had met her I opened the letter from Mrs. Page, and there it was. I knew that all along I had been a Brandon and that I should have had the same kind of childhood they had had, with love and care and maybe a chance to marry someone and raise a family of my own. It made me deathly ill to think how different all those lost years might have been had I known that I had a right to be where I was instead of thinking that I was a whim and an unpleasant one.

"Mrs. Page said that the birth certificate was missing, that some-one must have it, and that the someone else had known the truth. She was scared to death that I would tell what she had found, for she wasn't supposed to let me know. Poor woman, she's dead now and it doesn't matter. But I think that Effie had the birth certificate. She must have found it after her people died.

"I knew then that I was going to kill Effie. She had cheated me out of—not just the money, I didn't care about that—but out of my birthright. I was going to kill her for that.

"But she heard my testimony at the inquest on Sue Kennedy, and right away she was cautious again. She knew that I was trying to hurt her some way and she was on her guard. She shut herself and her sister up in that house and they wouldn't let me in. I used to go to bed early here and slip out of the window to see whether I could get into the other house at night. I still had the old knife I had killed the sheep with. I found it just where I had left it, in the birdhouse on the pole in the garden, and I carried it with me. Dan Warren bumped right into me in the garden that night while I told Elizabeth I had been out looking for lights in the other house. I struck at him blindly. I didn't know who he was till after. Then I came home, told Elizabeth the people at the other house were still up, took the pudding dish and the flashlight, and went back. The rest of my story about that night was true. I didn't know who had hit me, but at the trial I found out it was Anne.

"I was sorry that any of that happened, because it made it harder for me to kill Effie. The police were on the grounds every night, and twice I ran into them and could hardly get away. I knew that it was no use trying at night. I would have to do it in broad daylight.

"It was Elizabeth, really, who showed me a way to get into that house and do what I had planned. She had been taking sun baths in a suit she had rigged up from three scarves. That morning she had put them on me when we went down to the beach. After lunch, when she thought I was sleeping in my room, I left the house wearing the same scarves. I had white cotten gloves on my hands. I'm sure that Effie thought I was Elizabeth. Her eyes weren't good, and it's hard to tell much about a person's height when she's standing on a lower step, or much about her face when the sun's in your eyes. The minute she unhooked the screen door she knew she had made a mistake. I had brought the knife, but there was an ax on the porch.

I picked it up and killed her with it. Then I went back to my own room and pretended to have been asleep the whole time. Nobody seemed to think anything of the fact that three hours of my time were unaccounted for, and that they were the right three hours. Instead they blamed Anne.

"I didn't particularly want Anne to suffer for Effie's death, but I didn't see any way I could get her out of it without involving myself. Then I heard Mr. Lord say that there was fifty thousand dollars now to go to the nearest relative, and that made me think. Anne couldn't last long in jail, and after she had died and a long time had gone by I could suddenly claim to have found out I was her half sister and claim the money. It would mean an easy old age for me, and I thought I had that coming. I had not had an easy youth.

"The story about the dress was pure fiction, of course. It was the last bit of evidence they needed to convict her, and I supplied it. I tried to give it a twist to make it look as though I didn't believe her guilty, but I'm sure the right impression was made on the jury and the judge. I don't know what one thing made you suspect me."

She was standing near the door when she said that, and she waited courteously for his answer.

"You overdid the letters, Maggie. I knew two weeks ago that you weren't getting any. The mailman had told me about Mrs. Page's name on the return address of another letter, and I thought I would check on her too. When I found out who she was, it seemed queer that you should have cultivated that particular person without a motive. The Chicago police would have had the whole story from her a week ago, but she was too sick to talk to them. After she was dead they went directly to the records. They found that she had just been nosing through them, so they followed her track, and it was a hard one because of the hocus-pocus that had been played with the papers years before. They wired me the answer last night. And right away I knew we had another person with a motive and an opportunity for killing Effie Brandon."

She kept standing there, little and distressed, and I could have wept for her. "Don't cry, Elizabeth," she said. "They'd have found the scarves anyway. There was blood on them, and I washed them and put them in my drawer. I couldn't get all the stains out, and I was afraid to throw them away in case you'd ask for them back."

Lieutenant Stark moved toward her. "Well, Maggie," he said.

She was looking at me now, levelly, seriously. "If I had had a daughter, Elizabeth, I should have wanted her to be like you. You mustn't feel bad about me. If it hadn't been for you, I wouldn't have had those eight years. I can thank you for that. And I'm an old woman. I haven't too many years left."

She was out of the door and running across the lawns toward the lake before we could catch our breath. The lieutenant raced after her, but she had too good a start. She ran straight for the edge of the cliff that overlooked the beach, and in that split second I could picture the big gray rocks below.

She was only two paces ahead of him when she threw herself over, and I saw him cover his eyes for a moment when he first looked down at her. She was dead—her neck broken, her body battered—when they finally got to her. They would not let me see her, and her casket was sealed so that even at the funeral I could not look on her face again.

Well, a year has gone by since then, and I am at Brandon Oaks for the summer. Mrs. Moss keeps house for me now, and Nathan takes care of the grounds. The big house near the lake stands vacant, but Anne writes me that Dan is winding up his business in Detroit and that they will soon be back to take up permanent residence here.

I am not ashamed to say that I miss Maggie. She is buried in the little cemetery beside her mother, and I often take flowers there. The headstone is carved with her real name, Margaret Brandon, and I know that she would like that.

This place is very still now, and there is a lovely peace about it that was never here before. I have had offers for my own house, but I think I will not sell it. Lieutenant Stark says I couldn't find a better place to live or one as convenient for him.